THE
LEOPARD'S
WIFE

THE
LEOPARD'S
WIFE

PAUL PICKERING

SIMON &
SCHUSTER

London · New York · Sydney · Toronto

A CBS COMPANY

First published in Great Britain in 2010 by Simon & Schuster UK Ltd, 2010
This paperback edition published in 2011
A CBS COMPANY

1 3 5 7 9 10 8 6 4 2

Simon & Schuster UK Ltd
1st Floor
222 Gray's Inn Road
London
WC1X 8HB

www.simonandschuster.co.uk

Simon & Schuster Australia
Sydney

A CIP catalogue for this book is available
from the British Library.

ISBN 978-1-84983-016-4

Typeset in Palatino by Ellipsis Books Limited, Glasgow
Printed in the UK by CPI Cox & Wyman, Reading, RG1 8EX

Chui naye ana mke

Even the leopard has a wife

Kasai Swahili proverb, Eastern Congo

For Pascaline Niakekele
In loving memory

PROLOGUE

The boy had hoped that before dying at the hands of the approaching mob in the steamy afternoon heat, the bony Englishman, Smiles, might tell him more of the mysteries of the eight-legged sea creature, the octopus.

Nobody the boy knew had ever seen an octopus, not even his educated sister, who had gone soft-headed. She had fallen into a foolish love sickness for this white man and he had for her, it was disgusting. They made moany sounds and kissy-kissy ones like a red jungle pig taking its hind legs out of the mud. They had no dignity. No shame. They were happy as black-and-white hornbill birds and he was glad for them but ... The boy sucked on his hot, blue, safoe pear, just from the boiling water, the tangy, neon-green flesh sharp as the ideas flying around inside his head. He saw his sister linger by Smiles' side at the top of the grassy bank strewn with drying clothes as a dark line of thunderstorms threatened from upriver. The mob would kill his sister Lola too if they caught her because the stupid Smiles was not going to leave watching the boat and his precious, silent grand piano that they had cuddled under.

For Smiles to die here was better, far better than what her real husband, Chui, the leopard, would do to him when he had time from his army duties and battles. That thought was righteous and made the boy glad even though he liked the white man. The boy was nearly a man and had to be strong and aloof like the hunter.

The storm rumbled in the east, the band of grey and black across the horizon turning darker, and there was another flash. The rain would follow. The boy's mother had named him St James after the disciple Jesus had called his son of thunder. St James stared at the large brown expanse of the Congo River flowing past the ruined port of Kisangani, his home; he was sure there was probably an octopus or two in there, if he only knew where to search.

The mob, sniffing the air for anyone they thought was a rebel or a foreigner or a spy, came along the muddy path just above the slat-roofed food stalls on the lower bank, where fish was drying on mats. Heavy pirogue canoes drummed gently against one another and the scents of bodies and mud mixed with fish and spices and *chikwangue*, the fermenting manioc paste Smiles said stank like old socks. A trader from downriver was enveloped by the seething wall of bodies and a stall went over in a frenzied, fatal blur as the man was pummelled with sticks and eight-foot pirogue paddles. In the distance by an old mango tree not yet in flower St James glimpsed black smoke and smelt petrol and burning tyres.

He felt the drawing the white man had made of the octopus

safe in his shorts' pocket. The thing had eight legs and a beak like a bird. Did it whistle? Did it sing? Could a man turn into an octopus like men turned into crocodiles? Can men change themselves? The white man was dangerous because he brought hopes and dreams and Mozart music and wristwatch time and half-told tales of fantastic creatures that were more painful than whips if you did not know things. He brought more questions than answers. Perhaps that's why the mob was going to kill him. St James had had a clear picture of Smiles laid out on the ground and an old *sowcière* woman had told him his visions were the gospel truth. He watched the tall Englishman, who was very white with long black hair which shook around when he played his music and blue eyes and lips that were like a girl's with lipstick. He was white, really white, white as a drowned man. White as a maggot or a palm-tree grub. The mob stamped ever closer, carrying pangas that flashed in the afternoon light. Smiles should have run by now too. Anger blew through the market and the rioters began to move like one furious, scalded animal.

All wars lead back to Kisangani. St James knew that before he could walk and had watched the Ugandan soldiers rape and drown his mother only yards from where he fished. He had struggled in his sister's arms as the body floated away downriver to the sea. The wars may start somewhere else but this broken city in the heart of Africa was where they ended up.

The Englishman stood by the old bakery with the red brick chimney pointing up into the sky, anxiously watching Lola depart, her slim figure hurrying past a stall with blackened cauldrons of smoked-monkey stew. She wanted to get their papers stamped by the port official and had probably told him she stood a better chance alone. She wore her yellow blouse and green wrap-around skirt and her jet-black hair piled up like she was off dancing. One man, ambushed by her beauty, bumped head first into a pole. Why was Smiles letting her go unprotected? St James would never understand the white man. A limping boy ran after her, pointing: 'Rebel!' he howled. The crowd veered towards Lola.

St James gripped the boat rail tight where he fished. He did not expect Smiles to walk onto the red-earth road, shouting in French and waving his hands above his head: 'I'm the one you want! I helped the American who loves Bemba! I am the rebel!'

The Englishman seemed pleased to put himself in Lola's place. There was a grin on his face. For a second the mob were hushed. Then with a roar they swarmed down the riverbank, over the drying clothes, as Smiles ran towards the boat, turning to face them. A ragged man yelled in Lingala that he was going to tear the white devil's head and arms off and eat his heart. He had a panga in his hand and there was already blood on the wide blade. Smiles missed his footing on the gangplank, tripped and the crowd were standing over him, the rain-wet grass glittering in the sunlight. He was prodded first with a bamboo stick and kicked. He tried to raise himself up but his shirt snagged on a nail. He was caught.

All wars lead back to Kisangani.

Like the tide of water hyacinths bobbing ever upriver against the current. The clogging mats of stumpy leaves and blue flowers that choke everything. Stop you finding anything, let alone an octopus or truths. St James watched. Perhaps the mob would burn Smiles with tyres. But then he heard Lola scream out. His sister had not got away! She had not been able to leave Smiles! In that moment St James felt the earth shift and the future change as he made a choice he knew he was going to regret.

He saw clearly what he had to do, his hands shaking, as he pulled in his fishing line. It was all for the octopus, he told himself. All for the octopus.

ONE

As he faced the mob Smiles was surprised to recall the ambiguous fragrance of the quince he always kept in his dressing room and his first day in Congo and how he met her. How he had scrawled that last note to Dr Kaplan on the plane.

South African Airways
Flight SA 50 to Kinshasa
17, July 2008

My dear Dr Kaplan,

Many thanks again for helping this wretched pianist through his darker movements. I know that we disagree that my collapse at the Joburg concert with a suspected heart attack was all psychological. But I have done as you recommended and put down the story of my boarding school days, which you say are haunting me. My 'black book' is divided into small chapters and folded into neat brown-paper packets the nurses let me have at the hospital dispensary. More than that, I have had word from London saying the American Lyman Andrew, the man I helped ruin, has emerged from the shadows of jungle exile. He is to play at a charity concert in Kinshasa and I managed to get my agent to elbow me onto the list. I have to see Lyman Andrew after telling you the story. I have to make amends and hope he will forgive me as I owe him my success. I have to do this to know if there is any good in me at all. I realised you probably would not approve so I have acted first. I am nervous. It's like that moment of precious grandeur before the concert starts with my fingers poised above the keys. So will it do the trick, do you think? No more attacks? But this journey is more than medicinal. I have left a copy of my jottings for you in Joburg, which will be sent to you and have the original with me, safe with all my essentials in my precious leather music satchel, bought in lovely Florence, if there is something that I want to add. I expect I will be spending most of my time in a faceless European hotel but we can talk on the telephone when I get back to England. I hope you are not too shocked by my revelations. It is not pride that makes me think them unique even within your vast and terrible experience, Dr Kaplan. I am going to give this note to the stewardess now as we are coming in to land. Time to fasten safety belts!

With all good wishes,

S. Miles-Harcourt

'*Vous n'existez pas* . . . You have no visa, you do not exist!' said the large man from the customs service at Kinshasa Airport, with a Cartesian confidence and breath that smelt of violet cachou, his broken boxer's nose almost touching Smiles' right cheekbone.

In the top pocket of the man's dark blue uniform was a small, Barbie-pink lollipop and Smiles made out the word '*Papa*' on the wrapping. He hoped today was perhaps the official's birthday but when he tried to point to the page where the yellow oblong visa was clearly signed and dated the man ripped Smiles' passport along the spine and stood carefully on the pieces in his shiny boots, daring Smiles to try to pick them up.

The arrival hall was hotter than a Turkish bath and had a fetid zoo smell. Soldiers lounged against a wood-and-glass barrier, their Kalashnikovs pointed at the unmoving queue of anxious travellers waiting to have their papers stamped. All hung their heads as if facing the Last Judgement while an oriental man was pushed with painful intent against the greasy tiles of the far wall and began to hand over dollar bills. Next to him, a small African squatted, face in trembling hands, by a dark pool of blood.

Smiles bent down from the waist in a mixture of fear and anger, almost as if he were taking a concert bow, and several Belgian ladies turned in his direction and he wondered if he had been recognised. He was not a household name but much praised on the concert circuit for his Mozart and later Bach. His hat then fell off and the soldiers giggled and the women looked away.

It was an expensive panama hat and that was always a mistake in poor countries. It did not exactly fit him but had been a present from a woman who had not quite become his new wife, as had the linen suit which was impossibly hot and now resembled an old dishcloth. Like him, his lady friend had always striven for aesthetic perfection over the utilitarian. He surveyed the decaying building. He felt giddy and dreaded another breathless bout of fainting.

His shirt was wet against his back. Why had he come here? Why not leave the savage past alone? He felt a pulse hammering in his temples.

He gave the customs man his most radiant smile. One reserved for difficult conductors and composers.

'Please, Monsieur, I am a pianist. A concert pianist. Someone should have been here to meet me with a car. I am to play my new arrangement for single piano of Mozart's 26th at the Intercontinental Hotel. At the Peace and Reconciliation Concert. President Kabila and his wife will be there. There will be a collection for his Roi Baudouin orphans' fund. I am leaving for Nairobi in two days' time.'

He said this in a hesitant French that undermined all authority. But the man in front of him raised his eyebrows and took his foot off Smiles' passport. Smiles quickly snatched it up.

The official's eyes narrowed and his face softened into the kindly smile of a beloved father.

'The Intercontinental?'

'Yes. Absolutely.'

'The manager and I have an understanding. He is my brother. It seems your visa is in perfect order.'

The customs man clicked his fingers and a youth emerged from the crowd behind him. He tried to take Smiles' leather satchel but Smiles clutched it firmly to his chest.

'My nephew here is your protocol. It is our term for your guide in the airport. Only give him money. Now you will give me *mbongo*, money. I am the only exception to my rules. I am a great lover of the classical playing. I am liking *The Sound of Music*!'

Smiles handed over ten dollars and the official grinned, showing a gold tooth, and two hours later – the hotel sent a car – Smiles was heading through a traffic jam past lines of ragged concrete buildings with rubbish-paved sidewalks crammed with young men and women walking, selling, arguing and eating from plates with their hands at pavement cafés as he tried to stick his passport back together. His driver stopped frequently and boys tapped on the window, selling plastic bags full of water. '*Eau! Peu!*' they cried. A rancid old Pontiac drawn by a horse was holding up an air-conditioned Toyota Land Cruiser. The rust-coloured dust rose around teenagers with straightened hair, comparing their two-tone crocodile shoes at the base of a mango tree. A darting girl wanted to sell him a green-furred monkey whose tail was taped to its scalp like the handle of a handbag. Crowding into the roads, women with poker-straight backs carried sacks of concrete or trays of bananas and even a bleating goat on their level heads. The reds and greens and yellows of their dresses and shawls shouted through the haze. Smiles noted there was no one beyond middle-age.

When he arrived at the hotel, the manager at the desk looked at him nervously and shook his head, until Smiles thought it might fall off.

'Mr S. Miles-Harcourt? The famous Mr Miles-Harcourt? I am so sorry, sir, but your generous concert has been cancelled. Due to unfortunate human failings. And sorry unintended deaths, two days ago.'

Smiles stared at the man.

'Deaths? Is . . . is the other pianist here? Mr Andrew? Mr Lyman Andrew?'

The manager shook his head all the more.

'You have not been told? That is perhaps good. Too much news at once is upsetting for the soul. Your reservation here has been cancelled and you will please go to the Hotel Memling in town. The Hotel Memling is very nice and full of happy people. They will explain everything and what regrettably has happened to Mr Andrew.'

Smiles examined the manager's now-beaming face.

'What . . .? What haven't I been told?'

The man looked awed at the enormity of the question.

'Excuse me, sir. You must go to the Hotel Memling, sir. They will tell you everything there. I am sorry you have been inconvenienced. The Hotel Memling is a fun place with go-ahead, modern guests. You are lucky it is not the Hotel Invest du Presse. That is full of streetwalkers and whores that you may discover in your own bed at any time of day or night.'

Smiles sat for a long time by the too-blue pool at the Hotel Memling, where they were waiting news of his reservation. Around the pool was imported wooden decking. A stubby white Frenchman with a hairy back doing slow, hypnotic lengths stopped to receive a call on a mobile 'phone handed to him by his red-haired, freckled wife. The staff glared from the bar, motionless, until a waiter came over and said: 'Monsieur, your car is waiting.'

'I did not order a car.'

'You must go to the funeral.'

'Whose funeral?'

'The man who was playing in the concert at the Intercontinental? His name is Lyman Andrew. And the other man, S. Miles-Harcourt. A terrible accident, Monsieur. Perhaps a tragic shooting, or a bomb,

I do not know . . . Our television news is often vague and switches to gospel singing at difficult times . . . It is hard to say what has happened and so bad for business. Please hurry, Monsieur. The funeral will not wait and if there is trouble going to happen you do not want the roads to be closed. It is in Gombé cemetery, Monsieur. Where only the best people are buried. If you have dollars, Monsieur, I will watch your cases. But you should go now, sir. Gombé is very nice for funerals. It is where the massacres started last year!'

'But I am S. Miles-Harcourt.'

He was conscious of the rising desperation in his voice.

'So then you must go, Monsieur. There may be family members waiting.'

Smiles rose very slowly from the table. He suddenly did not feel very well. He was not sick. He refused to be sick. They must be playing a joke on him but the boy's eyes did not give anything away.

'Look, there must have been a ghastly mistake.'

The waiter shook his head.

'No mistake, Monsieur. The car has come for you and you must hurry. Cars are not ordered for nothing. It is a Mercedes! A Mercedes! You do not want to miss the funeral, do you, Monsieur? In a Mercedes!'

The dirty blue Mercedes shuddered asthmatically across the chaos of the town to a pleasant district by the river where the houses were bigger and there were flowering trees; flamboyants and frangipani and bougainvillea the Belgians had brought to pretty their colonial idyll. Smiles' attempts to engage the driver in

conversation led to a very Gallic shrug and a '*ne comprends pas
...*' as they weaved dangerously in and out of traffic. It should
have been funny. Seeking to put things right with his past, he
was presently going to his own funeral. He had not needed to
come and play in Kinshasa and everyone he knew had advised
against it. But he had forced himself to come.

'Do you know of an incident at the Hotel Intercontinental where
two pianists were killed? Were they shot? Was it a bomb?' he
asked the driver in his best French.

'Fifteen dollàrs, only new notes,' the driver replied, in English,
stopping the car by the entrance to the cemetery, where women
were reselling wreaths. Smiles dipped into his pocket and pulled
out three fives.

'Do you know what happened to a Monsieur Andrew? An
American?'

The driver sighed.

'If you will get out please, Monsieur?'

When Smiles did, the Mercedes drove off in a cloud of black
smoke and it was only then he noticed the light-green armoured
cars under the trees and the smart soldiers in camouflage uniforms
and bright-red scarves and sunglasses, watching him, the only
European on the street.

He quickly ducked past the wreath resellers and into the cool
of the cemetery and made for a crowd at the other side, holding
tight onto his music satchel. Here and there were more groups
of soldiers standing, reconnoitring the service, where a banner
was being unfurled showing the handsome face of a man with a
rifle who was not Lyman Andrew, although it looked a little
like him. A choir finished singing the wonderful *Missa Luba*

arrangement of the Sanctus that had been a favourite with Lyman Andrew. Smiles paused under a tree, listening to a Congolese priest, who had a stutter. Smiles had not heard a proper stutter since school – a boy from Kenya whose parents had been butchered by the Mau Mau. The service was a Catholic one and he did not know where to put himself as the priest intoned his name.

'. . . L-l-le musicien anglais, Monsieur S-S-Stanley Miles-Harcourt . . .'

The words sent a shiver through him. It was not only in South Africa with his stupid collapse on the piano in the second movement, prestissimo, of Beethoven's sonata no. 30, in E major, opus 109, with its intricate counterpoint, that he had begun to consider mortality. There had been his wife's death in the car he was driving. He could still smell her perfume and the leaking petrol. Death made him feel . . . old. Not that he was old.

He hated the name Stanley and had often thought of getting a solicitor to expunge it from the records. 'Do you see yourself as an explorer in the great Stanley's footsteps?' an interviewer had asked him when he had agreed to do a tour of Africa for his wife's charity. He replied he did not want to be compared to a woman-hating impotent whose main pleasures in life were undeserved publicity and shooting welcoming Africans with a Maxim gun. He then walked out of the radio station.

There was one large grave and three dark wood coffins side by side and he caught himself wondering which one was his. The imprecise roar of panic continued to echo through him. He could hardly breathe. He had the mobile number of the British Ambassador but did not exactly know how to begin. The

Ambassador would think he had gone completely barking mad. 'Do excuse me, Your Excellency, but I find myself at my own funeral. No ... I am quite well. You saw what happened at my last concert on television? Did you? And your wife thought I was drunk? How very amusing.'

Smiles experienced a cramping in his stomach and had actually begun to pray that he would not have to pull his white linen trousers down behind a gravestone when a hand touched his shoulder and so made him jump that he grazed the side of his head on a tree. He was looking into the manically smiling face of a tall and almost atomically eager Congolese, dressed in a shiny, light-blue suit and bright-red bow tie with sequins sewn into the edge and a black-belted raincoat thrown, Italian style, over his shoulders. He did not seem affected by the oven-like heat among the crumbling white stone tombs adorned with carved fruit and European angels around full-size front doors.

The man whispered to him with a conspiratorial hiss.

'It is not often one gets to go to one's own funeral. It is funny, no?'

'No.'

'It is. It is English humour.'

'No.'

The man glanced about him.

'You must come with me quickly. We do not want the *Garde Républicaine* to catch you.'

'Why?'

The man grinned a little wider. It was not a happy grin but one of astonishment.

'They will kill you. They will kill me.'

'Kill? Why on earth would they want to kill me?'

He took a step backwards. Why should he trust this bow-tied creature?

The man shook his head as if Smiles was being dim.

'Because you are already dead. The *Garde Républicaine* has a nasty habit of killing people it considers should be already dead. Come, we must hide a while. Follow me.'

Smiles sighed and allowed himself to be dragged into the shadows and through a rusting iron portal into what he realised, too late, was a tomb. It smelt strongly and unpleasantly of urine and decomposition. On a small platform in darkness at one side he half-saw, half-imagined, the pus-dried, fungal-haunted remains of what was left of a coffin and a twisted body. Insects bit his face and he tried to squash them but they crawled inside his shirt. His bottle of Deet insecticide was in his suitcase. Through a stone grille partially overgrown with creeper he could see the three coffins on the ground outside. Why were there three coffins? Who was in the third?

His foot brushed something which tinkled on the floor.

'Cartridge cases,' said his new friend. 'This is where the *Garde Républicaine*, the ones who wear the red bandannas, the president's personal army, fought the mai-mai of Bemba who is now on trial in The Hague, accused of genocide and eating pygmies and keeping them in his luxury fridges. Do you say refrigerator or cooler? Many thousands of people died in the shoot-out. Pow! Pow! Of course, it was nothing to the five or six millions who perished in our recent civil wars. I have the facts at my own fingernails if you want to know them. But do you know what? Both President Kabila and Bemba sent their children to school that morning so THEY did not know what was going to happen. It started over a beautiful woman. That is a fact. I am telling you this because my country is not . . . how you say in England? Like the home life of your own dear Queen?'

Smiles blinked in the festering darkness. His new friend was trying to joke but Smiles knew by the timbre of his voice that, wherever his real personality was hiding, he was scared too. He could always tell with musicians, in particular accompanying violinists.

'You don't say?'

'Oh, but I do . . . I do say.'

'You said a woman. Which woman?'

'There is always a woman. Always a woman in a story about human beings. *Cherchez la femme!* At least, that is true in Africa. It has to be.'

Smiles was tempted to say 'You don't say?' again, but he didn't.

His eyes became more accustomed to the tomb. There was a suffocating smell of old food and cheap perfume that had sweated into the whitewashed walls alongside the rot. He made out the remains of a stained mattress on the floor and a girl's electric-blue panties.

'Who are you? Why are you helping me?'

He could not quite see the features of the individual but was sure the face was above him. The young man was very tall. Too tall for their chosen sepulchre.

'I am Thérance, sir, at your service. I can speak English, Lingala, Swahili, French, some conversational Japanese from a pack of Nippon Airlines playing cards, and I have a degree from the Educational University, which is conveniently near by. I am a teacher but also an assistant and driver for the great international businessman, Celestine Mbando. He hired me after a British Council production I did of Gilbert and Sullivan. I like Gilbert and Sullivan, especially *The Mikado*. Celestine Mbando is the man who organised the unfortunate and fatal Peace and Reconciliation Concert, the man who spoke with your agent. He sends his condolences. Give me your mobile 'phone. My SIM card is finished and I must send a text . . .'

There was a noise outside and Thérance peered through the grille.

'Oh dear,' he whispered. 'I was hoping the Major-General would not be here. He is not a good human being at all in my estimation. He is the part of our country that we are trying to forget in yesterday. He is like the leopard who sits in the tree and will let no one leave the village.'

Treading on more spent cartridges, Smiles peered though the grille and saw a pensive man in a red beret, leaning over the three coffins as if he too was trying to guess the contents. He was not taller than any of the red-neckerchiefed guards around him but he immediately stood out. He took off his sunglasses and his face was noble, his voice soft.

'Which one is meant to contain my brother?' asked the Major-General, in a French that was clipped and slightly nasal and yet deceptively laid-back. It reminded Smiles of student intellectuals on the Left Bank. The Major-General launched into a short political speech about present dangers. The language was as impeccable as it was passionate: his phrases wound their way through subsections, qualification and the subtleties of a sophisticated intellect that had a hint of the revolutionary past about it, of every fibre of his being directed to an idealistic end he believed was attainable, and, above all right. There was nothing cold about him but he was balanced and precise and formidable. Smiles was not able to see his eyes but he knew from the public school he went to and the way the Major-General held his head what sort of rare man he really was and that worried Smiles.

The crowd melted away from the Major-General as he walked forward. Silence seemed to travel with his graceful movements and left a certain awe in his wake.

The blue-uniformed police had stopped the service and people began to move from the graveside and one man panicked and was running for the entrance. The priest said something in protest but the Major-General held up his hand.

'Break open the coffins.'

The words were almost gentle.

'No, Major-General. Please, you do not want to do that. You are committing a sacrilege.'

For a second a smile played on the handsome face.

'Sacrilege? Perhaps. But I must know if my dear brother is dead to mourn him properly. Not to know the truth, that is sacrilege. Our country is not in order. We cannot have anarchy in the after-life as well, can we, Father? Break it open.'

'*Oui, maintenant*,' said a soldier.

'"He is the very model of a modern major-general,"' Thérance half-sang under his breath.

One soldier produced a bayonet but the coffin had been too firmly nailed and the priest hung his head as a shovel was brought and then rocks and finally a small marble cross was torn from a nearby grave and used to batter in the top of the lid. The dark wood splintered. The lid was torn off and the soldiers reeled back from the choking smell of decomposition that Smiles registered even watching from the tomb. A small, female corpse wearing a black, Sunday-best dress, was shaken out onto the ground and, even though they were frightened, members of the red-hatted choir cried out and moaned in protest. A woman in a pleated white surplice held the side of her face and began to weep.

The Major-General was shaking his head.

'Ahh! There is a problem here. My beloved brother was a fine basketball player and more than two metres tall. He was open to new fashions but he did not, as far as I know, dress as a woman.'

No one spoke. The Major-General tapped the next coffin with his stick.

'Perhaps we will find my poor brother Fortuné in one of the others. It is like a children's game, *vraiment*? Open them up. And then put out arrest warrants for those who are meant to be inside. I want to speak to everyone involved. Oh yes, this is a good joke. But we will see who has the last laugh. Arrest that priest.'

A soldier stepped forward and hit the dignified, middle-aged Father with the side of his rifle and the man's face exploded in blood. The congregation began to scream.

'Now, that was not necessary, Corporal,' said the Major-General with his most charming smile. 'But, Father, you should at least know who your funeral Mass is for. *C'est vrai?* And I want to know the business of everyone here. That is my business. To protect you all.'

It was past midnight and velvety dark when Thérance and Smiles finally opened the metal door of the stinking tomb – Smiles heartily sick of Thérance humming `Three Little Maids' under his breath and asking him ridiculous questions about English, like when to use 'baby' in everyday talk. Did all women react well to the term 'baby', or just the young ones? If one used 'baby' did the girl think one was a rich and powerful American and what exactly was meant by the word 'dude'? And was the term 'get out of here', as used by Eddie Murphy, a command or an expression of confusion? A breeze had not removed the smell from the corpses, which had been left where they fell. Smiles wondered if he really was dead and this was purgatory if not hell itself. It was with sublime relief that he climbed over the crumbling wall of the cemetery even though he ripped his trousers on rusting barbed wire. They scurried across the Gombé district, dodging from tree to tree, like the stray dogs who began to follow their graveyard scent. Yet Smiles had never been so glad of the warm and perfumed darkness, or the night, or the silence.

TWO

Thérance paused nervously in front of a mansion. A patrol car was parked with its doors open and the police inside were drinking beer and a blonde-wigged girl sat on the back seat. Smiles dreaded Thérance turning around with another question. Inside the two-storey, white-walled building a more polite party was going on and Smiles could hear a string quartet and a piano making a moderate job of a minor work by Bach. Thérance stepped out into the light from behind a tree and walked slowly to the police car and, after money changed hands, Smiles, trembling a little, followed him through the security gates. The party was in the garden behind the house and he caught the haunting fragrance of wild patchouli he remembered from a trip to India, with Emma, his late wife.

As he caught up with Thérance he saw an obviously English face and heard the words, 'I am quite serious. My mother sent me a whole case of gooseberry jam!' and Smiles wanted to run towards the individual, who might actually be the British

Ambassador, break down in tears and tell him everything. There was a steely, reassuring authority in the voice and yet a note of kindness that spoke of cricket teas and cowslips on the village green. Smiles had been told the chap here was the absolute best. But Thérance held a door for him and he went inside the marble-floored house where the air-conditioning penetrated his wet shirt. Thérance led him upstairs to a room overlooking the gathering.

'You will please spend the night here, Monsieur Smiles. I will lock you in. Please do not try to go escaping. It will be very damn dangerous for all of us.'

He was about to protest but the door shut, the key turned and Thérance was gone.

Smiles took out his mobile 'phone and sat on the bed, trying to remember the number of a music-loving gay politician he knew in Chelsea who might get onto the Foreign Office for him, if he was sober. The 'phone's light came on but the connection he noticed was for Dieu.com and, after a video and gospel singing, a French voice told him that international calls were not allowed on this SIM card but one could always call on God.

'Thérance!' Thérance had stolen his card like he pilfered language.

Smiles walked to the window and looked down and the number of truly pretty girls amazed him. There were around ten in pink-coloured satin, dancing in a ring by a young couple in a flower-covered white gazebo, their stomachs held in and their backsides stuck out at an obtuse angle. It was at this point Smiles realised he was witnessing a wedding. The invited Congolese men were either dressed in designer suits and ties or in brightly coloured tops and trousers in the same African material; the female guests wore expensive Western dresses or lavish African gowns, mammy cloths and tall, expertly tied headscarves. The women fluttered their intricately painted nails and many of the men waved ivory cigarette holders. They all had a glass in hand, wrapped in a napkin, and giggled and shouted with their heads pressed together in a spirited combination of mayhem and an elaborate politeness that would not have been out of place in seventeenth-century Versailles; except he spotted one man putting a cooked fish down his trousers for later.

Over the wall at the bottom of the garden was the floodlit Congo River. The party seemed to be just warming up. There was a drum roll and a man got up and, after coughing and spitting, started talking very quickly into a microphone and Smiles caught the words 'honoured guest' as the youthful Major-General he had seen breaking up coffins that afternoon took to the stage.

Smiles stood away from the window.

He did not even want to look at the man. Smiles' throat began to close up.

Had Thérance brought him here as a trick? Were they going to break his door down at any moment? He was trapped.

He did not know what to do so he tried to concentrate on little things. He took his malaria pill (one of the essentials he had stuffed in his Florentine leather satchel) with only moderately shaking hands, undressed and slid under the bed's unnecessary mosquito net. On the loudspeaker he kept catching the words 'paix' and 'tranquillité', which the handsome Major-General managed to make sound fatal. Smiles thought of the words from the 23rd Psalm: 'Thou preparest a table before me in the presence of mine enemies.' He was glad when the lilting Congolese music returned and he fell into an exhausted sleep, a childhood prayer on his lips.

Smiles woke with the dawn filtering through his mosquito net and drew it back and padded over to the window. He saw the garden and river clearly now. Several canoes were being steered through the smoky pink light in perfect unison, four men in each, down the fast flow and he could make out where the river dropped away into rapids. He was even able to see astonishing grey-brown waves that reared up high as a house over hidden rocks.

These were the beginning of the cataracts and waterfalls between Kinshasa and the sea. Upriver, beyond Kisangani there were more falls, those 'discovered' by Stanley and, in between, the largest area of jungle on earth. This was a lost world, cut off from the trade routes; an immense, naturally rich backwater. Across the river in Congo-Brazzaville, a separate state that was once French Congo, were huge trees and hints of the wild forest. Below him the garden had tall tropical hardwoods and was blazing with colour. Birds darted among the flowers.

To his surprise there were even the hoops of a dewy croquet lawn and the multicoloured central stick he had not seen since school. For reasons he could not quite fathom, the croquet lawn annoyed him, angered him. He hoped at least the pantomime of yesterday was over and that everything was going to be sorted out. He dressed quickly, bemoaning his now-torn linen suit which was stained with God-knows-what from that tomb. A tomb! He tried to dismiss what had happened from his mind. Deep breaths, live in the present, he told himself. Smile! In the mirror of the bathroom he saw his very serious face was covered in insect bites.

He was going to bang on the door to demand to be let out when he suddenly had the idea of trying the handle. He must keep calm. The handle moved freely and he went downstairs.

The room he came into led onto a large veranda and was tastefully decorated with smoked-glass coffee tables and deep white-leather furniture. On one wall was the stuffed head of a leopard and on the other an African mask. The carpet was thick and gave to the touch of his bare feet. In the centre was a baby grand piano, a Bechstein. Smiles just could not resist, could not prevent himself from going over and pulling back the stool, sitting down and raising the lid and beginning to play. He launched expansively into the Mozart which he was meant to perform at the concert at the Intercontinental, with no thought at all except for the sheer pleasure of doing a task that he was familiar with and entering a territory within whose boundaries and rules he was totally at home; a place where he often hid. He was not sure exactly what made him pause but he felt a tingle on his back, as if he was being watched. He turned and saw her, sitting in the deep white armchair, and he did not know what to say. The power of speech had left him.

'Please continue. I do so love that piece,' she said, in scarcely accented English.

He stared. She was so beautiful. He felt himself a prisoner of her great brown eyes. It was a moment, an intense, soaring moment. As he looked across at her he felt quite dizzy, as light as a feather. The universe seemed to stop in time and the stars change their places. He had loved but this was a state beyond, only glimpsed through the music of others.

'You recognise it?' His words were a little too sharp. He had the impression she had been crying.

'I do,' she smiled. She had heard the music played by the priest in Yangambi and in Kisangani at an old lady's she visited when she was at the Lycée.

But Smiles did not resume his playing. He continued to stare at her.

'Don't worry,' she said. 'Like you, I am hiding from Xavier . . . the Major-General.'

Thérance had told her the Englishman was going to be difficult but she adored the delicate way he touched the piano and how his mouth turned up as he smiled when he first saw her. He was not the stuffy, middle-aged concert pianist she had expected. He did not seem old at all and she approved of the way the Englishman's black hair fell and the whiteness of his skin, which she wanted to stroke, it was so brilliantly white, icing-sugar white, the white of mountain snow on Mount Kilimanjaro she had only seen in films. He had such large blue eyes and his lips were so red. She felt for his helplessness, his obvious anger at not being in control of his situation, or Congo, or anything. She had never known an Englishman. His big, blue eyes had such long lashes, almost like a girl's.

'Are you a friend of Thérance?' he finally asked. She knew that he wanted something, anything, to say as the tension built between them. He was glancing at her legs and pretending not to. She wore a short blue dress and her long legs were stretched out in front of her. She had always been aware of the effect she had on men. A silk scarf was tied carefully around her neck.

'We have soon to leave,' she said.

'Now just a minute . . .' he began.

'We have to leave,' she said. 'Both you and I. Believe me, it is not safe here. You have been lucky so far. But if they catch you here with me . . .' She made the words as definite as she could. She liked the musician but hoped he was not going to be trouble.

'I must go to my embassy. It is close by, isn't it? Thérance said this is the Embassy district.'

She raised her eyebrows.

'Don't you want to see your friend, Lyman Andrew? Thérance said that's why you came to Congo to play the concert at the Intercontinental. They do not usually get the top musicians like you. They don't usually get anyone. The American will be so pleased to see you. I am sure you can spare the time. How long is it since you saw him?'

Smiles looked away and began to wind his wristwatch.

'I thought he was dead,' he said after a minute. His furtive manner puzzled her.

She shook her head. Her hair was a mass of tight black ringlets tied up at the back. She fluttered her hands.

'There was a small explosion which gutted the area where you were due to rehearse. The concert was meant to heal old wounds. Three kitchen staff were killed. Please excuse the deception about your death. We thought it was safer that way. It was said you had arrived on an earlier flight. It gave us time to get people out.'

Smiles had been about to explain to her he had presumed Lyman Andrew dead years ago before reading his name on the concert billing.

'Safer? Get who out?'

She stood up and stepped slowly over to the piano.

'Xavier's younger brother, Fortuné, and his aide. Xavier, was at the wedding last night and at that disgusting incident at the graveyard. I am so sorry about that. Xavier is an obsessive, unpredictable man. Though totally honest. He is not out for himself. I cannot believe he planted this bomb, though others do. Your friend Lyman Andrew did not arrive from the east, which was just as well. I am told he has a tendency to be outspoken. My cousin said the talk among the bridesmaids was of a coming coup d'état. Are you helping finance this? A coup . . .?'

Her eyes were teasing. But he was looking too closely to notice.

Smiles was gazing up at her in astonishment. She was the most beautiful woman he had ever seen. She was tall with a broad face and almond-shaped eyes which were very African but at the same time were delicate and almost feline. Her lashes were very long and her mouth wide and she looked as if a committee had picked her as the symbol of African womanhood. Her breasts pushed against the material of her dress and he could see her large nipples. The stupid words, 'The Queen of Sheba brought me spices, gold, and her skin scented with sherbets and quince', a phrase his father used to shout at his mother when she brought him a gin and tonic, echoed through Smiles' brain. There was a breathtaking sting of adolescence, the forbidden thrill of staring into dark eyes; and feeling he had known them for ever. He was perfectly conscious of what she was saying and at the same time not at all. She put her long-fingered hand on his shoulder and he positively trembled. The meaning of her words struck home.

'A coup? A political coup d'état? Me? Don't be ridiculous. I play the piano.'

She laughed.

'Don't shoot the piano player, eh? Well, I am afraid that's why Xavier and the government think that you are connected with Lyman Andrew, and even worse, with his good friend, Xavier's brother, Fortuné. Now that the opposition leader Jean-Pierre Bemba has been arrested for war crimes, those opposed to the Kabila government are supporting Fortuné. Xavier is on the side of Kabila until such time as he succeeds him.'

Smiles vaguely remembered reading about Bemba's arrest in the South African papers.

'Did this Fortuné come to Kinshasa to take over the government?' he asked, as she stood even closer to him. She wore an expensive French perfume.

She shook her head prettily. Her long, gold earrings caught the light. But she did not answer him.

'What's your name?' he said.

It seemed absurd he did not know her name.

'My name is Lola. My full name is Désirée Dolores Leila Mbanda, but my father always used to call me Lola. It means paradise in Lingala.' She turned from him and walked out onto the veranda. 'My father was a good and kind man who was killed fighting in the war against the Rwandans. He wanted me to marry the Major-General who is looking for you. He admired Xavier's strengths. He saw the good in him. Poor Xavier. He brought my family gifts. I was with him for a time but we fell out of love. I left him and went to his brother, Fortuné. He is . . . gentler. I had known them since school. I met Fortuné outside the concert before the bomb.

We have been parted for nearly a year. I was very much in love with him but . . . I do not know. It is all so confusing. And now Xavier is sending me poems. He says I am still his only wife.'

Smile's mouth had fallen completely open.

'You are his . . . wife?'

'In a sense. In the old custom. But I am a modern woman.'

'And he sends you poems?'

For all his eloquence the Major-General had not seemed the poetic type.

But tears had begun to roll down Lola's lovely face and Smiles was getting to his feet as the door burst open. She quickly wiped her eyes.

A debonair, middle-aged Congolese in a smart black African collarless 'abacost' jacket, the kind favoured by dictators, sprang towards Smiles and shook his hand. He then threw his arms around Smiles, chuckling and showing the large gap between his top two teeth. Smiles tried to pull away but the man held on and his twinkling eyes stared deep into his. The few lines on the African's face were from laughing too much and his shaved head glistened. He had an ironic slant to his wide mouth and smelt of musk and cologne and cigar smoke.

'Mr Miles-Harcourt! How good to meet you! My name is Celestine. There is not a moment to lose. You have met Thérance and Lola, I see. And this imp of Satan is St James, Lola's younger brother.' A lanky adolescent in a large blue basketball top and shorts watched Smiles with a coolness and a presence that unnerved him.

The youth went over and sat on his heels in the corner.

'Thérance says you are a fan of Gilbert and Sullivan?'

Smiles replied defensively: 'No. My luggage is at the Memling.'

Celestine put his hands together in a gesture of prayer.

'Aah ... I'm afraid not, old boy. Thérance checked and it's gone. Welcome to the kleptocracy which is Congo. All you have is that splendid leather bag of yours. And, of course, your talent. I have had such entertaining talks with your agent. But I must advise that if you turn up in any of the places one would expect, like your hotel, you will be as dead as boiled mutton. They will put you before a firing squad. I am not joking. They shot a Belgian birdwatcher last week because he was wearing shorts and boots and they decided he was a mercenary. Come into the car. We are going to pick up the rest of the crew.'

'The crew? Of a plane?'

Smiles glanced at the lovely face of Lola, hoping they were all going to fly out. He did not care about his luggage.

'A plane?' said Celestine. 'No, a boat. No one goes by boat. No one will expect it and therefore it's safer. We will go up to Kisangani and then to your friend, Lyman Andrew. He hasn't got a piano at the moment and we are taking him one. We are going to commandeer the one that was played at the wedding and stage the Peace and Reconciliation Concert upriver. In Kisangani. It's a rather good piano that I am sure you will approve of. Much better than this dwarf Bechstein. The one we will take was meant for the concert at the Intercontinental and I am going to let no one stand in the way of art, in particular Xavier. The Major-General thought everything about our concert was subversive and an affront to the government and to him. Lyman Andrew needs the piano, there are none suitable outside the capital, and he'll be so pleased to see you as well. I bet you never expected this sort of adventure! You must be excited! Don't worry, you will be quite safe. Safe as Piccadilly!'

Celestine twirled a Bombay cheroot in his beringed fingers.

There was a silence and underneath the flippancy Smiles detected a shared sense of danger.

'But . . . Kisangani is in the middle of Congo. It's nearly two thousand kilometres away. More than a thousand miles!' said Smiles. 'It's . . .' He did not say any more. Even he knew that Kisangani was the headquarters of Kurtz. It was the heart of darkness in Conrad's novel.

Celestine sighed.

'I was told by your agent you had nothing much planned for the month because of your health. He said there were to be no concerts in Nairobi. Our trip will do you good! And your health may suffer a permanent reversal if you stay here. Kinshasa is not safe for you, my dear. All the posters went up for the concert and there is your handsome and very white face on them, old chap. After the coup attempt by those Brits in Guinea everyone is a bit on edge. They'd string you up with your own piano wire. By the way, did you hear that motorbike this morning? That's the President riding his new toy. A Harley-Davidson motorcycle! A present from his good friend Michael Jackson. He tends to leave boring matters of state to the government or the army.'

Smiles began to wonder if the man called Celestine was right in the head.

His jacket and leather music satchel were brought from upstairs as he was trying to frame a 'but'.

'Are you coming, too?' he asked Lola.

She gave him a radiant smile.

'Yes,' she said, helping him on with his jacket. She was taller than him in her three-inch high-heels.

'I have to see Fortuné. There is much to be said between us. He might be at Mbandaka, which is a few days upriver. We may be able to get you out from there on a MissionAir flight. If you don't want to see your friend, that is.'

Celestine beamed.

'It is hoped we can play the concert on the radio from upriver. And put it on people's mobile 'phones and the Internet. A viral gesture for peace the government cannot argue with! Don't worry, my boy, you will be safe. Safe as Piccadilly!'

Lola watched Smiles closely in the back of the car as he tried to conceal his mounting fear and confusion. She assumed that as an important concert pianist he must have his life arranged and mapped out. The few white men she had met spent a lot of time on personal organisers and other electronic devices, which were then stolen. She imagined that other people arranged Smiles' flights and itineraries when he played in the safe countries where he performed for the rich and educated. She saw that he had pride in what he did. She felt like putting her arm around him. He must really love his friend to come to Congo to try and see him again. Lola noticed how Smiles swept his hair back nervously and she remembered the word 'foppish' from her English classes, though not in a bad way. They turned into the Matongé district and began to pass the clubs and clothes stores and music shops. The big Chrysler they were in halted outside a booth where two men's heads were being shaved, and a pink-painted club called Herman's.

'Go in there and wait with Lola. Lola, you know the way through the back if anyone comes in? No one will. Not here,' said Celestine and they got out and walked past the man at the cage-like door into the club. It was only mid-morning but still the end of the party the night before. A few girls were drinking at the bar on high stools and, above, the corrugated iron roof had started to cave in. On the floor were aluminium tables and chairs and round the walls were brightly painted murals of chubby-faced men. A couple were dancing, their hips glued together, legs spread apart and bottoms swooping near the ground. No one paid Smiles any particular attention even though he was surely the only European in the district.

One man smiled and nodded at Lola. She ignored him, and then whispered in Smiles' ear: 'Look, now they do the *ndombolo* dance. It means buttocks in Lingala and you have to stick out your bottom. It is illegal in Cameroon as part of the anti-Aids drive. Our last President, the current one's father, was going to ban it because he thought it was about his very fat backside. But his fourteen-year-old bodyguard shot him first. Mostly in the *ndombolo*. The pictures around the walls are of the heroes of our music scene. There is Papa Wemba. That's Itsy. I am sorry you are mixed up in all of this.'

He gave a little snort that amused her.

'So am I,' he said, and tried to laugh.

She laughed with him.

It was a long time since she had met a man with a self-deprecating sense of humour.

The waiter came and joyfully banged two very cold Primus beers on the table and, not thinking, she opened both of them with her teeth.

Smiles looked at her, appalled.

'People do that here,' she said.

'But your teeth?'

'Are very strong.' She giggled. 'Do not look at me like that!'

'I'm sorry.'

She held out her hand to him. She had painted her long nails. She wished they were already on the boat but she felt a wild sense of freedom with this stranger.

'Do you want to dance, Smiles? I like this one.'

He glanced round at the couple and shook his head.

But she was pulling him to his feet and he was on the floor by the *ndombolo* couple. Another couple joined them.

'Don't move your feet, Smiles. Stop it! People will think you are possessed by demons! Where did you learn such dancing? By putting fire ants in your shirt? That's it. Better. That's almost good.' And slowly he drew her body nearer as all the time she watched the metal grille which led out onto the teeming street.

Then she said: 'Please tell me why you came all this way to see an old friend, Smiles? Why is the American, Lyman Andrew, so very important to you?'

THREE

On that last fatal day in Kisangani, the boy, St James, opened the first handwritten packet of Smiles' papers and read them, after a fashion. St James' English needed work but the language was clear. He had seen Smiles with the completed papers, spread out on a table from his leather bag, when he got on the boat but here and there more recent, messier comments had been added in brackets. St James immediately liked the title, though. Did it mean that the man Smiles was a murderer? From what he had learned about murderers throughout the uprisings in 1999 and 2000 and then the civil war, he doubted that. He did not think Smiles could be a murderer in his human form. Perhaps he turned into an octopus and wrapped his eight arms around his victims. The man Smiles always tried to make jokes when you got to know him yet at heart he was serious. He was very serious about Lola.

My Confession:
Stanley Miles-Harcourt: black book, packet one

I am not quite sure why I am writing this down for you, Dr Kaplan. I do not think the cause of my collapse was psychological, merely over-work, and I am not sure of the importance you put on this one story. I will try to make it readable: criminals always have good prose style because they have no special regard for their actions or words. I think if it is told out of context, like this, the wickedness seems greater than it is ... And as the narrative took me over, to make it more readable for you, dear Dr Kaplan, I have put it down in direct speech as in a novel. You also have to understand that my story is set in a place curi-ously out of time with the rest of things (much like Congo) but I will tell the whole truth and now may have a chance to make amends with the man whose life I so thoroughly ruined. (Somehow, with the events taking place at the moment and because I have finally fallen in love, it is a duty I feel I have to perform.

It was in the Michaelmas term at my old school in Hertfordshire in the drifting, angry Britain which led up to Margaret Thatcher and I was fourteen and loved the school in my way although everyone said they did not. Even after what happened there I still remember the place as very beautiful, the soaring warm emeralds of the horse-chestnut trees, the dark strawberry brick and creamy Portland stone. Around a central quad, cloisters ran to four fairy-tale towers, identical to those of the Houses of Parliament and designed by the same architect. These in turn were dominated by a stone tower with a clock. The school was surrounded by acre upon acre of playing fields and gardens and woods and was run by the Universal Brotherhood of Freemasons for the sons of deceased Masons. We were there because we all shared the vertiginous finality

*of our fathers, or even both parents, having died. You were not allowed
to pay in any other way, for anything. Until I was eighteen all my shoes
were made by hand in the cobbler's shop.*

Our motto was `Aude, Vide, Tace'. Hear, See, Be Silent.

*(It was the sort of motto you would expect of a school run by a secret
society. It also said something of the somewhat detached English attitude to death and all emotion. I am sure even a hairy Boer like yourself can appreciate that, Dr Kaplan. And we were all exiles, orphans in
transit, prisoners, slaves, very much part of the present shifting post-
modernity but fetched up in a training ground for the imperial past.
We lost more boys in combat under the Union Jack than any other public
school. Dr Freud would have possibly said we were natural-born killers,
a den of sharp-toothed little Oedipuses, whose dreams were stalked by
the fear we had murdered our dead father and by the guilty rasp of our
mother's pubic hair and the snap of her suspender belt. Though on the
surface we were very polite, Dr Kaplan. We were famous for our politeness in the local shops and tea rooms.)*

We were in our morning break between lessons.

*'Smiles, you've got to swap from fagging for the housemaster to this
new man,' said a friend, who had smuggled us coffee made in the prefects'
kitchen into the tuck-box room as John Lennon sang `Imagine' on a
tinny old radio. The friend giggled.*

'The new Latin master? No one told me . . .'

*'Old Mr Reid's not coming back because of that fifth-former who set
fire to his balsa-wood model of the Colosseum when he wasn't looking,'
said a voice by the window.*

*'The new bloke's moving into the Colonel's old rooms in Derby
House,' said my friend with the coffee. I had a lot of friends back then.
'You have to clean his shoes and make his fire. I don't know what else*

*he'll expect you to do. Jammy change of slavery if you ask me.' He
laughed.*

'What's he like?'

*The other six boys in the room stared back at me. They were on the
verge of giggles, too. One was biting his lip.*

*'Oh, I'd say he was better than the Colonel. But . . . different. You'll
see. You have to go to him right now. He wants you to clean his kit, I
suppose.'*

'Is he going to be doing army?'

*They seemed to find this hilarious. I can see them now, reddened
faces, shaking.*

'What's so funny?'

*'You come back and tell us,' said my friend Pinky. Pinky Grey was
not my best friend, David Wace had been. A very dear friend. We had
a falling-out. He had taken something very precious of mine and . . .
(But that's not for now, Dr Kaplan.)*

*I slid off my tuck box, which still was perfumed with a quince my
mother had sent me, and went out of the door, closing it behind me and
heard another eruption of laughter. I didn't know what they were laughing
at but I did not mind. They were all my friends. It was the sort of place
where you had to stick together. And I lived up to my nickname, Smiles.
That's how I coped. That's how I've always coped. My smile never left
me from the first day. My mother said I was good-looking and my smile
was raised slightly on the left side where I had an ingenuous dimple.
It was a better defence than fists or running as here there was nowhere
to run and I was careful: my smile was never rebellious or insouciant
or sneering.*

*I wanted to please, much more than anyone else: it was almost a
curse.*

I had liked being the housemaster's fag. There were only two pairs of shoes to clean and he never wanted me to make up his fire as he enjoyed doing it himself. He was not part of the cadet corps, which was all-day army on Tuesdays and Fridays and voluntary, although if you did not join you were expelled.

The new master's study was at the top of one of the towers that formed the four corners of the quad. I passed Matron's room on the first floor and her dog, a sheltie, began to bark and bark as it always did. The Colonel had often threatened to shoot it but had gone back to his Scottish estates, where he went when his drinking made him see blue mice in the turn-ups of his trousers. There were two sorts of masters, the very good ones and those who were mad, bad or just useless and owed their job to the Masons. The fencing master had actually killed a boy in a duel at another school, so it was with trepidation I approached the new bloke's door, even though Latin masters were usually pretty boring.

The door to the rooms was open. Down a corridor there was a bedroom on one side and a bathroom on the other.

Ahead was the sitting room and study with one of the Colonel's massive stag's heads over the fireplace. The windows were closed and the place stank of spilled port and forgotten cigars. Then I froze.

A cool-looking, young black man was standing in front of me with an assured, radiant grin on his face. He had that casual assurance that boys from really well-off families with titles had; like a Moorish prince.

His denim shirt was open. He was wearing blue jeans and in his right hand was a knife. In his left hand a cigar. He tried to use the knife to open a window catch and then turned back to me.

At first he did not seem real.

He was too handsome. Like a male model from a Sunday magazine.

41

His face was perfectly proportioned. He reminded me of an actor I had seen.

Why was he trying to open the window from inside? Robbers don't usually try to break out.

Had he escaped from a mental hospital? (There were a lot near by, in between the boarding schools.)

There was no one black in our school or the village.

We had two Indians from Bombay but no one from Africa or the West Indies.

The man's skin had an almost purplish darkness, a deep blackness. But in a sudden burst of sunshine from the window it looked lighter, the colour of grey ash. His muscles stood out on his stomach and his chest, just like in the Leonardo book in the art school. He looked straight at me and his eyes were smiling as well as his curling lips. What was a black man doing in the new master's rooms? Had he broken in? Was he a pervert? A murderer?

I swallowed. I could shout or run but up here no one would hear me and he'd catch me on the stairs. He stood watching and I wondered if he was a friend of the Colonel, who was fond of Paris and once brought back a roller-skating waiter.

The man came towards me.

He held out his hand.

'Hi, I'm Lyman Andrew.'

The accent was American but nicely spoken. It was not like that of a gangster or a cowboy.

'I'm going to take over as temporary Latin master here.'

'Sir?'

'You don't have to call me "sir".'

I did have to call him 'sir', just like I had to keep the middle button of my jacket done up at all times or not sunbathe in long grass or wear swimming trunks in the swimming pool unless I became a school prefect.

The rules were the school and they were power. Whoever you were, if you stood in their way you were crushed. Often in sermons the head-master told us those standing in the way needed to be crushed, like in ancient Rome, of which he was fond. 'Carthago delenda est,' *he would exclaim in his shy voice.* 'Carthage must be destroyed.' *He meant it.*

I must have looked anxious.

He still held the large clasp knife.

So I smiled my biggest smile and he grinned even wider, showing his perfect teeth. The man had the most incredible smile that hung between his cheekbones like the moon on its side.

'The new Latin master?'

I very nearly said: 'Are you sure?' *but stopped myself. He had now taken my hand and was shaking it.*

'I was told to come up, sir. To be your fag. My name is Miles-Harcourt but everyone calls me Smiles. My first name is Stanley and I don't like it much.'

He stopped shaking my hand and looked puzzled. His expression changed and he cocked his head on one side, like I was taking the mickey.

I tried to explain: 'A fag cleans your shoes, sir, and runs errands and makes the fire and if you have a uniform I have to press it and clean your belt and brasses and your sword.'

'My sword? What?'

He laughed uproariously.

'I don't have a uniform and I certainly don't have a sword. My God! Where have I landed? For a moment there, the word "fag" had me confused. It means different things in the States. I'm from Boston. I just finished at Harvard. "Fag"?'

I pretended to laugh with him. My question was not so innocent.

'What does it mean over there, sir? In America?'

He regarded me carefully.

'I'd say you have a better idea of what it means in America than I have of what it means here.'

'Queer, sir?'

'Yes,' *he said.*

'Do you want me to do your shoes now, sir?'

Again he seemed surprised and a little moody:

'No. I never want you to do my shoes. I never, ever want you to do my shoes. I think grown men should be able to clean their own shoes or leave them dirty if they think fit. I don't like the idea of shoeshine boys. For me it has a connotation I think you are intelligent enough to appreciate. I just wanted to meet you. I need a friend to steer me around this place. Harvard has the same coloured bricks and stones but I'm sure there are many differences. My father thought it would be a good idea to come here for a term and decide what I am going to do for the rest of my life. I had quite a heavy year and he wanted me to get a bit of peace and quiet. I had a cousin who came over to England ten years ago to get away from the draft . . . I need a friend. Can you open this window? I didn't want to stink the place out with my cigar.'

I hit the window frame at the place the Colonel had showed me. It opened.

'A friend?' *I repeated.*

'Do I have to pay for fagging?'

'Pay? No, sir.'

'I mean what I say. I want a friend in this place.'

He was trying to communicate more than what he was saying to me.

44

But I was not sure what he wanted. Prefects just said straight if they wanted a boy to rub them up. He had a tattoo, a bird of some kind, just above his belt line and that was not a secret I could easily share with anyone or they would accuse me of having sex with him. I dreaded what they were going to say anyway ... A few of the masters and most of the prefects bummed or got sucked off or rubbed up by their YD – young delectable – fags and there was nothing the fags could do. A senior's word was always worth more than a junior's. I had been lucky. My housemaster was only interested in fives and tying elaborate fishing flies he never used as he had not got a fishing rod.

'It's warmer if you have a fire, sir. I can make one. For the draughts.'

He tilted his head to one side again. He put down the knife on the table and I felt relieved.

'I meant going to the army.'

'Sorry, sir, but I thought you weren't going to do the cadet corps.'

He sighed.

It was then I saw a shiny piano, which must have been brought from the music school.

'Do you play?' he asked.

I nodded.

'It's my best subject, sir. They can't stop me when I get in the music school ... We have a piano in the house day room but you are not allowed to play it except for special times like Christmas.'

He opened the key lid: 'Play something now, will you?'

I sat down and ran through of bit of the Brahms' Lullaby I had learned for an exam.

I stopped, embarrassed. He laughed sympathetically.

'My God, that was really good, exceptional!'

'Thank you, sir.'

'No, truly. The piano is my best thing, too. I am all right at Latin but I play the piano professionally and when I say you are good, you are good. Perhaps we can play together? I'd like that. I am going to keep the key for the piano in this little drawer in my desk. Feel free to come up here and practise any time. You have a real talent. Music as a form of self-expression is a basic human right. Only don't let anyone clean the keys. I hate them sticking. Well, we are going to be friends now, Smiles.'

The next day I sneaked into Lyman Andrew's rooms and searched out his shoes. He had three pairs of good quality, two black and one brown. One of the black pairs were brogues like the other masters wore and were new. The others were slip-ons, without laces, and looked fashionable and expensive. They were not as good as the housemaster's handmade Lobbs. But they were not meant to last for ever. There was the same Italian name in each of the shoes and Fifth Avenue underneath. I cleaned all of them thoroughly. First, I checked each of them for mud, of which there was none. Then I did them normally with the polishes I brought with me, borrowed from the housemaster, who I was sure would not mind. Anyway, he had two Lobb's polishing kits and was away playing fives against another school. The casual shoes had not been cleaned for a while. I paid close attention to the underneath, in the space between the front sole and the heel, which most prefects insisted on. Fags often got beaten for missing this. The shoes did not pong at all, only of the best leather. I then set about spit-and-polishing the brogues where you put polish on the shoe and then spit on a cloth and rub it round and round. You have to do that with the toes of military boots. But it brings up brogues nicely. I did not want Lyman Andrew to be at any disadvantage. I didn't think he had been in a boarding school before.

He didn't understand where he was, what sort of place he had come to. He never had the sort of mind that connected directly with the things around him or the dangers behind politeness. He saw everything through the prism of the ideal. I had never met anyone like him and have not since.

I searched in his wardrobe for a uniform, in case he had been joking around with me. Americans do. We had some American boys from a school in Georgia and they joked around. They joked around less by the time they went home.

The suits and shirts of Lyman Andrew were really amazing but he couldn't wear most of them in the common room, where the masters played billiards. He had several pairs of blue-denim jeans and white T-shirts. I had never seen a master wearing blue denim and T-shirts. He did not have a military uniform issued and I gave a sigh of relief.

I made up the fire next, which was easy, and then took the piano key out of the desk and sat down. The piano was a good one. The touch and the sound were totally different to our wrecked day-room piano. I improvised a bit of a crap Abba song I had picked up. We always had a piano at home when I was little and my father played by ear.

On the piano was a photograph of two people I took to be Lyman Andrew's father and mother and another with him at a concert. They looked really happy.

My father had died when I was nine and my mother had never recovered. He had brought her flowers at any excuse, like England winning a Test match, even though she did not follow cricket, except on the green of the little village outside Oxford where we lived, and only if he played. She made his gin and tonic and waited for the sound of his grey Jaguar scrunching up the gravel drive. One night he managed to pull his car under a street light and had a heart attack. (This final uncharacteristic *act of tidiness always makes me feel angry and suspicious. Like when I see croquet hoops abroad, Dr Kaplan.) Everyone said how considerate he was. In the war he had been a pilot and won the DFC but never spoke about those days. Mother listened to his favourite records over and over again, as if he might step back, absent-mindedly but without fuss, into her life for his gin and tonic.*

'The Queen of Sheba brought me spices, gold, and her skin scented with sherbets and quince.'

My parents were ghosts even in my imagination.

I packed up the shoe brushes and was about to leave when I saw a letter on the desk. The letter was 'From Paris and Martha' and 'To our dear son'. The supper bell made me jump. I only had time to read a bit.

'You take as long as you want, my boy, my good boy. I have no doubt of your noble intentions whatsoever. Take time out in the calm of this British school to sort out your thoughts and ambitions. Your record at Harvard was exemplary and your playing has never been better. But let this be a time of quiet for you. The Masons are good people. They organised the Underground Railroad to get freed slaves to the North. Lincoln was a Mason . . .' Where did the man think his son had come to?

There was a crucifix on the wall next to a picture of a very young Lyman Andrew in black tie. 'Playing piano at Carnegie Hall', it said underneath.

His parents had both written other stuff that I could not make out easily. There were a lot of kisses. I don't know why but I put my lips against the kisses.

My mother was a Christmas and Easter Catholic. But the reassuring smell of incense and the vice of dogma had not stopped her taking two bottles of yellow Nembutal sleeping pills, which she kept under the bed.

(Don't make too much of this, Dr Kaplan, as I got over it at school pretty quickly.) She badly wanted to join my father where he had stopped in silence under the street light. To her that tidy act was greater than God. But it was not to be. With her short-sightedness she took his equally sickly yellow lumbago pills by mistake. She said he was looking out for her from beyond the grave. My family were almost normal compared to other boys' parents. Kydd senior's mother had blown up his father in a potting shed with dynamite from the family quarries. And however strange matters were at any boy's home, there was always something odder at the school itself. (That is until I came to Congo, Dr Kaplan, you fucker, you total saint!)

Then the bell was calling, calling for lessons and I ran off.

St James sighed. There was so much that he did not understand. This was the problem with the white man. He told too little or too much and one was left wandering . . . lost. What were sherbets and quince? What was a tuck box? Was Smiles taught at school about the octopus and other matters? Why was he a servant to a black man? Was he a slave? St James' head felt full of jungle bees. Smiles' school was an enchanted world governed by strange bells and he put the papers back in their packet.

FOUR

Smiles felt so strangely protected, so very removed from his real life, dancing in Lola's arms. He was tempted to tell her why he needed to see Lyman Andrew again but it was impossible, even in the broader moral climate of Congo.

'Lyman Andrew . . . encouraged me a lot with the piano when I was at school. You could say he was my mentor.' He felt a difference immediately in how she held his hand. As if she could tell he was being economical with the truth. They sat down again and she had a delicate sip of her beer and smiled at him.

'I can imagine you as a schoolboy,' she said.

He laughed.

'Wearing a little cap and a blazer? Even now I am so ancient?'

She looked at him, surprised.

'You are not ancient.'

'Well, I used to be much younger. I had a scare recently when I collapsed in South Africa. But it was overwork.' He started to tell her about the suspected heart attack, the brass hand gripping where his shoulder met his neck, the siren of the ambulance and thinking he was going to die but the story was drowned out by the criss-cross guitar rhythms of the music. Instead he felt the breathless excitement of a school dance. 'Where did you go to school? Here in Kinshasa?'

He immediately regretted saying it.

She shook her head, watching him.

'No. I am from a village not far away from Kisangani. But there is no school there so I went to the next big village and to Kisangani and then to Kinshasa. I am still in my first year at the university here. I think they will allow me to repeat the year. After the trouble. I was too close to both Fortuné and Xavier and everyone knew they fought over me. The head of my faculty told me to stay away.'

'How ... how old are you?' Her eyes kept him guessing. At times they were very wise; at others focused on a distant panic he could not even imagine.

'How old am I?'

Lola was surprised.

She shrugged.

'Seventeen. I jumped a year when I was doing the *baccalauréat*.'

Lola liked the way Smiles showed what he felt in his face.

'You must be very clever.' he said. 'To go to university so early.'

He obviously thought she must be older to be the lover of Major-General Xavier and Fortuné.

'No. It's normal here. I grew up in the war years and could not go out and play. If my family was in Kisangani I had to stay inside all the time. The teachers would finish the syllabus quickly in case the school was blown up or they were killed. If we were in the village or fled to the jungle there was nothing to do. It was good to work and I learned my English from an uncle who had a job with the British Council in Nairobi. He is why I don't have much of an accent.' Smiles appeared sympathetic. Whatever his secret, he was a sensitive man but had no way of knowing about her life and the war. She thought of how she used to do her Latin homework by the light of a wick burning in a sardine tin; an oil lamp much like the Romans had, with the Ugandan and Rwandan invaders fighting among themselves over the diamonds and the coltan, the mineral in every mobile 'phone. For days the bullets splattered against the side of the house until her aunt and one of her cousins died of shock. She could still taste the concrete dust as she lay on the floor and puzzled over tenses and the use of the gerundive.

'If death grins at you, grin back.'

'What?' Smiles seemed alarmed.

'Something I was taught at school. Marcus Aurelius.'

'You were taught his "Meditations"?'

'For the *baccalauréat*. The war did not stop us.'

He took a nervous sip of his beer and then another.

'God, that's good.'

'It's the only good thing the Belgians taught us. That and kissing.'

'Kissing?'

'I am joking.'

He laughed and then she said: 'Will Lyman Andrew like the piano?'

He nodded.

'He'll be very pleased. Delighted. It's generous of Celestine.'

She shook her head.

'I should be very careful of Celestine Mbando and his man, Thérance. No one ever knows whose side Celestine is on. I don't think you quite understand the piano was lent for the wedding and the concert by Xavier himself from the Académie des Beaux-Arts, which he has spent a lot of time and money restoring. The piano is said to be valuable. To steal it for the concert upriver and the broadcast is an insult and very political. Fortuné, his brother, who usually cannot resist a gift, may not want it precisely because it is associated with Xavier. That's why I asked will Lyman Andrew want it?'

She saw fear overtake Smiles.

'Xavier will come after you?'

She did not answer him. Several men sidled hesitantly into the club and she guessed from the way they stood and stared awkwardly around that they must be the crew. She got up and led them to the table. '*M'boté, mama, malamu,*' they said. Hello, mama, how are you? Six more followed and then Thérance, Celestine Mbando and her lanky younger brother. She tried to give him a hug but he dodged away.

And then they sat and waited all day and into the night. Food was brought in and many Primus beers were drunk and the club became so packed they could not move. It was nearly three in the morning of the next day when the two-tone horn of an army van blasted through the sound system in the club and the blue lights played on the white ceiling and she could feel that Smiles thought they were coming in to get him. Lola held his hand under the table. He should not be mixed up in this, he really should not.

Then Celestine said:

'I think it is time now to be on our merry way. We should get to where we take the boat upriver during daylight. It's two hours by road.'

Smiles felt a surge of excitement as he walked, half-slid, down the mud chutes to the river at what the crew told him was the small port of Maluku with the dawn coming up downstream over Pool Malebo. The light was grey, and although it was very warm to him, the crew shivered and a wind was getting up, bending the trees along the muddy paths by the river, and the canoes knocked into each other with a deep, wooden noise. He glanced around for the boat.

'There she is,' said Celestine. 'We will go on that one.'

'But . . .'

'Look, they are floating the piano out to her, we cannot take it along the dock because it was all blown up in the war. And then they will use the crane to lift it onto the boat. I have told them to be most careful. You have not seen the piano, have you? It is a very good one. It should have never been allowed out of the Académie for the wedding.'

Smiles blinked at the dawn as he saw the jet-black piano, which had been lashed to two pirogues with ropes, being manoeuvred out into the current by paddlers standing in the stem and the stern of the canoes, each hacked out of a single forest log. They brought the instrument alongside a ninety-foot-long wooden craft with a roof of rush and bamboo matting and a bridge that looked as if it was falling apart. The boat had once been blue and white and was tied close to an old crane at the end of a ruined dock.

The paint was flaking but he was able to make out the name, *Le Rêve*, The Dream. He was going aboard a dream boat. The river was not wide here, perhaps only four hundred yards, and he saw the paddlers on the canoes slip ropes under the piano. After a small explosion, a cloud of smoke and a cheer the crane's engine clattered into life and, very nearly destroying *Le Rêve*'s thatched roof, the jet-black piano was winched up from the canoes and swung into place on deck in her bows. Another cheer followed and he was aware that people in the port were pointing at him.

'They want you to go and play. The crew have said it is your piano. They have never heard a piano. Not in all their born days,' said Thérance. 'You will play for them and they will be happy until they die.'

Smiles stared at Thérance, wondering if the piss was being taken, but then realised the man who had learned his English from Dickens, Gilbert and Sullivan and bubble-gum wrappers was quite sincere. Lola was looking at him too, so he picked his way along the dock to the boat and over the rickety gangplank and stood on the deck. He sighed. His shirt was already sticking to him in the heat. *Le Rêve* appeared to be an attempt to build a boat by somebody who had never seen one. None of the deck planks met and, much worse, he could see that their supporting timbers had only been roughly hammered with four-inch nails onto the ribs, which came up from the keel. It was a dirty skeleton of a boat. A ghost.

Yet even as they sat in port he could feel the river making her creak and talk. He had loved boats ever since his father had bought him a model schooner as a child. He ran his hand along the black satin varnish of the piano, which was altogether different.

It was perfection.

He knew at a glance that the piano was one of those rare creatures that should have been pampered and cosseted in a concert hall by an army of tuners and conservers and humidifiers – it was undoubtedly very old – and never dragged through the mud and sewage of a small port on a tropical river where it was starting to rain. A boy popped over the side with a piano stool covered in red leather as if on cue and Smiles sat down and opened the key lid. He gave a low whistle when he read the name of Zimmerman in gold letters. From the shape he could tell it was a French-made instrument from the company started in revolutionary days and not the lesser firm founded in Bavaria in the nineteenth century using the same name. It was made at a time when the piano was just evolving from the harpsichord and might have been one of those confiscated from the aristocracy during the Reign of Terror. Now it was here. He hardly dared breathe on the delicately yellowed ivories. The piano was priceless and already steeped in blood.

He had no doubt that, especially for Bach, it was probably one of the best in the world.

Fear started to rise in Smiles' stomach again, but a small army of children was now sitting around the side of the boat and he was expected to perform. He was conscious of Lola standing near him, her perfume cutting through the smell of diesel from the winch and the dank smell of the river.

He began to play the bouncing, looping, rubber-band rhythms of Gassenhauer from Schulwerk Vol. 1, Musica Poetica, by Carl Orff and in a moment there was a cry from all of the children and some of the adults and they ran up the bank and stood under a tree in the warm rain, not quite sure whether to look terrified or pleased. He stopped and then started again and slowly they came damply but joyfully back. He had trained first at the Royal Northern College in Manchester, then at the Royal College of Music in London and finally at the Musikhochschule in Vienna. But there was no substitute for seeing the sheer delight of those new to piano music.

The Zimmerman was bliss. The tone as rich as marzipan and the notes seemed to play with the lightest of touches.

The children grew in confidence and soon were touching the side of the piano and then jumping up and down on the deck. Then all of them vaulted over the side as the boat pulled away backwards into the stream and, with the wind behind, forced her way upriver.

A single boy had been left on board, his ear pressed against the wood of the piano, a huge smile on his face. He suddenly realised his mistake and the crew fell about laughing as he ran and stood at the rail and shouted while two other little boys jumped into one of the huge pirogues and paddled with remarkable speed after the boat. The child leapt onto the canoe and immediately started arguing with his friends but then grinned and waved gratefully at Smiles.

Smiles stopped playing and the roaring silence hit him.

He half-rose and sat down again as the reality of his situation began to dawn. The wind had turned astonishingly cold and the rain was making the piano keys wet. To the left and to the right he could see both banks quite clearly rising into misty hills, almost mountains that reminded him of Scotland, while the river, where the waves were forming white horses and the canoes were now using great square sails to make them race upstream against the current, was like the English Channel. One of the crew began to wipe the piano with a cloth and then covered it with a tarpaulin.

'We do this for the weather. You play again later. You play very well, Mr Smiles,' said Thérance, as the boat was buffeted. 'It is quite cold. Here is an extra jacket. Marie who takes care of everything on the boat has got you a change of clothes from Aid America. They have very good clothes, designer labels, even the wonderful Gap!'

As Thérance said that, spray from a breaking wave hit Smiles' back and he stood and, so as not to appear concerned, walked down the length of Le Rêve on the rough deck, steadying himself when she rolled and the timbers groaned. Lola and St James were deep in conversation. She looked up and even behind her smile she had that quizzical expression he was becoming used to; people changed towards him when they heard him play as if the music made him an outsider, a kind of magician. St James just stared at him. Smiles was a little wary of the detached boy on the awkward edge of adolescence.

'Ah, Mr Smiles,' said the woman called Marie. 'You must play for us every day. Music is good. Music drives away the devil.'

He laughed.

'I thought he had all the best tunes.'

'No, he does not!'

Marie was sitting on one of the sea lockers that ran the length of the boat. Below a bright-yellow turban she wore a dress of the same canary colour. She was counting a moulding roll of Congolese francs and spoke good Baptist English.

'These are your clothes. I hope they fit . . . I did not have enough time. But if they don't, you just tell me and we alter them. This stupid girl is my maid, who has worms and is fell pregnant again with child. I think it a great thing that you take piano to your friend upriver because he dedicates his life to helping the poor mothers raped in the war.'

Smiles was brought up sharp by how the journey had been sold to the crew. As if it was Smiles' personal whim. But he just patted the pile of clothes.

'Thank you, Marie. I hope we can keep the devil away.'

Beyond a curtain he wandered down four makeshift steps, the nails left sticking out, to a half deck, where the boys were already bailing water from the leaking hull and the cook was cutting meat directly over where three outboard motors were powering *Le Rêve* through the tea-dark water.

He got a splinter in his hand as he climbed the ladder to the bridge. At the top were a pile of trussed live green pigeons with red bills and two tortoises beside what at first looked like fire-blackened babies.

'Smoked monkey! Good for when you weak. Not feeling well,' said the captain, who was at the wheel. He was a compact man with a bitter face. Behind them Smiles could smell something cooking in the galley.

'Bad weather! *Il y a du vent!*' At the last word the captain's face lit up into a smile as he pointed at a sandbank he was being blown towards. The boat's wheel was from an old Buick and the only other control was a throttle lever tied up with string. The chart, in the form of a book, was the original survey of the river done by the Baptist Missionary Society in 1902. There was no compass or clock and beside the captain was a fragrant white cup of what Smiles took to be palm wine. The brown-grey river spread out in front of him as the wind tore along the straw matting and they turned for the coast of Congo-Brazzaville. There was no echo-sounder. At the front of the boat he saw a man take up a long pole and push it down into the water.

'*Mittakenamittake!*'

'He see if water under the boat,' said the captain in French, then handed Smiles the wheel and, after vaguely pointing out the heading, disappeared with his wine. Smiles swallowed and gingerly steered along what he thought was the channel as if playing a difficult sonata, while the man with the pole kept uttering the same mournful cry.

'*Mittakenamittake!*'

Surprisingly, the boat's steering was light and, on the bridge, he could feel her bending to the power of the river like a living creature and a new Africa spreading before him. He was beginning to enjoy himself when the captain came back with another brimming cup of palm wine and one for Smiles. From below Smiles heard a shout.

'Toilet at the back, mama, shower at the other side.'

Lola climbed up the makeshift ladder to the toilet with the buckets of water outside and looked down into the space beneath in the middle of the boat, where three small outboards stood side by side. Two were already being stripped down among the pulpy fronds and blue flowers of the water hyacinth. She cursed Celestine: she knew that Fortuné must have given him more money than this. The buzz of the engines and the smell of the oil and the blood from the butchered goat funnelled out of the enclosed space. She stood up and went into the toilet, which, as she suspected, was a hole over the outboard's wake. She paused with a bucket of water until the mechanic tried to peek and drenched him. After another minute she lifted up her dress and took down her knickers to pee. Flies buzzed around her nose but it did not bother her. She remembered long journeys in the big canoes as a child and, of course, the war and fleeing deep into the bush so fast her bare feet bled. She pulled up her knickers and shrugged down her dress. She had to descend the ladder and collect her wash things to go up the one at the other side of the boat to the shower, which was another hole in the floor, with a plastic bottle of fresh water to tip over your head. She watched for the boys peeping but there was nothing. Lola felt a quiet satisfaction.

She slipped off her shoes, dress and knickers and hung them on a rusting nail. The framework of the shower was rough, dark wood and the corrugated iron which made up the walls was rusting into holes. She lifted the shower bottle and shivered as the cold water splashed down her body and through the hole and then she began to soap herself with a lavender-scented bar she had been given in the house in Kinshasa. It smelt so simply chic. It was from France. The owner of the mansion had an apartment in Paris on the rue du Cherche-Midi. She wanted to go to Paris one day to climb to the top of the Eiffel Tower and sit in the cafés and go to the fashion shows and buy every dress! To take discreet blond-haired lovers . . . She soaped her body some more. She liked to bathe. It always made her want to sing. As a small child in the river under the old village tree in Bokondo-Rive she would play in the water and splash and sing. She did not want to go to Paris for good. She lifted up the bottle again and tipped it over her body and her hair and wondered if they were looking at her from below. She did not care really. Everyone washed in the river and the river washed everyone: from when you were a baby to when they carried you out. She got soap in her eye and reached for the new towel and wiped her face. She scooped up the shampoo and began to massage it into her hair. Lola became suddenly aware of a broken piece of mirror on one wall. She admired her tightly curling hair that she took so much time with and her breasts. Her thoughts flitted to Xavier, who was never going to forgive her or his brother . . . She paused. She massaged the shampoo into her hair more vigorously and then rinsed it, pouring the water over herself. It felt so good. She stood rubbing at the thin strands of pubic hair and wrapped the towel around her. It was going to take at least two weeks to get to Kisangani in this boat and she would have plenty of time to think.

And there was the delightful but slightly sad Englishman, fading almost like a pencil sketch in his whiteness and the creases of his suit.

It was stupid, she knew, but she had begun to feel something for him the moment she saw him tentatively enter the room in Kinshasa and go over to the piano with an expression of relief and wonder on his face, and then to be able to play music like that, to be a kind and thoughtful man who dedicated himself to the arts . . . She wanted to protect him. The Englishman showed everything in his eyes and, even though he was older, they were wide for her.

What she did not understand was why a man like Smiles came to Congo at all. The white men who came to Kisangani, even the priests, especially the priests, all had an angle and nothing in their eyes. The next moment she was thrown against the shower wall as the boat hit a sandbank.

'Are you all right up there, mama?'

She ended up on the rough boards of the floor but she was still thinking of the Englishman.

'*É loke ezaté*,' she called back, pulling the towel around her. 'No problem.'

When she had dressed she saw they had come to rest on sands under the brown hills of the northern bank. The sandbank was part of the land, white, fine, wet sand strewn with water hyacinth and bamboo rhizomes and pierced by lilies.

'It's OK, mama,' one of the crew said in Lingala. 'Captain stop on purpose. Our launch is bashing a hole in our side. We got to make repair.'

It was then she noticed, concerned, that Smiles was already on the sands, spinning around like a madman with his arms outstretched. She had to go to him quickly, or the crew might think he was possessed.

FIVE

Lola ran barefoot down the gangplank onto the white sands and in the wind, which had started to lessen as the sky brightened, Smiles was whirling around and singing. There was something familiar about the song.

'Do you know this?' he asked her.

'Yes . . . but . . .'

He was singing the words of the Mass. He was stamping his feet to a rhythm.

'It is the Sanctus. The *Missa Luba*. The Congolese Mass. Lyman Andrew loved it. I never expected Congo to be all white-topped waves in the river and mist on the hills.' He reached down and took a handful of sand. 'The music was in a film about a school like mine.'

Lola drew an arc through the sand with her toe.

'I don't think you realise the dangers here.' She was going to warn him that the crew might think he had been taken over by spirits.

But he interrupted.

'Oh, I do. Believe me, I do. I saw the faces of the people in that graveyard when your husband, Xavier, showed up. My God, the people were all so frightened of him. Even the priest.'

He gazed at her.

'This sand here is so white. I never saw that on a river before.'

Lola picked up a handful and let it blow away. She had not expected him to mention Xavier.

'There is a lot of quartz upstream which holds all the gold and the diamonds. The things that people fight over. The things they have always tried to take from my country. Perhaps it will be different with a new American president.'

He shrugged.

'People go to war for the same things throughout history and not just treasure. Xavier and Fortuné fight over you. You are their Helen of Troy. I am on a boat with a face that launched a thousand ships! My God. Please don't look like that. I was joking. I am so sorry. That was an awful thing to say. You have your own dreadful war still going on.'

She felt her smile curling up at the sides of her mouth. She knew very well about Helen causing the Trojan War and he was not being patronising like most white people. She took it very much as a compliment.

'No, it isn't an awful thing to say,' she said. 'I don't care if I never hear of our war again. We all just want to forget and move on . . . No one has ever called me Helen of Troy before.'

'She was the most beautiful woman in the world.'

'I know. I just never thought of her as from Congo.'

'You should have.'

There was a banging from the boat. Thérance was at the top of the gangplank frowning at them and drumming on the roof of the deck. He would not follow. He was from Bas-Congo, near the sea, and did not trust the river people or the river spirits and would get off the boat as little as possible in such a place as the sandbank. He probably believed that if he strayed too far from the boat the spirits would break his bones before they bleached them and turned him to dust.

Smiles was laughing at the day. He had forgotten his fear and where he was.

'I used to play on the beach a lot with my father. I woke up so early and demanded to be taken down to the sea to build elaborate sandcastles. I actually pulled my father's eyelids open . . . Open the eyes, Papa! We ran around on those sands all day long and looked in the rock pools for crabs and put them in a bucket but let them go in the evening for their teas. He sold pictures for a living and he adored art. And my mother. He was a deeply happy man and always began the day in a good mood, especially on holiday. Which is why I love beaches and the sea, I suppose.'

'I have never seen the ocean.'

Smiles picked up the delicate shell of a freshwater mussel.

'I don't know why but I am most at peace down by the sea.'

A fisherman mending his nets on the sandbank came towards them with a wide grin, muttering something in Lingala.

'He says he will let us take a ride in his canoe,' she said.

'Gosh. Please.'

They walked to where the rough-hewn craft rested. She giggled as Smiles climbed aboard like an excited child and took the big paddles in his hand. She stepped in and moved around him as the fisherman pushed the boat off. The wind was dropping now and the day was suddenly very warm.

'"Sanctus! Sanctus!"' Smiles half-shouted, half-sang into the breeze as they paddled a circular course and returned. When the fisherman helped them back on dry land, she felt very close to the Englishman. She saw that Smiles was about to produce money but she stopped him with a hand on his. She took five hundred Congo francs from her own pocket, about a dollar. The fisherman rattled off a gleeful string of words in Lingala.

'What did he say?' Smiles asked.

The fisherman had told her to look after her white husband carefully as he would take her to Europe and buy her electricity to cook with. That he was going to take her to Belgium and they would have many fat children and that it was a great thing to see two people so deeply in love.

'Oh, he just wondered if we wanted to go around again,' she said.

When they climbed back on the boat they ate a lunch of corned-beef spaghetti Bolognese and in the calmer water the captain tried to make up for lost time as the temperature rose. Smiles went for a shower and she heard laughter and one of the boys came and told her the Englishman had dropped a bottle of water on his foot. He then put the same clothes back on and sat in an untidy heap in the shade at the front of the boat, trying to catch the hot breeze. Yet there was a grin on his face: he appeared to be relaxing into the country as the banks started to get wider apart and the massive trees came right down to the shore.

At dinner they ate chicken in a peanut sauce and he suddenly said: 'I saw a boat pass with soldiers. I thought the war is the other end of the country?'

Thérance shrugged his bony shoulders.

'Against Bemba. The war is over for the moment. He's in jail, but here and there the mai-mai, the local chief's militia, fight with the government Forces Armées. In Kinshasa the mai-mai even have their own party. Or some anti-government rebels fight the mai-mai and the UN. Or all three fight each other. And there is General Nkunda near Goma, who is supported by Rwanda. The Bemba supporters like Fortuné want peace but the government say no. It is confusing.'

Smiles sighed.

'And those rebels are not the same as the rebels who came from Rwanda? The Interahamwe? The ones who fled from Rwanda after the massacres there?'

Smiles regretted the simplistic words as soon as he said them.

Celestine drew himself up on his wooden chair.

'What happened and is still, to a lesser extent, taking place in the east of our country is complicated, so very complicated, and it's spreading west. It is unhelpful to take it out of context. At the start there was the killing of the Tutsi in Rwanda by the Hutu. Then, aided by Uganda, and possibly the United States, the Tutsi rebels in southern Uganda invaded Rwanda and the Hutu, who were responsible for the genocide of a million Tutsis and others, fled into the Congo forests as the Interahamwe – literally, those who kill together – and fought with the pro-Mobutu forces against Laurent Kabila, our incumbent President's father. This became our ghastly civil war with Uganda, Rwanda and America on one side and us, Angola and Zimbabwe on the other. Some would say it was about our precious metals. Whatever it was, five and a half million and more died, mainly hacked to pieces with pangas.

That, in our population terms, is equivalent to the First World War in Europe. I gave a well-received lecture on this when I was still allowed to teach at the university.'

It was obvious to Smiles that teaching was a joy to Celestine. Thérance interrupted.

'The Interahamwe are very bad. They chop up women. Even babies. They are enjoying this very much and are happy in their work.'

Celestine held up his hand and Thérance smiled and was silent. Celestine then continued.

'When I think of our current epic tragedy I always remember the Czech author Milan Kundera and how he talks about a great war in fourteenth-century Africa, which has no significance because no one notices. Like a tree falling in an unexplored forest no one hears and therefore makes no sound. Silence . . . Silence! And Kundera points out that if no one notices in the so-called civilised world and turns our poor war into a moral abstraction, a case of right and wrong, the horror will repeat itself for ever. The law of endless return beloved by Nietzsche. We are caught in a myth. It has been happening to us since King Leopold. This is the true horror Joseph Conrad spoke of. The West, the so-called civilised world, creates a charnel house, a river of blood, so outsiders will be too scared to exploit our riches and the countries who pay the killers will plunder what they want, by and by.'

At this point Lola pretended to yawn but Celestine went on unabashed.

'If we are too bloody lazy to understand, the past will be our future. A cease-fire was called in 2002 but, to quote Dante, there are still areas which are 'beyond the sun'. He struck a pose as he said this and a fly spoiled it by biting him on the neck and he slapped at the creature angrily. It all made Lola smile and she examined Celestine's well-manicured hands with two gold rings on the left, one on the middle finger and one on the little finger, and a single diamond on his right the size of a jelly bean. When the politicians and businessmen came to see her father, those who talked and quoted and jumped out of their seats with rhetorical flourishes, spilling precious Scotch over old copies of *Libération*, they always wore the rings, the men who never fought. Her father never had a gold ring to his name, spoke little and did much. She thought that was what had attracted her to Xavier. He never announced what he was going to do.

He wore no rings at all.

On the first night they put up tents on the boat, tents one could stand up in and Smiles marvelled how they fitted under the sunshade roof and, as he unzipped his own, he saw the silhouette of her body against the coloured lights that ran under the eaves. Inside, his tent was so hot that the sweat dripped off him. He went to sleep to the chanted prayers of the crew and, for the first time in many years, he added his own. He had loved being on the river beach with her today and gliding across the grey-brown water in the heavy canoe, but now his fears returned to him. He imagined Xavier following him upriver and finding him with Lola. Smiles tried, unsuccessfully, to put the thought out of his mind and reached into his leather music satchel and took out a knife. It was something he had been given at a celebratory dinner in Rovigo in Italy after playing a concert in the town. He unfolded the knife and laid it on his bare breast. It was very small. It looked like a hunter's clasp knife but in reality it was for eating pears and Parmesan cheese at the end of a meal. He was intending to defend himself against a battle-hardened Major-General and his troops with a fruit knife.

He heard Lola moan suddenly and softly in her sleep only a yard away from him. Smiles was both reassured and excited by her presence even though he knew it might prove fatal.

He folded the silly knife shut and put it back in his bag.

He awoke to Marie singing her prayers, which lasted for half an hour, as the crew came to life around his tent, some saying prayers of their own, others not: all seemed to gargle and spit their toothpaste with exaggerated relish. There was a procession to the lavatory and then he heard everyone washing their hands in the bowl and using a cup to rinse them over the side.

'That way no tiny snails that give you river blindness go back into the bowl,' he heard her say.

Smiles lay under the mosquito net, luxuriating in the cool of a dawn which was already becoming hotter. And this morning, even after opening his satchel and looking at the packets of 'jottings' he had made for Dr Kaplan in South Africa, Smiles was more than a little delighted with the beauty and strangeness of Congo. He was on an adventure and the ones he usually had were drab and hurried and with women in hotels followed by stilted mobile-phone calls afterwards and then blessed silence. He got up and dressed just in time for the tent to be taken down around him.

The cover of the foam mattress he had slept on was wet with his sweat.

'The Englishman pee his bed! Pee his bed! Pee his bed!' shouted Marie, triumphantly holding the cover up for everyone to see and repeated the charge as he politely objected, until Lola, who had already showered and was wearing jeans and a red T-shirt, came to his aid. She said something low and inaudible to Marie, whose face changed immediately and breakfast was served.

'It is the way of Congolese to joke all the time, especially about toilet matters,' Lola said, as Thérance and Celestine joined the table with the rest of the crew.

The day was bright and hot and the wind had stopped. The great river was still comparatively narrow, perhaps a quarter of a mile across, perhaps more, sweeping past them in a light-brown, eddying stream, while the clumps of water hyacinth on the surface appeared to travel in the opposite direction, as if swimming. Smiles had noticed from maps that the river became perversely many times wider upstream.

'Oh yes, we Congolese are great jokers!' laughed Celestine. `When Mobutu died in exile in Morocco they say he closed his eyes two days before and everyone thought he had passed on and there was silence and a little crying. Then he opened his eyes again and said: "If that pathetic attempt at mourning is the best you can come up with I am going to stay around a while . . . I obviously did nothing bad when I was alive if no one will talk about me when I am dead!"'

Lola reached for the Belgian, two-tone Nutella.

'He was no joke. He tried to send this country back to the Stone Age. He encouraged corruption. He had my grandfather tortured and killed. He had my grandfather's eyes torn out.'

There was a silence around the table.

'He gave me a book at my school prize day,' said Thérance, beaming and trying to lighten the mood. 'It was *The Wind in the Willows*. He said it was one of his most favourite books. He said he liked books where people become animals. Especially the character of Mr Toad, who knew driving too fast was very bad for him but could not stop.'

The leading hand among the crew, a hunter from upriver called José, grunted.

'Mobutu would have a job driving anywhere in Congo now after he let the roads go to hell ... The forest deer cannot pass on them they are so overgrown. All we have is our river.'

'He not lead himself into temptation,' giggled Thérance.

Smiles noticed that Lola was staring hard at the bread roll on the plate in front of her.

'What Mobutu did led to the present wars, or have you forgotten? That is where government by one strong man leads,' she snapped, and everyone glanced at her. Smiles saw she was trembling slightly as she sipped her *café au lait*.

She rose and went to sit on her locker at the side of the boat and the crew started to talk again in Lingala and eat the bread, omelette and dried fish. Smiles walked to the bow and took the damp tarpaulin off the piano. A cockroach scuttled one way across the lid and a large hairy brown spider ran the other. Smiles lifted it carefully and propped it open; just in case there was anything worse inside, nestling under the delicate hammers or lurking behind the strings.

The sun came from behind the clouds and the light was almost blinding. From memory he played a theme from the ballet *Pulcinella* by Igor Stravinsky and, lured by the Zimmerman's magic, a small crowd of boys gathered on the bank to hear him while the boat cast off. The crew all stopped and watched him for a golden moment as the sun shone in their faces, as if the music were beatifying them, and then went about the business of the day as they headed upriver. In the distance he could hear ragged cheers from the children he had left behind and from a barge they passed at its mooring, so crowded with people that an old woman was tied onto a cane rocking chair for safety. People were climbing on top of each other to get a better view of their boat and hear the music. Then the crew were pointing.

A corpse floated in the water.

A man had probably fallen off the barge drunk or there had been a fight over an inch or two of space in all this vastness.

Water hyacinths had started to gather around the body and with their spikes of blue flowers looked like a funeral wreath as the bow wave nudged the traveller out into the current, where he spun around and began his journey down to Kinshasa ahead of the rest of his marooned village.

SIX

Smiles played most of the morning and afternoon as the banks slid past. Clumps of trees turned to stands of jungle and there were hints of a higher forest. He saw a brown and white eagle with large yellow talons glide over the boat, skim low and gaze at the piano. It made a sudden turn, flapping its wings in surprise at the exotic sight and sound of the instrument. They passed palm-thatched huts where fat, brown, long-horned cattle ran joyously loose on the beach. Yet the village they pulled into was much bigger and darker with brick-and-corrugated dwellings. It had an air of enforced regimentation he did not like and, here and there, he noticed that houses had been destroyed: their walls stood in ruins like bad black teeth.

In a large tree on the bank he saw the hanging nests of weaver birds and caught the yellow flashes of their breasts through the green leaves and, when the engines were switched off, there was a quiet only broken by the occasional shout of Marie and the twittering of the birds.

'Belgians built this. This once village for coffee. Finished now,' said José. As they landed a group of men with shaved heads and maroon scarves came towards the boat. They wore AK-47s slung around their thin necks. They walked with a swagger.

'They the chief's mai-mai, his militia. *Mai* means water. And very magic water,' Thérance said, with a small giggle. 'It is often word used for the rebels, also. These men are also rebels in that they are for Mr Bemba. They certainly not Interahamwe, don't worry. They against Rwandans and all that. The witch doctor sprinkles magic water on the fighter so that the bullets will turn away and the ends of the enemy guns bend. It true! There was a woman, a sorceress, who worked for the Interahamwe and was captured by our army and now does magic for the government that can make roads and rivers bend and come round on themselves, so you start to arrive back before you even going. Like in the physics of clever Mr Einstein! But you do not believe such things, do you, Mr Smiles?'

Looking at the three men on the beach, Smiles doubted they needed help from anywhere. They were very tall and supremely fit but their stern faces cracked into a smile as Marie passed them a bottle of Primus beer each and told them to help put up the tents.

'*Oui, mama,*' they said, pausing to stare at Lola and then at the piano. The beach began to fill with children who stood as near to the boat as they possibly could and watched every move with wide-open eyes. Marie tossed them sweets and empty plastic water bottles, which the children fought over.

'The children can store palm oil in them and make lamps with coconut husks or a sardine tin and a raffia wick and then do schoolwork in the dark . . . I was in the dark with all my school-work.' Lola smiled.

Smiles opened the piano and started to play a little Beethoven and the entire beach went quiet and even the mai-mai stood still as the notes mixed with the woodsmoke from the fires and the bleats of the goats eating the reeds. None of them moved for twenty or more minutes until he stopped and then they cheered and sang.

Briefly, up at the top of the bank under a tree, Smiles glimpsed a figure in crimson red but the man vanished. Then Smiles went down the gangplank and onto the beach with the crowd reaching out their hands but not quite touching him.

'The village think what you have done is magic,' said José. He grabbed Smiles' shoulder and they both froze. Smiles had stepped on the empty rusting casing of a landmine in the sand and mud, the side covered in Russian writing; the explosive stolen. He gulped. They pushed on in trepidation through a herd of goats, which, like the children, did not seem to be troubled by the possibility of other, live, mines. The crowd was following him now among the small compounds full of chickens and thin pigs and people came out to show him their children.

Thérance caught up with him.

'This is a fine village of four thousands human beings! They like you, Mr Smiles. They like your playing. They think you a high priest of harmony.'

With Thérance and José he walked around the huts and up to the rise on which stood a reed-and-clay shack church and the villagers brought him chikwangue, the fermented-bean paste. From the rise they gazed down to a valley and the start of thick jungle.

'We go down there,' said a boy, and after a mile on a track which allowed only two people walking, or a bike, he stepped onto an ornate bridge over a small river that was big enough to take a truck in either direction before shrinking back to a bush path, like the absurd bridges Potemkin had built in the middle of nowhere for Catherine the Great to show her the richness of his conquests in the Crimea. Dark trees overhung the river and the skull-white bridge and white water lilies shone against the black stream. Suddenly, the children and the adults who followed him huddled to one side, as if the span were about to fall into the water, and he turned and Smiles saw the red man he had glimpsed in the village.

The man stood solemnly at the other side of the bridge, nodding.

Smiles blinked. The man had red-velour carpet on his head, a pretty red blouse and a wrap-around skirt. In his hand he carried a staff crowned with strands of blond hair.

He came towards Smiles and his eyes were large and pale. He then began to sing `Frère Jacques' and Smiles could not help himself.

He burst out laughing.

The man's features contorted with rage.

'Give me *mbongo*, at once!' he shouted in French.

It must have been the heat, or the adulation of the crowd, but Smiles found he could not stop laughing. He was not in control of his facial muscles and the expression of the man was one of total anger.

Thérance pulled Smiles away.

'He is the chief,' Thérance said sternly. 'He demands *mbongo*. His money tribute.'

They started walking back.

'I'm sorry. I thought he was the village idiot,' said Smiles, tears running down his cheeks.

'Often an easy mistake to make,' said Thérance wearily. 'But he is mad with us. We must give him his tribute later . . . He can be dangerous . . . He the power here.'

'Look, I really am sorry,' said Smiles.

When they got back to the boat to prepare the evening meal, no sooner had Smiles jumped down from the gangplank and onto the large lorry tyre on the boat deck meant to break one's fall, than it started. At first it was one or two flies sizzling in the dying heat as the mist came off the water and then in a few minutes the boat was filled from stem to stern with biting insects, flying termites the crew said, which were crawling under his shirt and in his eyes and ears and hair.

He opened his mouth and they were inside, biting at his tongue and going down his throat.

Marie's maid was screaming.

More and more insects wriggled and swarmed over every flat surface.

The more Smiles brushed them off, the more they came. The boys rushed to the side of the boat, trying to draw the mosquito blinds, but Smiles, helping them, saw there was not a single insect on the beach or in the village and the children and the grown-ups watched while the red chief stood alone under the mango tree.

'He send them . . . Chief send them. You make him mad, Mr Smiles. Give me ten dollars. Marie, give me some bottles of beer,' shouted José.

Smiles reached into his pocket and handed over the notes, which vanished under thousands of insects, as did the beer.

José ran down the gangplank and up to the man under the tree. In between wiping termites out of his eyes, Smiles saw the chief take the beer and the money and walk slowly away. Smiles was now up by the piano, which had been left uncovered and under which Lola had retreated beneath several blankets with only her amused eyes visible. Smiles was worried that the insects might get into the mechanism and ruin the instrument. But there was a sudden dank smell in the air and he felt the temperature drop as, from the front of the boat where he stood, the termites began to retreat along the deck and then were gone altogether, like a puff of smoke.

He examined his hands and face and the bites were bloody and real.

Lola came out of her cocoon.

'It could be worse, Smiles,' she laughed. 'He might have sent crocodiles.'

'The chief? You really think it was the chief?'

She nodded and Thérance said: 'You must be careful now, Mr Smiles. We are beyond your two-and-two-makes-four world.'

Lola watched, fascinated, as the Englishman pushed the fried bananas and rice and beans and tough river duck around his plate. He had not said a word about the termites but she saw that it bothered him, had fractured his mood. Her brother, St James, had collected the termites which had remained on the deck and had a mound of them in front of him deep-fried with sugar; in the markets they were often sold by the spoonful. It had never occurred to her not to accept village magic when she was growing up, but if one were brought up in Europe, where they claimed these happenings did not occur, she saw it might be a worry. The sunset hung over the river in a great golden bow. Three men standing in a canoe paddled into its reflection. When she was thirteen and doing her *brevet* exams a Dutch father at the mission had told her the problem in Congo was one of beauty. He said everywhere he looked there was so much living, growing beauty that he was left speechless and uncomfortable before it. He had lived in a little gatehouse and one of her girlfriends became pregnant and he had to leave. But she knew that his words were sincere and she experienced what he had meant when she stood alone in the deep forest on her father's hunting trips as a child, many miles from anywhere, at the mercy of nature. Unlike the guilty priest she loved those moments when the leaves turned greener and the trees grew higher and the drip, drip of the water was inside her and became her heartbeat. She was sure that the musician, Smiles, would feel the power, hear the jungle's tune, when she took him there. He had just eaten half of a piece of fried banana and put the rest back on his plate.

'It is better if we sleep ashore tonight. Cooler,' she said.

'OK,' Smiles replied.

Marie laughed.

'I afraid he not get to toilet in time and do pee pee in bed again because too polite to pee in river.'

Lola looked sharply at her.

'Sorry, Mr Smiles . . . I joke.'

There was a silence.

'Well, I want to sleep on the beach and I am sure Smiles will be there to protect me,' Lola said. He had put on his borrowed Aid America clothes, which must have once belonged to a truly super-size American and he looked even more the schoolboy.

'Do you actually, totally believe that the chief sent those insects?' he asked her again softly.

She did not answer him.

But José said: 'On the river we believe people can turn into crocodiles. Some men can transform themselves and kill their enemies in their huts and then go back to the river and swim off. Or they become hippopotamus and destroy the house and the vegetable garden of their enemy. Turning into a hippo is best if you want to mash up a garden.'

'Have you seen this?' asked Smiles.

José inclined his head very slightly.

'And winds . . . I have seen a friend who had so much anger in him we go out into the forest and he turns into a wind and blows me off my feet and flattens the jungle around us. I was scared more than I have ever been. And then there was calm and he did not have his anger any more. You have to be careful if you are hunting crocodiles and hippos now because they are so few after the war and often they are people who have transformed themselves. It is hard to find a crocodile who is only a crocodile . . .'

Lola noticed that the words were having an unnerving effect on the Englishman.

But then Celestine coughed.

'And I have heard people change themselves into leopards. What kind of person does that?'

Lola was holding a napkin and her hand tightened on the cheap cloth.

She glared at Celestine and he was smiling but was the one to look away first. She stood up quickly and the Englishman watched bewildered as she picked up a bottle of water and her things from her locker and, cleaning her teeth on the way, spat outside her tent and went in and lay down in the dark.

Lola did not like Celestine Mbando and the way he teased her about Xavier, the leopard. His nickname had been Chui, the leopard, in Swahili, after he had gone to school in Kisangani.

She still missed Xavier. He sent her poetry through her cousin and it was good poetry, in French and English and Swahili, although few people realised Xavier wrote those passionate words between his military reports. At the same time she knew he still hated her because of what had happened with his brother, Fortuné. That tortured, easy thing, love.

One evening she had begged Xavier, in his spartan rooms, to leave politics and the army. He was becoming another man. They had argued so violently she thought he was going to kill her.

'So get out, then, why don't you go? You stupid little girl! You do not understand. Go on, get out!' He had picked up her bag and thrown it at the door. A man had come in and then closed the door again.

'Get out!' yelled Xavier.

'I am going,' she said, and had picked up her bag and run from the house and his compound.

She had gone to his brother, who did not live far away, even though the two were politically opposed. She had known Fortuné at the Lycée and had regarded him as just a friend, but one she could always confide in and capable of cheering up a dead man: almost family and better than that because what she said did not get back. His house had an emerald-coloured pool and there were deep settees and soft music.

They had drunk a bottle of Cristal champagne (Bemba had sent him a case, trying to get Fortuné on his side) and soon he was kissing her; he was all over her, telling her he had loved her for years but it was so obvious that she loved his brother and he had no chance. And she started to kiss him back. A small kiss and then more and more. It sounded so awful when it was told like that, the way women would tell it, while washing their clothes in the river. She suspected Xavier had other women; there was a girl who worked in his office, she supposed for no other reason. Lola knew he had had an affair with one of her classmates. At first she felt in control making love to Fortuné and then so desperately sorry. But she had remained at Fortuné's house for days and she still did not know why. Almost as if she wanted Xavier to find out.

She sighed.

It was too late now to think of what she and Xavier might have had together ... She had not stayed with Fortuné although he was so nice to her and much more predictable than his brother. She had gone instead to an aunt who had her own compound on the airport road, which was where the violence that started in Gombé cemetery spilled over, with the people running and screaming and those who were following them turning into that spirit of violence that people call animal.

It was painful for her to use that word because the Belgians had always called her people animals.

She saw the anger of Xavier become the leopard on the streets of the capital and the dusty roads run with the blood of women and children. She had to flee for her own life.

He had come to her in the night, the door of her bedroom burst open and she expected to die. He stood there shaking.

'I know. Fortuné came and asked for my blessing to be with you! Bemba's gangsters have been using him. They wanted me to fight them and lose. But you are what the fighting was for and I won! My brother has fled but I will find him. I will find Bemba and all his henchmen. Bemba is a man accused by the courts of cannibalism against the Pygmy people, for God's sake! I will kill Bemba! I will kill them all and I never want to see you again.'

It was dark then and there was a full moon, huge over the city, shining through the bedroom window.

She remembered looking up at the moon as the sirens blared into the night and then she went for him with her fists and her nails.

'You don't get it, do you, Chui? You still are blind. Even after all those people you killed today.'

He held her wrists and said: 'Your lover is alive. He is no longer my brother. But I will find him.'

She had spat at him and cursed him but he just stared at her and eventually he let her fall. She was there on the ground by his boots, slumped in the moonlight. She hated him. She hated him more than anything. He was the sort of vicious man her father had said they were fighting wars to get rid of for ever.

Yet Lola knew, at that moment, if he had lifted her up she would have gone with him, gone with him anywhere.

She ran her fingers under the belt of her jeans and touched herself and felt a rush of warmth.

In his poems he called her his wife. She did not want to be the leopard's wife and she did ... Her soul was cut in two. Xavier had stayed for an hour that night, just standing there, over her, and she had begun to sob. One of his men then came and he departed without a word . . . Fortuné, who had fled, had sent her flowers. Flowers!

All from a very expensive shop that was owned by the Bemba family.

She pushed down her jeans.

She saw the face of Xavier in front of her and arched her body. She loved to kiss his lips, forehead, cheekbones . . . His eyes were so deep and sensitive when he was alone with her. Whenever she thought of sex or felt hot she wanted him and his muscled body on the single white linen sheet of his hard bed in his house in Gombé. He used to take his clothes off quickly and she loved to feel his taut stomach as her hand went down to his thick penis but first he would kiss her thighs and his tongue would probe between her legs with such tenderness. Whenever she remembered such things, she was his, a man she hated and detested after the many violent acts he had done. And now they had fought in her name in the graveyard in Gombé.

Lola both wished Xavier dead and with her for ever.

The magic was not all the Englishman had to understand about her country. The magic was the easy part. There was love, always love and beauty, but why did there have to be killing?

SEVEN

As he fished under the blue sky of Kisangani on that last day, St James took another packet of papers from Smiles' confessions book. He was fascinated that Smiles had been the same age as St James was now and sent away from home without a single member of his family. That was hard, like the stories from Dickens his sister had read him. And St James was interested in the American black man in a white world who was the Lyman Andrew who was meant to play at the blown-up Peace and Reconciliation Concert. But mainly in Smiles.

My Confession:
Stanley Miles-Harcourt: black book, packet two

'I am really mad with you, Smiles. I told you not to clean my shoes. I tell you one simple thing like that and what do I discover? You not only have cleaned all my sorry footwear but I can see my face in those *battleship brogues my mother bought me. I thought this was a disciplined school.'*

Lyman Andrew had caught up with me as I came back from games. (I always thought of him as Lyman Andrew, Dr Kaplan. Not just Lyman or Mr Andrew.) I knew he had been in London all day. He had not been at a special assembly that morning.

I hung my head. It was always good to hang one's head when being told off by masters.

'I am very sorry, sir.'

Then I looked up and saw he was joking.

'That's a good shoeshine. You are a professional.'

'Thank you, sir.'

'I thought I told you not to call me "sir", either?' He laughed. He then shot one hand into his jacket pocket and brought out a fifty-pence piece.

'Here, have this. Go and buy some tuck. At the tuck shop. You see I am learning your strange, native language.'

I stared at the money.

'Go, take it. It won't bite. What's the matter? You don't look well, Smiles.'

I still hesitated.

Then I took the coin and put it in my pocket.

'I'm OK,' I said, even though I wasn't.

'Now you can show me around.'

'Can I get changed first, sir?'

'Of course you can, Smiles. And no more "sirs". And there's a few things you can tell me.'

'If I can.'

'Is it true that every last one of you has lost your father or both parents?'

His eyes became terribly upset and serious when he said this.

'Yes. The only way to get here is for your father to die and have been a Mason. Then you don't pay for anything.'

'Was it just your dad?'

'Yes. He died of a heart attack and my mother ... Well, she just missed him. She's OK now though.'

I found even that hard to say.

'I am so sorry,' he said, as if it were his fault. There was a long silence and then he changed the subject.

'So, what's the school gossip at the moment, Smiles? What's been going down?'

I looked at him incredulously.

'What?'

I remembered that he didn't know what had been said at the special assembly.

'You don't know, do you?'

'Know what?'

'What happened at the assembly this morning. I'm surprised no one has told you. A boy has been killed. Not at the assembly, I mean ... before. A third-former. David Wace. His body was found on the school rubbish dump.'

'Killed. How? Was he a friend of yours?'

'He was my best friend. My best friend ever.'

I paused. The words caught at the back of my throat and I thought I was going to cry. We had been told not to talk about it. Everyone was scared, really scared. Like when you think there is something behind you in the dark. I managed to get the words out.

'The gardener found him. David was cut up ... His ... heart torn out of his chest ... And they burned his bowels ... That's what was

said. I had been on an exeat with him to the village and I left him up there . . .'

My mouth was quivering.

He thought I was joking around with him. Like I was about to laugh.

'This isn't funny, Smiles.'

Then I began to shout at him.

'It's true, sir! Honestly!'

'OK . . . OK . . .'

I started to talk more quietly.

'The headmaster had to tell us because the story was getting around. The masters are frightened the school may be closed. It's because this is a Masonic school and Masons are accused of doing things like that to people who don't keep their secrets. They are searching for a knife. If you have one, I should get rid of it.'

From the moment I said the word 'knife' there was a greater bond between us, because I obviously hadn't spoken to anyone about his clasp knife. It was strictly forbidden to have the smallest penknife and gossip went around the school in minutes. He had a funny expression on his face like he was about to say something sympathetic. It was almost as if he felt responsible now for what had happened to my friend David Wace.

He put his hand gently on my shoulder.

Lyman Andrew trusted me. No one else had informed him about David Wace, no one had told him about what was being called 'murder'.

'Jesus Christ, to think that happened here . . .' he said. 'That happened here, in this place? I can't believe it. Here?' He was almost in tears. It really got to Lyman Andrew and to me.

I was shaking like a leaf and thought I was going to be sick.

St James had a fish on his line and put the papers back in their packet and the packets back in Smiles' satchel. And such a killing! He wondered which tribe these Masons were from.

EIGHT

The sun was in Smiles' eyes as they swung into the port of the city of Mbandaka three days later. He had been giving the boy St James a piano lesson. The boy was quick and very eager to learn but cool and guarded in a way Smiles had never seen in a thirteen- or fourteen-year-old. St James had caught sight of the logo of an octopus on a letter in Smiles' bag and asked what the creature was and sat in rapt fascination, shaking his head slightly, as Smiles drew a bigger one. He had wanted to go and find one immediately and was disappointed to hear that they only lived in the sea. Then an argument in Lingala between Celestine and the captain broke out around their heads.

St James whispered to Smiles: 'Celestine wants to go to a mission place outside Mbandaka to ask a priest where Fortuné and your friend Lyman Andrew have gone.'

'They don't know?'

St James shook his head.

'They maybe here and you see your friend and we give him

piano. But captain say the people in the port are crooks and are always confiscating boats for no reasons.'

Smiles was glad the boy was confiding in him.

'Have you ever met Lyman Andrew?

'No. I like Fortuné, though, he make me laugh. He very kind, he bought me a basketball, a real one from America, not the kind you make of forest rubber and a plastic bag. They don't bounce. They only good for football.'

'And what about Xavier? Did you meet him?'

St James paused.

But just at that moment the rain lashed down and they were both covering the piano with the tarpaulin and then the boy disappeared. Smiles had seen a change in St James' eyes at the mention of Xavier and it was not fear. The look was somewhere between respect, affection and awe.

Their boat idled offshore, then the sun came out again for a few seconds as the rain splashed on the water and there was a rainbow over the forest canopy. Everything shone as they nosed into the port. The buildings of the waterfront had once been impressive but many were ruined or burned out and rusting iron barges lay on top of each other, as if discarded there by a giant's hand. A colonial villa had one side missing and, surrounded by grass and reeds, there were several paddle steamers with stern wheels and high, narrow funnels. He was looking at a landscape after a forgotten battle. Their boat came almost to a stop as the captain tried to find a gap between the pirogues and then, losing patience, pushed several of them up the bank as he edged in and men began to shout from the shore. Moored next to them were two iron barges, each bigger than their boat, with another whole exiled village on board, heading downstream to Kinshasa, except they had no engine or power. Every inch of both barges was covered in people. On one a skinny girl stood naked, laughing, on the very top of all the belongings before throwing a purple wrap around her body.

Women were washing their babies in the water and a slick of sewage floated around the rusting sides.

On the bank of mud, rotting vegetation and pieces of driftwood, the traders had laid out their wares. The citizens of the barge were bargaining for fruit and vegetables. Then it started to rain again.

'Those poor souls,' Lola said. 'The pusher boat will have left them here and they have to find another one and pay more money. That is how it always is and, if they survive, if they have any Congo francs or dollars they will lose them all in Kinshasa. They think Mama Kinshasa will be the end of all their problems and she usually finishes the exiled off. They are from Kivu, where the war is.'

Celestine was peering out at the riverbank. A woman was fanning a fire over which she was cooking sweetcorn.

'We must go ashore while it is still raining. I know the lazy bastards that run this port. If they see you on the boat, Smiles, we have to pay them huge bribes. Come. We'll take a ride and see a friend of mine and perhaps even find Fortuné. Who knows, your friend Lyman Andrew may be with him.'

Smiles stared at Celestine.

'But I thought he was in Kisangani, far upriver?'

'There is a place he may have stopped here . . . And, if not, the person we will meet knows where he has gone.'

Lola was staring at him, too.

'Fortuné . . . here?'

'It could be, Mademoiselle,' said Thérance. 'It could be. Come on, we will get a taxi. And we can show St James the biggest crocodile in the world. You would like to see that, wouldn't you?'

Smiles could see that the boy did not care for Thérance's easy insincerity.

'I would rather see an octopus.'

'Well, who knows?' Thérance offered a string of encouragement in Lingala. 'Come on, let's go to the taxi,' he said, his thin black raincoat blowing out behind him like a cloak as he skipped down the gangplank. Smiles followed more slowly, praying he would not fall into the filthy water.

They squelched up the sloppy, sodden bank through the mud and raw sewage and Smiles turned around wondering if he had covered the piano well enough. He swallowed hard. He had had no idea that he might see Lyman Andrew so soon. They got into the back of a taxi, a minivan with water leaking through the roof.

Lola sat in the back and looked out of the window as they passed a Baptist church. The rain clouds were low and the day dark with an almost biblical sense of foreboding. She did not quite know what she would say to Fortuné, what she felt about him now. He had often attempted to call her, though not since the bomb had gone off in the kitchens of the Intercontinental. She did not expect to see the American, who, it was said, had once lived in what was left of the Hotel Pourquoi Pas in Kisangani, which had been grand in the days when Katharine Hepburn and Humphrey Bogart had made *The African Queen* and now was full of snakes. The

American was Fortuné's newest hero and had stayed upriver, helping refugee women in the bush. Fortuné insisted he loved her and they had begun arguing in the Intercontinental car park. She said she did not want to see him any more just as the bomb had gone off and the air was suddenly full of brick dust and the smell of explosive.

'This is my brother's work!' he had shouted.

Fortuné had then kissed her and he and his people were spirited away and everyone was told he was dead. Lola had at first been so pleased when she learned of the Peace and Reconciliation Concert and that there was going to be a truce between the brothers.

The only trouble was she did not believe a word.

Xavier was not a man to forgive or forget.

Celestine Mbando must have known that and she trusted him less than a crocodile.

Before they got out of town they stopped by a liquor store and then a pharmacy where soldiers were sitting outside on nursery-school-size chairs, drinking Primus beer. Celestine went inside.

'He get pills and booze for the old Father,' laughed Thérance.

They bumped along tarmac roads for a hundred yards before hitting a dirt track where they had to stop for two oncoming military jeeps and a straining lorry as the reeds, papaya trees and elephant grass closed in on either side. Women with huge loads of firewood or leaf-wrapped packets of *chikwangue* waved at them as they went by and little by little the forest took back every trace of civilisation.

The old mission was perhaps twenty kilometres outside Mbandaka but it felt like so much more to Smiles, over axel-breaking roads as the rain drummed on the roof like a thousand demons and ran through a hole onto Smiles' trousers. Then all at once it stopped.

They turned through what had been an elaborate entrance in between brick walls, but the gates were now missing, and drove up a sodden track more or less completely overgrown with grass to a low range of buildings. On either side of the track were broad-leaved catalpa trees with large white flowers. Children were hanging from the branches and, as Smiles got out of the minivan, a priest in late middle age with a trimmed grey beard rose from his rocking chair and approached and the children swarmed down and ran over to the taxi and watched.

'Greetings, Father Lieven,' said Celestine.

'Greetings. To what do I owe this honour?' The Father shook hands. His were soft with closely bitten nails. He regarded them anxiously. His voice was reedy.

'Fortuné told me he was going to try to come here. Perhaps the American, who I believe is known to you, is now with him?'

The Father gave the slightest of nods. He seemed trapped in his own domain. On the table where he had been sitting was a compendium of Dashiell Hammett's hard-boiled detective stories.

'The commandant in Mbandaka has been replaced with a man who is very loyal to Kabila. Yes, I remember you, Celestine Mbando. Come in and sit down, my friends. I only heard that there had been a small explosion in a hotel lavatory. That's what they said on the radio and blamed a lightning bolt. There are more and more of these lightning bolts. It is getting far too Old Testament for my liking. I suppose total peace is impossible in this life.'

Smiles noticed an expression of almost spiritual panic in the

Father's eyes as the children took to the trees again. They obviously had an affection for him but did not want any of the religious gifts he had to offer.

'Has Fortuné come here, Father? We will not betray you.'

There was a sudden excitement in the Father that echoed his penchant for detective fiction.

'Fortuné spent a night under my roof and then went upriver to meet the American.'

'Not to Kisangani?'

The Father pursed his lips.

'No. The town is still divided. Fortuné is elsewhere and as far as I know the American never came downriver. I must go and talk with a man Fortuné trusts and if he gives his permission I will tell you, as best I know, where they are.'

Thérance smiled.

'We are taking him a piano. To play the Peace and Reconciliation Concert.'

Father Lieven smiled weakly.

'It may be hard to take an accordion where they have gone. If they are in the jungle. It brings me such sorrow that intelligent young men who should be working hard for their country are engaged in this fight of Cain and Abel.'

He turned his pale gaze on Lola.

'And why is she here?'

'I was with Fortuné at the hotel.'

'Perhaps you should stay away from them both,' said the priest.

But Lola looked back without blinking.

'Perhaps I should.' She then walked slowly away along the cloister in the direction of a sign which said '*Bibliothèque*'. Celestine and Thérance stayed with the Father but Smiles followed her and so did St James.

Inside, the mission's famous library was much bigger and higher than it seemed from the cloister. The shelves reached twenty feet into the air and had to be climbed by old, half-broken ladders. There was a recent book by a Belgian politician on the ten million Congolese who died under the 'free state' of King Leopold but mainly there were mission records and those of a leper colony near by. Smiles searched for anything showing a picture of an octopus but did not find one. The collection was more concerned with the past world and the next.

Before they all left, Smiles went back and found the Father alone. He wanted to use the toilet and the Father gave him a key and pointed to a door. Smiles went inside and realised it was the Father's room. There was a rusting white iron bed and a torn mosquito net and a plain wooden table and a chair. At one side of the room was a dusty washbasin with no taps and at the other, a simple wooden cross by a photograph of a young priest whose eyes had none of the doubts of Father Lieven's. The toilet was a hole in the ground, which even the fat flies avoided, and there was a shower fitting above. When Smiles tried to fill a bucket from a standpipe there was a vibration from the tap but no water and large cockroaches rose from the hole like monks summoned by the mission bell. He went out again and the Father was there, staring down at his sandals.

'Walk with me to that old church. We do not use it any more. There is no congregation, except a few pigs. The people from the village ask when I am going home. They won't even come and mend anything for me now.'

The sun swept across the lush grass.

'It is such a beautiful country,' sighed the priest. 'Are you a Catholic?'

'My mother was.'

They skirted a boggy patch of ground.

'I have one of your recordings, you know. Beethoven's late piano sonatas.'

'I am flattered.'

They stood before the church and Smiles could see it had been burned out inside. The Father was muttering something under his breath and it was hard to tell if it was a curse or a prayer.

Then he said: 'Lyman Andrew came to see me on many occasions. He was eager to learn about the work of the Fathers in collecting the old Congolese tribal music that became the *Missa Luba*. I was surprised when I knew he was doing this Peace and Reconciliation Concert. I almost thought he had stopped playing. He told me why he was here, why he came to Congo. To do good works. I worried about him. We learn to worry in our trade about those who are too earnest.'

'And did he mention me?'

The priest nodded and then stared at Smiles.

'You have had trouble of late. I know, I can see it in your face, my son. Take my advice and do not go upriver. One thing I have learned here is not to trust too closely. The Congolese moral narrative can suddenly fly off in an unexpected direction. In the mission in Kisangani there is a room with paintings of all our martyrs who trusted too much and were butchered and, in a few cases, eaten. A few in the recent war. You will meet so many delightful people but there are forces running through this land which no one can seem to control. Do not trust Celestine Mbando or his man. Celestine has lived too long to be honest and that girl is exactly the sort of person I am talking about. I told Fortuné I did not want to be part of this any more. My order, the Sacred Heart Fathers of Ghent, now read about Bemba in The Hague and would not understand how I could back a man on trial for such war crimes. My advice would be to take a plane from the airport back to Kinshasa and demand your ambassador. To remain up here, or to go any further, is more dangerous than you can possibly imagine. For your immortal soul as well as your earthly body.'

NINE

'Where are we going?' Lola asked in the taxi, when they took a different road from the one back from the mission to the port in Mbandaka and, as the rain increased, were quickly axle-deep in liquid mud, skidding down a rough track.

'You will see,' said Celestine mysteriously and Thérance gave his toothy laugh.

'Are we anywhere near the local airport?' asked Smiles.

'The airport, the airport!' said Thérance, as if it was a great joke. 'He wants to go to the airport!'

Celestine shook his head. He was in the front seat.

'The airport will be closed because of the weather. And anyway, the police will be looking for you. Do you want to go to prison?'

'I want to see my ambassador. I want the SIM card I lent you, Thérance.'

Thérance pretended a look of wide-eyed surprise.

'I gave that back to you in Kinshasa. In Matongé. It must have been taken from the table by a thief. You can try mine but there will be questionable reception. Do you know His Excellency's number?'

Smiles had the number, but it was on his SIM card. He was angry now as much with himself as Thérance. He was beginning to feel trapped again and did not know what to do. The minivan taxi oozed to a stop in front of twelve-foot metal gates and a man dressed in dark green and black with a Kalashnikov shook Celestine's hand through the window.

'Here we are. This is the famous botanical gardens,' said Celestine expansively, as if they were his. 'You can spend the night here while we sort things out with the boat. Then pick you up.' Smiles was about to protest but he felt Lola's hand pressing on his leg. 'We will never get the boat out of Mbandaka if they see Smiles or you, Lola. Everyone knows you . . . Now, I promised to show you the crocodile, St James. I think he is the biggest crocodile in the world. I believe he has eaten many people.'

They drove about a mile into the park and there was a slimy pool in a concrete pit six foot deep fenced around with flimsy chicken wire only three feet high. Everyone got out of the minivan and St James leaned against the wire, watching the immense fifteen-foot creature with its intricate brown scales and intelligent green eyes, which, in its stillness, seemed a far more natural part of the encompassing prehistoric forest than they did. Women came towards them with blue buckets on their heads full of live catfish and Celestine insisted on buying some and St James throwing one. The reptile suddenly lunged forward and for an instant its jaws were wide open, displaying rows of three-inch teeth, and the catfish disappeared, unchewed, down its red gullet.

'The mai-mai round here throw enemies to Papa Ngando,' said Celestine.

'Do not try to frighten the boy.' Lola put a hand on her brother's shoulder.

'I am not afraid,' said St James, never taking his eyes off the crocodile, now motionless again.

The rain started once more and they got back into the car and bumped down the road to the river where several four-by-fours were parked and there was a restaurant under a high bank of trees, taller than any Smiles had yet seen in Congo. A pair of hornbills flew raggedly up into the branches and as he gazed across the river he could see the grey storm and lightning flicker on the far bank. A party of sorts was going on in a little covered shelter near the water, from what French he could make out, the celebration of a *baccalauréat* pass and a couple were doing the *ndombolo* dance to Lingala music from a laptop computer, the girl in her white Lycée shirt. The waiter came over and Celestine ordered beers and a Fanta for St James, who had already run down to the river. Thérance brought four tents out of the car and put them on a table under another shelter and drew up a chair.

'This is a civilised place. We all spend the night here.'

'Shall we go for a tour, mama, please?' One of the little boys from the bar popped up to be their guide. 'I will show you the beautiful gardens with trees from every corner of the Belgian Empire,' he said. They laughed and the boy looked confused. 'I will show you my grandmother. She is still alive.'

Lola and Smiles went with the boy, who wore a blue Bemba T-shirt, leaving St James playing on the river beach. They met their thin-limbed guide's grandmother, who was in her forties and had no teeth, in a damp brick house black with smoke. She looked at Lola with such longing for chances she never had. Chickens and pigs wandered into the house and the stone floor was covered in dirt in a way never permitted in Lola's village upriver. She could not stand it any longer and gave the boy a dollar and pulled Smiles away. 'Come on, we will explore on our own.'

Further from the river, great trees were set in grassland, an eerie landscaped European parkland for which there once was scientific purpose. The buttress roots of the trees were taller than a man, forming dramatic triangles out from the trunk like the fins of a rocket. They sheltered at the base of one tree in another sudden rain shower and Smiles checked that the packets of papers and music he carried in his leather satchel were wrapped up in a plastic bag.

She had been thinking of Xavier and Fortuné and looked into Smiles' open face and said: 'Have you ever been totally and completely in love? So that you cannot think of anyone else? That your every waking minute is full of them? So if they do not speak to you in the next hour, you will shrivel up and die? Have you felt like that?'

His expression was one of confusion and then pleasure.

'Yes, I have been lucky enough, once. With one person, I mean. She was very special to me.'

'You have been married? You are married?'

She did not know why, but she never thought of Smiles as married. She imagined him only devoted to his music.

'I was married.'

She saw a shadow cross his face. Then he leaned forward and

she expected him to kiss her but he did not. She wanted him to kiss her, to take her in his arms, but he just stood there, his hand on her shoulder and an electricity went through her. She loved that look of longing and uncertainty in his eyes.

'I suppose I was married . . . am married. Xavier still regards me as his wife. He paid the *dot*, the marriage tribute, to my remaining uncle.' Lola sighed. 'Tell me, Smiles, why does it always hurt?'

'One person is always more in love. That's what I have found,' he said.

A tiny piece of leaf or a flower petal had fallen onto her forehead and he gently picked it off and continued.

'The gods are jealous of us, of all that emotion and pleasure and wanting. Our every breath becomes governed by the other. Then, when one goes away or dies, we are left trying to find them again, trying to recreate all that beauty and passion.'

In Congo men did not talk to her like this.

But then the boy who had showed them his grandmother limped towards them, shouting and waving his scraggy arms.

'Mama, mama, come. Your friends are going. Mama, your friends are going. They are taking your boy!'

She sprang out from between the tree's dark roots.

'Going? Stop! Celestine! Stop!'

She ran faster than Smiles did and was back at the café to see the minivan driving off at great speed down the track and rounding a stand of trees. St James was leaning out of a window.

'Stop! Stop! Where are you taking him!'

She started after them but the man from the café overtook her and grabbed her arm.

'Mama! Don't do that, mama. The sun go soon. You never catch them. They say they come back. They come back with boat tomorrow.' He spoke in Lingala and she saw the young people who had been celebrating had gone and two of the humpbacked tents from *Le Rêve* had been pitched above the beach. Across the river there was a flash and a deep rumble of thunder as a dark cloud drifted towards them. Smiles caught up with her.

'They have taken St James with them' was all she said.

She and Smiles sat under a shelter and watched the storm across the river.

The light faded to a watercolour world of greys and greens.

Eventually she said: 'I think we should get into one of the tents. Please would you come in with me?'

He nodded.

How could she be so stupid as to leave the boy with Celestine Mbando and Thérance?

Terrified, she thought of the crocodile and those snapping jaws.

She sat opposite Smiles, taking in his face in the failing light and listening to the quiet and the night noises. In a tree near by a large owl began to hoot. Smiles had such delicate features for a man and he sat cross-legged and hesitant on the small foam mattress that was in the tent. The evening felt cold and then it came to her. The owl hooted again, this time louder and more insistent. She saw clearly what was going to happen and she was pushing Smiles off the mattress just as she pushed her whole family out of the door one morning in Kisangani when the Rwandans launched an attack and they had brought heavy weapons to bear on the houses in the wealthier part of town. She had herded the children of her sister towards the emerald stand of forest and could still remember the surprise on their faces and her sister's youngest daughter breaking her arm and still crying for a doll when the house next door exploded in fire and smoke.

She shoved Smiles again violently and was unzipping the tent.

'Get out, come on . . . *Allez!*'

'Look, I was not going . . . to attempt! I thought you were scared! I do want to kiss you but I understand . . .'

She laughed.

'No, not that, you fool! Quick, hush, keep low. I think they mean to kill us. They are coming to kill us!'

'Who?'

She did not say anything but he grabbed his bag and followed her blindly into the growing darkness and they half-walked, half-ran until they reached a ruined house. Lola guessed it would be the pro-Bemba mai-mai coming for them. She thought of trying to go to the home of the grandmother but her sons might be mai-mai too. Perhaps they intended to kill or kidnap her because the men who controlled the militia thought she was in touch with Xavier and had been involved in the hotel bombing. Or it was Celestine's work.

She and Smiles crouched against a wall deep in shadow and stayed there as the night got darker and the thunder and lightning came closer. When she was very young storms and warfare had become tangled in one long explosion in her mind. There was a flash and then an almost simultaneous bang and she felt he was about to say something, probably to tell her that she was being hysterical, imagining things, when the next flash silhouetted a ragged line of figures close by, heading for the river. It was only for an instant but she felt that every angle, every line of their bodies was evil, intent on the kill. She could see the guns slung over their shoulders and one man swung a panga, the blade white in the intense light. The tense and hunched progress then vanished again into the rainy darkness.

She tried to see where they had gone.

It was not long after, on the cusp of another detonation of thunder, that there was a burst of machine-gun fire and she was suddenly holding Smiles in her arms, as tight as she could, desperate to protect him rather than give in to the shaking fear that almost consumed her. At that moment the clouds shifted towards them and a wall of water hit the ground.

The hot rain was so heavy they could hardly breathe or see.

Once she thought she heard a man passing near by, searching, then a child's cry. They were so near. She could smell the *chikwangue* they had been eating. Sticks broke underfoot only a yard away. But the darkness and the torrent of water hid them.

She then heard one man begin to shout.

'Mama Lola, you come out now . . . You come out now!'

They spoke in Lingala.

'Mama Lola, come out now and death will be quick. Do not make us come and find you.'

'They know your name,' whispered Smiles.

'No, they are cursing the heavens. That's what Lola means.'

She prayed and prayed they did not have St James.

'Mama Lola, I see you in the pictures in the paper . . . I want you! We all want you. We have the boy. We have the boy and you can get him back. We will spare him. We do not want him. Come out now, Mama Lola. Come out for the boy. We make him squeal like a little pig.'

She knew if she showed herself they would kill her anyway and there was no proof they had St James. She tried to put him as far out of her mind as she could. To turn her mind to the sky, her mother used to say. She and the Englishman had to survive; she was not going to let these demons cut up the musician, an educated and sensitive man.

Then Smiles was breathing too fast, the short spasms of breath she knew were dangerous. When she had been caught once in the fighting in Kisangani a neighbour had died that way, and she kissed Smiles' wet face to calm him, soothe him.

'It will be all right, *chéri,*' she whispered in his ear. 'Breathe slowly . . .'

There was a flash of lightning that lit up everything as bright as day. She saw a green lizard on a leaf. There was a figure further up the path and she was sure he must see them and open fire. She pushed Smiles down into the mud.

The soft, hot darkness surrounded them again.

They crawled deeper into the wet bushes by the crumbling ruin for the night and wrapped their arms around each other like children lost in a wicked fairy-tale forest. She felt his heart beat and his body relax as he slipped away into the sleep of exhaustion while she watched and listened. She was glad to have him so close. She did not expect him to protect her. It was the same comfort and sense of purpose an infant would bring. She brushed his cheek with her lips and wondered if his wife was dead or had left him.

The night was so long she scarcely dared believe it when the birds and the monkeys and the frogs began to call and the first light showed over the inky-black trees. She shivered in his arms and he awoke, fearful, but she put her fingers to his lips. They waited where they lay until the truck with the botanical-garden workers laboured out to the café. Only then were they confident enough to venture out into the open and stumble stiff and cold down to the wrecked tents. The garden workers were putting on their park jackets and the normality of the scene somehow made the night worse. The man who ran the café shook his head but there was a ghost of a smile on his face. He was old for a man around here, like the grandmother, in his forties. He picked up a piece of canvas and peered through the bullet holes. Smiles snatched it from him and let it drop. Lola trembled.

But her voice was angry.

'Get us two *cafés au lait*. Now.'

The man shuffled off, his oversize rubber boots dragging against the long grass.

'Will they try again? Will they come back?' Smiles asked.

'Not now. The mai-mai will wait until it gets dark. Come, we must sit in the sun and dry out.'

'Who were they? I mean, which side? Why?'

'I don't know. You never know. That's Congo.'

She moved two chairs out so they could sit down and held his hand hard as the sun warmed them. Over the river she could see for ever across the forested plain. The sun was hot on her face and she closed her eyes.

They cannot take the beauty of the world away; they can only kill you, Lola, she said to herself, as the sun rose higher and she forced a joy into her limbs the way she had after the bullets hit the walls of her house in Kisangani.

'We made it through the night,' she said to him, suddenly

anxious again for what had happened to St James. But she realised that if she let her imagination run away with her she would freeze up. Lola had seen people die from using too much imagination.

The café owner limped back towards them with the two coffees on a tin tray. Gobbets of milk powder floated on the top but she did not care.

He did not ask them for any money.

'Can you give us a lift to the road?'

He shook his head.

'Best you stay here and wait. Wait for your friends and the boat. They will come back here by boat if they are going upriver.'

And she knew from the way the terrified man looked at her that when the darkness returned so would the mai-mai with their guns and pangas to kill her, to use her and to kill the Englishman.

She felt anger at her powerlessness. It was all because of her love, her lost love of Xavier.

Lola inhaled the damp air of the river and watched two boys paddle a canoe out in midstream, standing, and then swing it with the current downriver. They were far away but she was on her feet waving to them and they waved back, smiling, and were gone, borne on by the huge force of the great brown stream she had known since she was a child and to whom she prayed first and deepest and who she believed would rescue her, if she was worth rescuing.

She saw another pirogue coming towards the bank and then veer suddenly away, the occupants paddling fast, a woman turning and holding up her hands and crying: '*Té! Té!* No! No!'

The bank fell quickly to the water's edge and there was a ridge of red pebbles.

Lola let out a low moan. She brought her hands up to her face and Smiles rushed to put an arm around her.

'What is it?'

She pointed up the stony beach.

A boy's body had been cut to pieces and left in piles of flesh along the shore.

A black wading bird was pecking at a foot.

Why hadn't she protected St James? Her mother had taken her place when the soldiers had wanted to rape her. 'Take me,' her mama had said.

Lola then saw a single poor shoe and felt a warm wave of relief and guilt.

'The ... boy ... The boy who showed us his grandmother ... Smiles!' She recognised a torn piece of blue Bemba T-shirt that had not stopped his killers. 'He must have been watching our tents when they came for us.'

Smiles did not say a word.

TEN

On that final afternoon in Kisangani, St James reached for another packet of Smiles' papers which he had addressed to Dr Kaplan in South Africa. St James sighed. It was a sad truth in his country that nothing got to where it was going through the post and, if he did not read it, the story would go to waste and not be told. To put letters in postboxes was pure silliness. All you did was make sure that the present went to the children of the postman. Everyone had wanted to be a postman until no one was sending any letters any more because they had all been stolen. The best way was to send a parcel in one of Xavier's jeeps. No one stole from Xavier and he stole from no one. He had a magic trick which could make a sweet appear in your top pocket or come out of your ear. Except that was not really magic and was different from people turning into crocodiles or a rushing wind. It was said Xavier turned into a leopard sometimes or a rushing wind and St James believed the stories up to a point. He was frightened of Xavier. The postmen would be frightened of Xavier. If Xavier's men stole he made them disappear. He shot them. St James did not think the Englishman Smiles appreciated whom he had made an enemy of in his silliness and kissing with Lola. Perhaps there is a deafness to the world that comes from too much playing of the piano? St James opened the neat packet.

My Confession:
Stanley Miles-Harcourt: black book, packet three

One Friday at school we were doing army corps and everyone was jumpy because of the killing of my friend, David Wace. I had been questioned about it by the police, who were now from Scotland Yard, the famous Scotland Yard, Dr Kaplan. A detective with dirty fingernails had showed me a picture of David at home with his mother, laughing on a lawn. I told them how I had walked with him to the village. I thought of his untidy fair hair and his blazer he hadn't brushed and an argument we were having. He was not like my other friends, I really trusted him. I shivered. I could not stop thinking of him. How he put his tongue at the corner of his mouth when he was going to cry and how I had done my best to stop him being bullied. He was too sensitive for a school like this one and he only ever fooled around when he was with me. It did not seem possible he was gone. Tears were starting to well up in my eyes and I blinked them away. We were all lined up in the dark-khaki battledress of the First and Second World Wars, which was as uncomfortable to wear as a hair shirt. But that morning I was almost glad of the distraction from remembering my friend.

That Friday my boots were not well polished. I just could not concentrate. I had done too much piano practice the day before at Lyman

Andrew's and then there was the school musical. So I had to get up in the middle of the night and do my prep in the dorm bogs. I totally forgot about my boots.

The Company Sergeant-Major, who was the head of Devon House, the next one to mine, came and screamed in my face: 'Look at your boots!' and when I did, 'Don't look at your boots!'

He stood very close and ugly as he shrieked at me, bending down, hands behind his back, his face below mine. His breath smelt of the milky coffee we had at break times. Prefects did that. They came at you and yelled in your face so everything else vanished. I could usually cope with the abuse but, as I had been up most of the night and was upset, it startled me. We were at attention and my heavy Lee Enfield .303 rifle was held at my side. The shouted orders made me jump and my hand slipped in the trigger guard. I tried to catch the dropping rifle but the sharp metal foresights caught the prefect in his left eye. The rifle clattered onto the ground.

The prefect let out a howl of agony and rage.

He staggered away. I thought I had knocked his eye out and blinded him. His beret fell off as he reeled around and everyone was looking at me astonished, as if I had done it on purpose.

He straightened up. His eye was all right but his cheek was bleeding.

He came back and slapped me straight across the face with his hand. I was seeing stars.

The prefect then began to hit me with his swagger stick: the black stick that had a metal core and a silver end which all the sergeants and officers carried and the prefects used for beatings. He was going wild.

But the next thing I knew, he was being pulled off.

'Do you want to try that with a person your own size, you bully? I guess you don't. No human being should treat another like that, ever.

Is that clear? We have had one body in the morgue, we don't want another.'

The prefect mumbled something inaudible.

'Is that clear?'

'It is clear, sir. Quite clear.'

'Good.'

Lyman Andrew had the prefect by the ear, even though the boy was every bit as big as he was. There was more surprise than fear on the prefect's face, as if the grass had suddenly turned purple and the sky green. Lyman Andrew let go. The prefect glanced over to my head of house, Anderson, who was an officer, wearing a Sam Browne belt and a jaunty smile. Anderson made a little 'OK' gesture with the thumb and forefinger of a leather-gloved hand.

'I am very sorry, sir,' said the prefect to Lyman Andrew.

Lyman Andrew nodded his head. But he seemed sceptical.

'I don't think you are. I don't think you are for a moment and you probably never will be if you imagine life is all about payback.'

The prefect looked confused. He knew he was being told off but was not quite sure what about.

Lyman Andrew then turned and stared at me for a moment, smiled, and walked away.

The trouble was Lyman Andrew kept doing things like that. He stopped all he thought unfair or cruel, when most masters would not get involved if the prefects had murdered a convent full of blind and crippled nuns. He even complained to our puzzled housemaster about prefects beating boys:

'Your housemaster told me, "That's what they do, Andrew, the prefects. They beat boys," and went back to tying one of his fishing flies. He argued it was best to leave it to the prefects and not make a fuss. They

don't like people interfering,' Lyman said a few days later, as he was teaching me a piece of Mozart.

'What century is this place living in? The young are treated worse than slaves and the old have absolute power. I mean, I can see the logic when you were all going to be soldiers or administrators in a far-flung outpost of the British Empire, where cruelty was part of the trading system. But surely all that is history?'

A week after Lyman Andrew stopped the prefect hitting me, I had half-an-hour before I was meant to be in the dormitory so I went across to the changing rooms. It was break time from prep and, though I did not smoke, I wanted to see a couple of friends who might be sharing a Player's No. 6 behind the oil tank. It was dark but not freezing cold. The new heating-oil tank for the shower blocks was behind the changing rooms. A brick wall surrounded the room-sized metal tank in case of explosion. There were signs that said `Danger, No Naked Lights. Strictly No Smoking'. But if you slipped between the bricks and the tank there was enough room to light up and talk in private. It was currently the safest place to smoke in the school from a prefect point of view. But when I squeezed inside there was no one.

I got out again and, making my way around the changing block, I noticed a light at the corner.

Anderson suddenly stepped out of the shadows. He had been waiting there and had obviously spotted me going behind the oil tank. I saw his feet first and then his face. He leaned against the wooden side of the building very casually.

'Congratulations! You have been caught smoking, Smiles.'

Anderson did not have a handsome face. His eyes were small and his jaw too square but he always looked amused. Not just laughing at a *joke but cosmically amused as if he could see how everything fitted together and it was all so funny. He was Scottish but his accent was the languid, upper-class drawl all prefects affected. Fear pinched the top of my solar plexus and I wanted to run into the welcoming dark but it was much too late.*

'Excuse me, Anderson, but I don't smoke.'

We always had to say 'excuse me' when addressing a prefect for the first time.

'Cheek and insubordination, too.'

'Where are my cigarettes? I have to have cigarettes to be able to smoke.'

Anderson sighed. He reached into the pocket of his blazer and took a step towards me:

'I have them here.'

He showed me a packet of Player's No. 6. He took one out of the packet, lit it and blew smoke in my face. He then dropped it at my feet.

'Pick it up, Smiles, there's a good chap.'

I hesitated.

'Disobedience, Smiles? I thought we had an agreement, you and I? That you were going to keep out of trouble.'

That meant 'gating' too. Not being able to leave the school grounds for a month.

I bent down and picked up the cigarette and handed it back to him. He took it and stubbed it out on his shoe and picked up the dog-end.

'Gosh, smoking, insubordination, disobedience. And I have two chits already from other prefects saying that you have been running round with the middle button of your jacket unfastened. One might almost think the gods were out to get you. What have you done, Smiles?'

I never broke small rules. Three chits and you were beaten. In front of the whole house.

'You have been a naughty boy, Smiles. I think it's all because of that new master being a bad influence on you. He's popular with the little chaps because he treats everyone as if they were worthy of an opinion. Dangerous. But he's not a softie. He insists on decency. And people actually want to go to his Latin classes, which I regarded as a punishment, and the school musical he's taken over is oversubscribed. What happens to such a paragon in a school like this? And he's an optimist. I admire that. I heard him say to the head that it was so refreshing to work in an institution where there was no racism. The head did not know quite what to reply . . .'

Anderson paused.

'We must not let you stray, Smiles, especially in the circumstances.'

'No, Anderson.'

'We must correct that. We have to be cruel to be kind. Remember our agreement? How I helped you? Is that a tear I see in your eye, Smiles? A quiver in your lip? For yourself, or someone else? Go and change into your pyjamas and see me in my study off the day room. I have not beaten anyone in a while. Chaps seem to avoid being beaten by me. Do you remember when I beat your good friend, Wace? Last fortnight? Made him blub, didn't I? Made his little botty bleed? You miss him, Smiles. I can see you miss him.'

There was absolutely no point in saying anything more. I was crying inside, but not for myself. I was crying for poor David Wace. I had been beaten a few times by masters at the junior school but never by a prefect at the senior school in front of the house at prep. As soon as they saw you enter the day room in your pyjamas they knew you were going to be beaten. Once in the prefect's study you were out of sight but prep was silent and they could hear the slight whistling sound the swagger stick made in the air and the thwack as it landed. (I bet this is the sort of stuff you are dying to hear, Dr Kaplan.) Everyone, even friends, waited for you to cry out or blub and then you would be punched and kicked in the dorm that night and your bed would get tipped over for ages afterwards without warning because you were a filthy coward.

I nodded to Anderson and walked away.

I went up the tower stairs to the dorm and was quiet so as not to make Hag Large's sheltie dog bark. (We called all the matrons hags, whether they were nice or not.) I nearly stuck my foot through the leg of my pyjamas, I was shaking so badly. I then put on my dressing gown and slippers. All were school issue.

When I opened the door of the day room, the silence of prep had changed.

That silence was as loud as the roar of the Colosseum. I think that's why silence wakes me. My worst moments at school were in total quiet.

I tried not to look at the boys as I walked through. One of my friends gave me a nod but others grinned and made throat-cut signs.

'Settle down, or you'll be next,' said the junior house prefect.

I walked to the study and knocked on the door.

'Come.'

I turned the brass handle and went in. I closed the door behind me.

Anderson was not at the desk in his study but in his old leather armchair. He was holding his black, silver-tipped, swagger stick.

'You know why you are here?'

'Yes, Anderson.'

'I'm not certain you do ... Are you sure?'

He was playing with me. Trying to make me more afraid.

'Yes, Anderson.'

'Well, you must be an even brighter chap than we thought. Now, take off that old dressing gown. What an awful school dressing gown. That one couldn't even have been chosen by your mother. Take it off and hang it on the door. Yes, that's right. On the hook. Are your hands shaking, Smiles, or is it chilly in here? Now, let's have the pyjama bottoms next. And the silly old top as well. We don't want them spoiled with spots of blood. Matron would tell me off, wouldn't she just?'

I froze.

We were always beaten in pyjamas.

I found it hard to breathe. My lips were trembling.

'Do as I say.'

'My pyjamas?'

'Your pyjamas and your slippers, there's a good chap.'

I took them off. I hung them on the door too. I stood before him naked.

He sat there tapping the swagger stick against his knee, staring at my body.

'Now, Smiles, I want you to bend over that desk. Put your hands in the middle of the desk and get right up on tiptoe, so that nice little botty of yours sticks out.'

I did what he said.

I have never felt so exposed and vulnerable in my life.

He got up and walked around me. For a whole minute he made no sound.

Then he touched me with the swagger stick on my bottom and I flinched.

'Good . . .'

Anderson then stroked the tip of the swagger stick against my neck and ran it down my spine, pausing at the crack between my buttocks. He took it away and I tensed for a blow.

I jumped when the stick touched my skin again, gently, side on to my backside. He then pushed the stick between my legs so it rested against my belly and lifted me up further on my toes. My legs started to shake. I tried to concentrate on a book he had open on the table. It was Crime and Punishment *by Fyodor Dostoevsky.*

'Ready to receive your due?'

'Yes, Anderson,' I said, struggling to control my voice.

I closed my eyes.

The swagger stick came down, pausing in between each blow. The sound was very loud.

But the stick did not come down on my backside.

Anderson had turned to his armchair and had hit the cushion six times.

'You can get up now,' he said in a loud voice. 'What do we say, Smiles?'

'Thank you, Anderson.' One always had to thank a prefect who beat you.

'Thank you, Miles-Harcourt.'

He came closer to me. He saw the confusion in my face.

'You see, I have not forgotten our bargain . . . I do want something from you, of course. Can't be doing a favour for you without you doing one for me. Or this can be repeated every week with your poor botty standing in for the cushion my blind godmother embroidered.'

'No . . . Please . . .'

He paused and sighed.

'No, Smiles, I do not want that. At least, not at present. What I want is for you to come to one of our meetings and we will discuss things further, at a certain time and place. A meeting of the Eumenides, the 'kindly ones'. A little society based on the Furies of Greek mythology,

the avenging deities Alecto, Megaera and Tisiphone, who used to torture criminals and such with the stings of conscience and the odd famine and pestilence. A classical education is such a delight, don't you think? You probably know our little band of prefects as the Mau Mau? But we are quite civilised savages. I'm sure you will be enlightened. Now, not a word to anyone, or we will be meeting back here a lot more often. And before you go, put a little of this horse liniment on your botty. Makes it look a bit more respectably rouge, though I usually cut. I don't want to damage my hard-won reputation for unspeakable cruelty, now, do I?'

I put my clothes on and hurried back through the silent day room, trying to look as if I were fighting tears. I would rather he have hit me.

Under the now pearl-grey sky of Kisangani St James had a fish but he did nothing at all about it. He could feel it wriggling, all its life between his two fingers on the line, but he did not pull it in over the side and put it into the bucket. He took a breath of air but it was no good, he was dizzy, giddy at what he had read. St James had always assumed white boys never got beaten and certainly not in such a way. He had heard stories about how the whites used to beat the people in Congo with *chicottes*, the whips made from the hide of the hippo. He had once seen such a whip in the museum and when he had been growing up his aunt and his uncle had hit him with a leather strap. But although the schoolboy Smiles had not been hit, this was far worse. This was humiliation. With the threat of further punishment hanging there like a curse. The man Anderson frightened St James and he was glad he did not go to school in England among such people. But he wanted to know more. That was the trouble. You always want to know more, be it about an octopus or a murder.

ELEVEN

Smiles sat close by Lola, his arm against her arm, writing in his journal (she was trying to get a signal on her mobile) until the light began to fade and the shades of pink glowed across the river and were reflected in the water. It was difficult to imagine how the crime, which littered the beach, even though he had tried his best to cover it with Primus-beer crates (he did not know what else to do), could be committed in a spot so beautiful against a blameless young boy. Yet his school had been serene and beautiful in the same timeless way and his friend, David Wace, every bit as innocent. Why was it always that one thought beautiful things were superior? The beauty that surrounded them was no help now and seemed to be mocking them. They must do something, they could not stay here and wait to die.

'We ought to try and walk out of here. The café owner was wrong.'

She turned to him. All the workers had gone.

'There is only the one road, Smiles, and the men from last night will be waiting on it. The gardens are ringed with marsh and jungle and small rivers. Under Mobutu it was like an open prison for his political opponents. Our only hope . . .'

It was then, as she lingered on the word 'hope', that they heard the low sound of an engine in the distance.

He held his breath and he thought he was going to burst.

Lola ran down to the water's edge.

She was jumping up and down and shouting and waving her arms.

Around a leaning stand of trees, out of the rising evening mist, the boat emerged, wraithlike, a sudden impossible vision with St James yelling to them from the bow. Smiles thanked God. The captain, smiling, was bringing the boat close and José was getting ready to tie up but Lola kicked off her shoes, picked them up and waded into the water.

'Don't land! Don't land! Whatever you do, don't land! Men tried to kill us last night! Throw us a rope!'

The captain let the boat drift and Lola caught the rope and athletically pulled herself up to the deck as Smiles ran in the shallows after her, tripped, fell, and then picked himself up clutching his bag and flung himself at the rope. He was shaking as he was hauled aboard and sat by the piano at the front of the boat, touching the black mahogany and trying to get a hold of sanity again. His hands were muddy and wet against the polished wood.

'Go! Go!' Lola was calling up to the captain from the front of the boat while a debate started among several of the crew about the tents. 'Go as fast as you can! Leave the tents.'

She hugged St James.

'My sweet, you're alive! I'm so sorry I left you.'

'Of course I am alive.'

She almost smothered him and he broke away embarrassed. But she grabbed hold of him and began to hug him again.

'Did they hurt you?'

'No. Nobody hurt me. Men tried to kill you?'

'Was it soldiers?' asked José.

'Was it mai-mai sent by Xavier?' asked Marie.

'They were not soldiers,' said Lola, watching the high trees of the garden vanish around the long bend. She started to recount the terrible night and Marie put her arms around Lola, glancing accusingly at Smiles as if he should have done more. Slowly the whole crew followed suit, except for the cook, who patted Smiles on the back and said: 'Praise the Lord you not dead, Mr Smiles.'

But there was no great alarm or surprise because they all expected and were used to such things.

Lola sat down in a chair.

'Where are Celestine and Thérance?' she said abruptly.

'They were arrested,' said St James.

'What?'

'They were taken to Mbandaka prison by the *Garde Républicaine*,' continued St James. 'They stop the taxi and drag them out in the rain. They do not want me, they too busy beating up Thérance for talking smart to them and singing his stupid Gilbert and Sullivan songs. So when we get to the jail outside town they put me on a cart going into Mbandaka and I walk back to the port.'

Lola sighed.

'I thought they betrayed us,' she said.

'They probably will. The soldiers were hitting them good when

I left. They were promising to tell everything, they are not brave. And they know where Uncle Fortuné is. They said the name of the place. It is a place known as Pendé, where there is an old Belgian house and what was a plantation where he and the American feed women who are escaping from North Kivu and the war and teach them to sing and gather coltan. It is not so far upriver from our village at Bokondo-Rive and the jungle is so thick it is impossible to attack.'

Lola drew herself up.

'Unfortunately, "impossible" is a word his brother Xavier does not use.'

Everyone went quiet after that and the cook brought them coffee and warm rolls. Smiles then watched as Lola collected frangipani flowers that the crew had been feeding with other greenery to the tortoises. She threw the blossoms one by one from the back of the boat, the sun hanging in a great crimson ball over the river like an accusing god. The sky was now layer upon layer of strawberry light above the water and the forest, windless and suffocatingly hot. As she scattered the flowers Smiles heard Lola saying a prayer but could not make out if it was Catholic or Baptist or African. He realised the little ceremony was for the boy in the botanical gardens. Smiles mumbled a Hail Mary to himself and went and stood by her. There was nothing else to say.

The boat was still taking on water and the captain tied up that night in a small creek and Lola and St James slept in the remaining tent. Smiles spread a bed mat out on the lockers and net curtains were strung partially over the top in an attempt to keep out the mosquitoes. He found himself being ridiculously jealous of St James and, as he strained to hear what she was whispering to the boy, what stories and reassurances, he realised how deeply he felt for her, how much he wanted to kiss her, wished he had kissed her in the tent before she had led him into the bush and safety. He did not care if a thousand warlords were prepared to commit their armies and fight to the death to win her. His journey was not just about his past and Lyman Andrew. His river had become wider. He felt all the emotion that had nearly killed him while playing, that he had blamed on exhaustion. Except when he thought of her, of Lola, all he felt was alive.

Lola slept late in the morning and the crew let her. She was woken by the boat moving under her and Mozart coming from the piano. Smiles played the notes so happily and she could see the sunshine through the thin fabric of the tent and his outline at the piano. It was eight o'clock with the sun already hot and Marie began singing along to a hymn on her mobile 'phone, trying to drown out Smiles. Then St James yanked down the zipper.

'C'mon, Lola. We are going to land. We are going onto an island.'

She pulled on her jeans and T-shirt and picked up her wash things from her locker and quickly cleaned her teeth and rinsed her face before asking the captain what he was doing.

When Lola came back from the bridge she put her hand on Smiles' shoulder. He had come to the end of the movement he was playing.

'That was lovely.'

He smiled.

'So are you. Why are we stopping?'

'The captain wants to repair the boat at the next village. He says he has to put in two new planks at the side or it will sink as the current gets stronger. But he does not want us on it as he does not know who the village supports at the moment. So we are going to be marooned on our own desert island. Do not worry, it's a friendly place, no mai-mai here.'

Smiles turned around.

'Look, I'd rather stay with the boat, if it's all the same.'

St James was standing at her shoulder.

'I am not getting off the boat again, sister. I am not getting off the boat until we reach Kisangani.'

'We should not test our luck,' added Smiles. 'Should we?'

Lola did not say anything but watched as they nosed in towards the right bank where there was a white sandy beach and three huts, roofed with straw, on a finger of sand and reeds, but no people.

Beyond the sand was a thick wall of high equatorial forest, dark and green, unlike the solitary trees in the botanical gardens, and under the top layer of vegetation there were toddy palms and she caught the smell of palm wine over the rot and river water. Mother-of-pearl cloud covered the whole sky and the island seemed to hang between earth and water, not part of anywhere.

José was in the front of the boat calling out the depth, stripped to the waist and sweating. A white heron flapped up over the water ahead of them. The far point of the island disappeared into the haze.

The engines stopped and they glided silently in.

They came to a gentle rest on the shore by a reed bed and a

collection of ancient, brown canoes that were broken into pieces. Lola half-climbed down the side and leapt into the water. Smiles scrambled after her, trying not to fall. She looked round and saw him following her up the beach when they heard the engines thrown into reverse.

He turned.

'No . . . I thought we were just having a look . . .'

Lola pulled him back as Marie threw a large canvas holdall and Smiles' wash bag onto the beach. The boat had already moved away out into the stream and José was singing: '*Mittakenamittake!* Clear water below!'

St James was waving to both of them from the bows with a quizzical expression on his face. In a moment they were alone, standing by a reed-and-palm house built on stilts. There was a ladder up to the house's only room, raffia screens for privacy and a rush-matting floor. The roof was coated with jungle rubber against the rain. There was nothing else except for a small carving of a man with the shell of a snail embedded in his head.

'Do not touch that. It is a fetish. It protects the hut.'

He nodded.

'Against floods?' he asked.

She grinned at him.

'And against crocodiles and the hippo who looks for a mate.'

'Do they come here?'

'All the time.'

'Really?'

She burst out laughing.

'I am only joking.'

'Good.'

She gave him a kiss on the cheek.

'They used to. I remember when there were hippos in the river above Kisangani. Above Ubundu. But then there were the wars and people had guns and shot them so you do not see them on the big river any more. Unless it is a person who has turned into a crocodile.'

She grabbed his hand playfully and he jumped. She was staring right at him and her great brown eyes filled the room. She kicked off her shoes.

'I . . . I left my journals, the stuff I've been writing on the boat. My leather bag!'

It had been an extravagance Emma had bought him in Florence, from a man she knew who had a workshop near the railway station.

'They will take care of them.'

'And my music?'

He had begun to put down music. Just the basic themes. But it was the first time in years he had tried and now he wanted to write more; to write for her. He had never done that, written for a woman.

She gave him another, more lingering kiss on his forehead.

'They will respect your music and the piano. St James will watch over them. No one will touch them. He will not read the journals.'

He shrugged. Her nipples showed through the pink T-shirt.

'I don't care if he does.'

Smiles did care. But he doubted if what he had written would make sense to the boy or if St James would talk to him again.

'It's stupid things from my school about Lyman Andrew, who

I thought I would never meet again when I wrote them. This doctor in Johannesburg thinks Lyman Andrew is very important to me. I am not sure now. The school I went to taught you to be cold and uncaring.'

She shook her head and smiled in such a way it made him tremble.

'You are not uncaring, Smiles. You are one of the most caring men I have ever met.'

She did not stop smiling at him.

He blinked nervously and then she was kissing him on the lips. Her tongue gently probing between. He was so excited he could not breathe and he was terrified. His stomach was seized with a cramp as he stared at her closed eyes and the incredible, that was the word, beauty of her face. He was shaking as she drew back and stroked his hair.

'There . . . isn't that what you meant to do? In the gardens?'

'Yes.'

'I wanted it, too.'

He was going to make a nervous English joke about a gang of armed men seeking your violent death being the enemy of passion, when she was kissing him again and this time he took her in his arms, he was not scared any more. She was kissing him at the same time as unbuttoning his shirt and pulling it off his shoulders and then shrugging off her pink T-shirt and rubbing her skin against his. She hugged him to her breasts and her nipples traced across the flesh of his chest and he shuddered and bent his head and licked and sucked each one in turn. He was losing himself in her now. She was lifting up his head and kissing him again and she was tugging at his belt and his pants and he had a moment of sheer panic as he scrabbled at the stupid knots of his Aid America baseball boots until she finally released them and he was naked on the rough mat.

'Smiles . . .' she murmured.

She knelt in the hut before him and wriggled down her jeans and bright-green panties and eased them off. She rocked there on her heels.

How could she want him? He had never seen anyone so beautiful and he wanted her as he had never wanted anything on this earth.

He was going to write her symphonies, all the pretty works were going to be dedicated to her, laid at her perfect feet. He understood why men fought battles for her. He quickly pulled her to him.

TWELVE

Smiles woke ecstatically happy, happier than he had ever been in his life. He watched a pale-pink gecko in the roof of the hut as the immense light of dawn flooded through the side slats like the greatest choir he had ever heard. All the transcendent works of music, of Handel and Wagner, were not able to add to that moment for him. He felt joy at this world that only days ago he thought he would be leaving in a shameful, shabby death no one would ever record. But now!

His mind danced along her every caress like the reflections of the water on the roof of the hut.

A hot wind blew through the straw matting and he looked out at the river and she was there, naked, her hair let down in ringlets around her face, her breasts and belly shining in the light as she washed herself in the flow.

She reached up into her hair and took out what looked like a bone and started to brush her teeth.

Smiles had been warned not to wade in or drink that water.

She seemed to crave it, she cupped her hands and drank and drank. She was so delicate and yet so tall and strong and he had no doubt that he was totally in love with her, this woman of wars and water.

She came running out of the river and the sun made the droplets on her body glisten.

She held out her arms. Lola looked as if she was going to embrace creation.

It was as if they had stepped outside the world.

Then she ran up into the hut and kissed him.

'I borrowed your toothbrush.'

He was shaking his head. She looked puzzled for a moment.

'I was just thinking how beautiful you are.'

She laughed.

'I was once Miss Young Kisangani, when they were trying to cheer people up after the fighting had stopped. I was hauled through the streets on a broken Toyota truck which had no petrol. I was dressed in flower petals and dreaded it raining. But everyone applauded, even the old priest from the cathedral.'

Lola ran her hands over his chest as he lay blinking up at her. She could not get over the paleness of his skin in the morning light. It was as if he had never been exposed to the sun, like those fish she had read about that live in the caves of Mexico and are all white and blind as bats.

'I thought you said you were brought up in a village?'

She nodded.

'But my father worked for an Indian in Kisangani from when he was a boy. A man called Balraj who had come from the coast and was a lovely, polite man who knew many things. In the massacres and confiscations of the Mobutu years, when everything was given to us Africans, he put his property in my father's name and only left when the Zanzibari woman he loved was killed by a stray bullet. I used to try to pull out his chest hair as a child because I thought he was turning into a monkey and told him so and he would laugh and read me the *Jungle Book* stories of the Bandar-log and Shere Khan and the bad cobras who try and kill the mongoose. He went 'home' to Calcutta but wrote and wrote to us, saying that he wanted to come back. Then in the war there was nothing. His money paid for me to go to the Lycée and will pay for me to go to university.'

It was in the white shirt of the Lycée, as a little girl, she had first noticed Xavier and his brother. They were the two most handsome boys in the school and the day she saw them they were arm in arm.

Lola chattered to Smiles the way new lovers do. She told him how her father had met her mother in Kisangani when she had come in with tiger fish from her village of Bokondo-Rive downstream. She was from the small tribe of the village and he was of the Mariènde, who were from North Kivu and more warlike than the people of the river. A group of villagers had come over to seek greater prosperity in Kisangani and avoid raids from Uganda.

Lola did not tell him that one of the families was that of Xavier and Fortuné with four other brothers and a sister who were now dead and that Xavier and Fortuné also learned all they could from the Indians of the richer Domaine district and quickly became the town sophisticates. The two brothers had dominated the basketball team and she shut that out of her mind too, as Smiles reached for her and they made love.

Afterwards she said: 'Come on, get dressed. We will go and see if there is bread at the village.'

'I thought we were alone?' he said.

'We are, it is about ten minutes away.'

'But we can stay on this beach? While we are here?'

'Yes.'

Smiles was on the beach for about ten minutes, lost in contentment, the village and bread forgotten, when he looked up and there was a man standing by the tall reeds near the broken canoes, wearing an old coat and clutching a silent, staring child. Moments later Lola was by Smiles' side and the stranger held out his hand and they both took it. They were not as alone as Smiles had imagined and he wondered if they had been watched. The man, beckoning them to follow, then set off towards a path through the swaying green elephant grass and reeds and they had to jump over a small river which divided their island from the forest. Once on the land proper the track turned to mud with hairy palm trees at every twist and turn. As he climbed over a rotten log Smiles grabbed one and several long thorns went painfully into his palm. Through a thicker patch of jungle and a spray of dark-red ginger flowers they came to a village of charcoal smoke and little children and barking hunting dogs, one of which took hold of Smiles' right jeans leg and began to shake it, playfully.

Their guide shooed the yellow, sharp-faced animal away.

By one of the huts a beaming woman had taken a tray of rolls out of a mud oven.

They were handed one each and a beaker made from bamboo.

'Drink. It is all right. They have their own ways of purifying the water on these islands. They run it through charcoal into a clay-lined well. It is so cool.'

He drank and she took the beaker from him. The water was very good and he inhaled the smell of the warm bread before biting into the roll. He was famished.

Lola sat on the ground with the woman who had baked the bread. She was in her twenties and already surrounded by children. One sucked a ragged nipple.

'You stay as long as you like here, mama. My husband bring you fish and maybe meats. I like your man. He is a white man and not an albino. He is the first white man I have seen here. The first real white man. Is he too hot? He looks too hot. My husband take you to the forest and show you the palms and you get palm wine.' And all the time Lola and Smiles were being passed bits of meat and fish and pungent *chikwangue* paste beside the smoking fire as more children came out of the forest and stared at them wide-eyed and eventually began to sing and dance a welcome, over and over again, their voices cascading into each other.

She saw with amusement that the little ones were reaching out to take Smiles' hand. One even ran up and touched his face and then darted away again, examining his finger and showing it to the others. In the end they were satisfied Smiles had not been painted like the dancers at a feast.

Lola took another roll. There were only a few huts in the village but more and more women appeared and three men, one with

139

an ancient shotgun and a green pigeon and a hornbill in his leather belt.

Smiles had eaten too much of the bread when the man in the coat they had first met, the chief of the Eleko tribe, led them through the forest to another little village and another, where they were fed more rolls and whatever else the people had. Then they struck out into the forest and the singing children who followed them became silent.

The forest was dark but not in any way cooler. The air was close and steamy and so hot it stung his lungs and made his sinuses hurt. He had not gone a hundred yards before he wished for a canteen of that cool, filtered water.

They scrambled over fallen logs and at every turn there was a loose piece of palm that scratched his hand or stuck in his shirt like barbed wire as the temperature made him feel giddy and heavy. There were shallow pools of open water covered in bubbling slime and he saw bright-green frogs dart away from the surface. The highest white-barked trees soared to the canopy sometimes a hundred and fifty feet above, spreading out in parasols of leaves, but the vegetation around him was close and there were many toddy palms and great gourds left at the base of them full of white, frothy palm wine, which had been tapped high up on their trunks.

The chief offered him some to drink from a gourd.

He hesitated and the man smiled. Smiles tipped the gourd up and drank deeply.

The wine was sharp and perfumed and creamy and strong.

'That's so good, thank you.'

He handed the gourd back to the chief, who smiled and did not take a drink.

Smiles realised that the whole forest reeked of the pungent wine and almost immediately he felt light-headed.

Lola laughed.

'You are brave, Smiles. It is too strong for me. They take the wine out to passing boats and to nearby towns. That is how they make a living and trade for flour and fish hooks.'

They were on their way again as another man joined them, barefoot with his jeans cut in a fringe at the bottom and without a shirt. He was not big but his arms and chest were perfectly sculpted with muscle. At the man's waist hung a panga and ahead of him the chief sang out and from the forest two other voices sang back. When they came to a fork in the path the chief did this several times and Smiles realised the man was fixing his position on the earth in song.

Smiles then sang out the first lines of Ode to Joy from Beethoven's Choral Symphony No. 9.

'Freude, schöner Götterfunken,
Tochter aus Elysium,
Wir betreten feuertrunken,
Himmlische, dein Heiligtum.'

It could have been written for Lola. A true daughter of heaven and this was her shrine. The notes carried on the heavy air and after a puzzled moment there was an answer back in Lingala.

He was part of a musical map and found the sensation as exhilarating as being called back for an encore.

Before he expected, he was back at the first collection of huts and Smiles watched as the palm wine was stored and not drunk.

They were given a whole tray of bread and no one would take his dollars.

He then walked back with Lola and they sat on the beach, which had only their footprints from that morning, and watched as a white-headed fish eagle soared over the river, looking for prey.

He had begun little by little to hear music in his head, music based around the river, of the cry of the *profondeur*, of the chief in the jungle, of the eagle above them.

He felt such a delight in being with her it made him far more inebriated than the palm wine.

'I want to stay here for ever, for ever and ever,' he said.

'No, you don't.'

'Perhaps love is only possible where there is no time.'

She laughed.

'Then the whole of Congo is the place to love.'

He shook his head.

'I mean here . . . Why can't we just stay here? To live like this for ever? To wake up to the sunshine and the dawn and the river? To leave all the cities behind and all the people with guns who want to kill? Look, there is a kingfisher.'

She followed his gaze to a greeny-blue-and-white bird she probably knew by a different name.

'Don't you want to take me to London and Paris?'

'You would be the belle of the ball,' he said.

She jumped up. He grabbed her hand and whirled her around in a sandy waltz.

'We can take one of the witch-doctor aeroplanes.'

'What?'

'The poor people on the river who cannot afford to fly take the witch-doctor aeroplanes. They even report the crashes in the papers. People believe in them, Smiles.'

'I want to take you everywhere.'

She stared into his face.

'Let us not start making plans, Smiles. Because you know what happens?'

'No . . . ?'

'The *ngando*. The crocodile comes and drags our happiness away.'

He opened his mouth but she closed it with a kiss.

'Let us enjoy our world outside time. It cannot be for ever. You know that, Smiles, don't you? It cannot be for ever, can it?' And then she kissed him again and giggled and they ran laughing around the beach together.

That night she awoke and saw the moon was on the fetish in the corner of the room and she felt its eye on her and every nerve on her back tingle. The light illuminated Smiles' body, which looked frail in the night, and she found herself crying for him, against unimagined dangers, against his fate. Silently she moved off the mat and down the ladder and onto the glowing white beach, and went and sat beneath the weaver-bird tree with its curling roots and watched a star fall to earth. She held out her arms and prayed as her father used to: 'Please, Lord of all, do not hurt this man, Smiles. He is not a warrior. Please do not test him. He is a maker of music and a good and sensitive man. Do not cause him the pain of the body, even at the moment of his death. Do not let anyone lay hands on him or cut him or shoot him with bullets. Grant me this, Lord, and I will be dutiful and never leave Congo.'

She thought of her father and honoured his memory. He too was not a warrior in his soul even though he was Mariende and had fought when he had to. In Congo there were too many warriors and not enough musicians.

Lola stared up at the stars for a long time and then her gaze fell to the river and at first she was very afraid but then her fear vanished, and so did the large crocodile which she had seen clearly in the moonlight.

There was nothing there now but the black-pearl surface of the river.

She smiled and went back to the hut where she lay next to Smiles and listened to his untroubled breathing and gently blew loving thoughts into his dreams.

THIRTEEN

A week or it may have been more passed and he treasured each day, every moment on those white sands with her, listening to the music that was playing in his soul once more. He was in love with Lola and to his surprise and delight she was in love with him.

They had been seemingly freed from what was past and what might be in the future. He had never realised love was so bound up with time. Music he knew was composed of all the combinations and nuances of time but now he saw how one has to stop time for the wellspring of creativity to burst forth. He had been running for planes to become a better musician when all he should have done was sit on a beach under a mango tree with a beautiful woman.

'Did your wife leave you, Smiles?' Lola asked suddenly, appearing next to him on the beach. She could walk so quietly. He never heard her coming or going if she did not want him to.

'In a way.'

He regretted how he said the words. They must have seemed almost flippant.

'Did you fall out of love?'

'She died.'

It was still painful to him, even here on the beach.

'Smiles. I am sorry. I did not mean . . .'

She held his arm.

'We were having a difficult time, I suppose. She might have left me. She often said she was going to but never did. She was a gifted writer but a much better alcoholic and very nearly made me one too. She was American, from Massachusetts, with a gift of converting people to her sins. There was something in her Puritan soul that said every bit of happiness has to be paid for, so she drank. Her name was Emma. I was driving my car, an old Jaguar. My father had always had Jaguars and we were having a stupid argument about it not being modern and safe and such and then she grabbed the wheel and turned it to the side of the road. We hit a tree, an ash tree. We were not far from where I have a cottage that belonged to my parents. And the car turned over and . . . she was dead, lying there quite still with her lovely red hair all over the place. Then someone was smashing the window and pulling me out and I smelt all this petrol and the car went up in flames. There was nothing anyone could do. That's what they said.'

He picked up a little stone and threw it towards the river.

'That's why I had been working so hard. I suppose I blamed myself. No, that's not quite true, the emotion built up when I played, only when I played. I collapsed in South Africa during a concert and they thought it was a heart attack but they could not find anything wrong. The doctors made me see a psychiatrist, Dr Kaplan. He said I felt guilty about my wife and, when I told him about school, about Lyman Andrew because I did not help him. That's why I came to see him and . . .'

She kissed him on the cheek gently.

'You cannot feel guilty for what you did as a child. You must learn to let go, Smiles. It is impossible to make amends, if that is what you are trying to do. There is a point where we have to turn away. To look away, or go mad. You do not hear people talk of our war here, do you? That is why. We want to begin again. We do not talk of the colonial times. A few politicians, perhaps, but the people do not. It is the better way. And I do not agree with white people's idea of trying to make everything all right when you have done wrong, or that you should never be happy again. A priest at our school said atonement was only the other side of the coin from revenge and that they were both driven by the sin of pride . . . Let's step into the future, Smiles.'

He put his arms around her and hugged her to him.

'You make it sound so easy,' he said.

She rested her chin on his shoulder.

'It is. Only we do not believe strongly enough.'

He wanted to tell her everything about school and Lyman Andrew but they were kissing and making love and then she got up and smiled down at him.

'I have to go to the village. Give me some time, they are planning a surprise for us. Give me time and then come. Just before it gets dark.'

*

He sat out on the beach and watched her walk gracefully up to the path, her hips swinging, her long arms at a slight angle to her body. There was a spirited happiness in that walk, the girl who was fought over by armies and brothers. He tried to imagine her in Europe or the United States, waiting for him in a sanitised hotel room with its ninety-five TV channels and ice-making machine. Or what would she make of his friends in England, who would, no doubt, expect her to be slightly stupid, uneducated, and then be offended when she was not. What of the differences in their ages, which did not seem to matter here, where he was the only white man and the white men she had seen were mostly old. And if they were prepared to kill hundreds of people in their rivalry over her what would they do to the musician who tried to spirit her away? But he looked out at the afternoon light dancing on the water and thought of what she had said. He was not going to spoil the time they had. If she had not pushed him out of the tent in the botanical gardens in Mbandaka then both of them would have died that night.

He chuckled to himself.

What was happening to him now was an encore. He must enjoy it. He must.

Lola watched from one of the far collections of huts as the men heated the skins of the drums in the fire to get them pitch perfect. These were drums like Smiles had never heard before, she was certain. Few white men had seen these drums, and survived. The tribes on this part of the river had once lived by piracy and canni-balism and their villages were so dispersed among the jungle as to make them less easy to attack and empty houses, like those on their beach, were often left there to confuse prying eyes. The drums, the *lokali*, were made from the trunk of a tree, like the canoes, and their sound could reach to the other side of a river, to recall hunters if there were intruders, or to direct an attack. There was one huge drum and one smaller one. The larger was four metres high and the smaller one three and a special high stool had been put by the fire for the man who was to play. Tonight the drums were not going to talk to the other villages. The village was going to dance. They were going to dance for the Englishman who they liked and the women realised she loved, they told her so whenever they could. She knew it was true but as they smeared her face with colour, put white circles on her breasts, garlanded her hair with flowers and tied only a simple raffia skirt around her waist she felt even further from him, that these days were all there would be . . . She pulled away. In her schooldays she had spoken out against men who championed more 'traditional' culture mainly because they wanted women barefoot and pregnant, back in a smoke-filled hut surrounded by fighting children. It was why she refused to be manipulated by Xavier and Fortuné, although Xavier in particular had always been against sentimental returns to 'the African village' and did a very funny party-piece impression of a drunken, sex-crazed, witch doctor his soldiers would not believe: 'Tek it from me, devil child, I can cure you of the problems virginity brings.'

Here, in this village, in Nganda Saisai, there had been no break with the past and she realised in some panic what they were doing. Another girl was to be wed and this was a wedding dance and she was going to dance for Smiles. In a way they were going to be married! The thought both delighted and scared her. Xavier had said she was married to him and had given the gifts to her uncle but there had been no feast. Her mind swung to the moon and back on the matrimonial technicalities of a roast pig or two.

The villagers tied a garland of special leaves around her neck and gave her herbs to eat and palm wine to drink.

Lola thought of Smiles' white body in the moonlight. All of this meant she was his.

She felt hot in her throat and the women laughed. They had given her whatever drug they gave girls on their wedding night in the drink and the herbs. She sucked air down into her lungs. The night prickled on her skin and raised her nipples as she was led down the steps towards girls who were dancing with the bride, the other bride, who kissed her on the lips and she felt a fire between her thighs.

The drums were suddenly considered to be in tune and were raised upright and a man climbed up the stool and swayed there perilously over the coals of the fire. He began to beat on the highest drum and another played the smaller one and a boy hit against both drum sides with sticks and the striking of each hand travelled up the inside of her legs and played on the lips of her vagina and her clitoris.

The other girls, they were so much smaller than her, began to move. She knew the dance, it was known up and down the river, but at first she felt drowsy. Then the rhythm of the drum overtook her, was inside her. The drum was within her and try as she might she was not able to stay still, and it was as if a hand grabbed her belly and she jumped and a warmth spread up over her. Her knees were jelly. The drums grew louder and men and boys began to dance too, now standing, now on all fours, running beneath her legs, as the dance turned them into crocodiles.

It was then that she saw Smiles at the other side of the clearing and the drumming stopped and she fell to the ground, panting.

Smiles had heard the drumming and smelt the smoke of the fires for a long time but had waited until night approached, then walked down the path to the collection of huts and had been led by a bare-breasted girl to the next village. He had read somewhere that the secret ceremonies on the river were conducted in the dress of the ancestors rather than the Western clothes the Belgians had brought with their missionaries and their whips and their porcelain toilets. He stood at the corner of the clearing, clutching the girl who had led him by the hand. The coals of the bonfire glowed in the damp night but at first he could only see the drummer perched highest up on his stool amid the movement of the dancers. Then Lola, standing head and shoulders over the village girls . . . She took his breath away and he staggered slightly and they were giving him palm wine as he stepped around the embers.

A torch was lit and he could see her dancing towards him, her hips bucking and her breasts wet with sweat. The girl who had brought him was pushing Smiles forward and then the drumming stopped and Lola fell down, as did the girl next to her.

A man came from behind him, naked except for a headdress and a loincloth, and picked up the other dancer in his arms and tossed her up in the air and took her to a nearby hut. There was screaming and ululating and the drums started again for a moment and then fell quiet; a silence that seemed to drift from the river like the mist.

Smiles was being led forward to claim the girl he loved. This was a kind of marriage. This was marriage! She was holding out her arms to him. Those long, beautiful, welcoming arms. This was the fulfilment of all dreams; more than he ever deserved. He began to walk towards her and then there was an intake of breath around him.

Suddenly, in the woods beyond the forest, there was an awful growling.

At first nothing happened and then the noise came again.

Lola looked terrified.

The men of the village called to each other around the fire and then they were rushing to their huts. Dogs were barking as the men ran naked after them into the bush, chasing whatever it was that had dared to interrupt the wedding dance.

And somewhere in amongst it all he thought he heard laughter.

Smiles raised Lola to her feet and led her back to the beach and the hut as they heard baying and the sound of shots in the night.

'I love you,' he said, but he could tell the noises in the forest upset her.

'What is it?'

Lola began to cry. The tears ran down her painted face. She was shaking and then she almost tore his clothes off and clawed at his body in a violent and terrible lovemaking and as he shouted in orgasm he passed into an instant and bottomless sleep.

Lola lay awake, watching and listening to the dogs and the hunters. She could feel the leopard's soft fur and its fatal hot breath on her neck and the horrible realisation she wanted to give of herself.

Had given herself. Lola pulled the flowers out of her hair and the necklace of leaves from her neck. The tribe had taken her over the way she had seen men and women taken in the streets of Kisangani and Kinshasa, turning into animals as they ran amok. Part of her wanted to stay here for ever and be part of the dance. Another part felt so afraid she could run out over the river in the starlight. They had meant well in arranging the wedding dance with Smiles, who was curled up in a happy dream. She wondered if he understood how close the tribe were to the forest. How far she and Smiles had been taken and the spirits they had raised.

There were mysteries she did not know and made her tremble.

She heard the frantic dogs again out in the darkness. They would never catch the spectral creature who growled all the fear and wonder of creation into the savage night.

FOURTEEN

In those final hours as he fished and waited for his sister and Smiles to return to the boat, St James read another packet of the Englishman's writings. He had to know more about the murder and the terrible punishment hanging over Smiles. Yet he felt he must puzzle over every word, one page at a time. His sister said to cheat and go straight to the end of a story showed a market thief's impatience and a lack of education.

My Confession:
Stanley Miles-Harcourt: black book, packet four

Lyman Andrew always reminded me of a cat at school, Dr Kaplan, especially in the way he moved and how his independence was always informed by the prospect of death at the jaws of the pack, or should have been. A couple of weeks after Lyman Andrew stopped the prefect hitting me in the army-corps parade, I agreed to go and time him running. The cinder track at the back of the school was below the terraces of a classical open-air theatre, scooped out by boys during the war with picks and shovels and bare hands and was one of the best in the county. After the murder of David Wace we were forbidden to go there alone. From there you could always see the smouldering rubbish dump, where the third-formers hunted voles, which was also beside the back fence and now strictly out of bounds. That cold morning I remember smelling the smoke and wondering how far the police were in their investigation. I had found a picture of myself and David Wace in my tuck box, taken at the junior school, and could hardly bear to look at it.

Lyman Andrew asked permission from my housemaster, who was a bit puzzled and said that athletics was a warm-weather sport, until Lyman Andrew told him that he was being considered to run for the USA team in the four-forty yards and had to keep himself in practice. The housemaster had not known whether to be impressed by what Lyman Andrew said or be embarrassed by what he might call 'boasting'. He glared down at his shoes as Lyman Andrew innocently produced a letter from his inside pocket from the United States Olympic Committee.

This made the housemaster breathlessly angry.

'I wasn't questioning you, old fellow, no need to pull rank. You can take Miles-Harcourt, by all means. But get him back for classes. He's a bit of a swot and we need our swots. Sport is necessary but where would England be without its brains? And don't practise too hard as too much preparation is contrary to the Olympic ideal. We don't want anyone thinking a master at this school is any sort of professional.' The housemaster then rushed off, one shoulder held stiffly higher than the other, which always happened when he was annoyed.

Lyman Andrew was open-mouthed.

'He was joking, right?' he said to me.

'No ... I'm afraid not. He wasn't joking at all.'

'You mean you're not meant to win?'

'No. You are ... absolutely ... It's ...'

'What then?'

'You're not meant to show you ... actually enjoy it.'

He laughed.

'God, I'll never understand you Brits ... I suppose the imperial power must not show the natives he rules that there's any pleasure in it. I always wondered why those white men looked so grim shooting tigers or having tea. They learned it in school.'

He was not being serious.

Lyman Andrew reached for his bag but I got there first and carried it for him. It was a leather bag with 'Harvard Track' written in red on the side.

We walked together on that chilly morning down to the circuit, which was covered in places with golden leaves. A spinney ran along the back and a huge oak tree had turned yellow. Lyman Andrew pulled off his grey tracksuit and began bending and stretching for ages and then took his running blocks out of his bag and carefully nailed them in place. Next, he slipped off his plimsolls and put on a pair of immaculate leather spikes. He reached back into his bag and produced a tin. Inside was a stopwatch and he handed it to me.

'I will just jog round and get warmed up first and then you can start to time me. I'm gonna be slow. I know I'm gonna be slow.'

But when he began to power round the cinder track he became something much more than his fitness or strength. He was an unstoppable force and it was beautiful. As he came off the last bend he threw back his head and gave himself totally to the day and all creation in an explosion of energy and ... innocence. It was strange to think that of a master but that's what he was, an innocent. I held the watch tight. Lyman ran faster and faster and I timed him as he dipped under the fifty-second mark and then got faster still. He was smiling and gulping air but there was an irrepressible joy on his face. He knew he was running well and was in tune with everything around him. It was as if he had a right to win, a right to all records and laurels and he did not mind anyone seeing the pleasure he took.

'What was my time?'

'A whole second better!'

'Good boy!' he said, as if I was responsible.

He stared dreamily over at the school buildings and the clock tower, rising like a little city above the trees.

'You know, I may quibble at your old customs but you are damned lucky to be in a place like this, Smiles. An honourable place.'

I did not reply. I did not quite know what he meant.

We walked back to his rooms. Breakfast had already started and I was going to slip into one of the prefects' kitchens to make myself toast and marmalade and a cup of coffee.

But then Lyman Andrew said: 'I like to have pancakes when I've been for a session. I put them in the oven earlier. I guess they'll be all right. We eat them with bacon and maple syrup. The syrup was first made by American Indians. They used to tap the maple trees and it just runs out. Do you want some?'

His eyes shone. It was as if we were going to have a secret feast.

I nodded and ate the doughy pancakes that were not at all like my mother's and the combination of sweet syrup and crispy, salty bacon was amazing. It was like feasting with a visitor from Venus. It was delicious. I kept lifting the pot of syrup and inhaling the sweet foresty smell and he laughed and ruffled my hair.

While we were eating he told me his family first lived outside a place called Birmingham, Alabama, but they had moved to Washington and then Philadelphia, where the Declaration of Independence was signed, before going to New York, which he liked best, and they were now in Chicago. It was obvious that even though he felt some things were bad there for black people, he really loved the ideals of America that all men are created equal and have a right to freedom and happiness.

Then he looked me in the eyes and said: 'What do you want to do? What do you want to do for the world, Smiles? How are you going to change the planet? We can. We all can.'

He called me by my nickname now, all the time.

Usually, when masters asked you what you wanted to do, they meant a job of work like banking or being a solicitor. How you were going to make your money. What profession you were going to try and enter. Changing the planet made me think of the endless, green-black, American forests, inspired by the bitter-sweet syrup.

He stared seriously over the vanishing stack of pancakes in the middle of his dining table. Then he burst out laughing.

'I don't have a clue either. My father wants me to do a law degree for safety if my playing is not good enough or I don't get the breaks. My mother just wants me to play the piano. In a bar if need be. She says I should follow my heart and white people make the laws and always will. And then there's the running. I suppose I could just run away from it all.'

I laughed too.

I think we were totally together in that moment.

We were good friends now.

'I could just keep on going.'

'Fast,' I said, and then we both could not stop laughing.

He helped me to a few more pancakes.

'It's nice to have a lot of choice,' I said.

He nodded slowly.

'You know, I never thought of it like that, Smiles. That's a good way of looking at the damn problem. A very good way indeed. My father calls me a dreamer because he is scared I'll get hurt but I just want to help get rid of all the shady deals and the ugliness. To change the world. He does, too. He went on his fair share of protests in Alabama when it was really dangerous and the white boys threw peaches stuck with broken glass. He's always told me that we are put on earth for a very short time and we should try to conduct ourselves with as much dignity and courage as possible. If we all do that everything will get better. That will be great, won't it, Smiles? And not much to ask on a sunny morning? To stop the petty cruelties and fears that hold us all back. To change the world.'

'It will,' I said.

The trouble was, when he stopped talking I was not so sure.

The pancakes were getting cold now.

Lyman Andrew was nodding to himself and smiling and I began to fear for him right then and there. I think that was when I began to love him.

His kind of honesty was dangerous here.

I had a lot of friends but I did not tell them my innermost thoughts, even Pinky Grey. You did not give out stuff which could be used against you. I knew everyone in my year who was in my house and they were all my friends and at the same time they weren't. You had to stay deep inside and look after yourself. The school was not what Lyman Andrew saw on the surface. He saw what he did because he was a good man.

'I hear you got beaten the other day?'

I shrugged.

He probably would not have been able to comprehend the truth.

'It's about time we put a stop to that caveman crap. I've already talked to the headmaster.'

Then he jumped up and went over to the piano, which he had left open.

'Hey, do you know how to play blues runs? I learned all that side of the piano from a great-uncle who used to work in a honky-tonk. Has anyone ever shown you?'

'No.'

His fingers ran down the keyboard in a way which made my spine shiver.

'Well, besides the classical stuff this is good to know. Some say it's the biggest advance since man began to string notes together. Sit down.'

I perched on the stool next to him. I followed what he did and he seemed pleased.

'And this is boogie-woogie. It's even easier.'

His hands began to move about the white and black notes and a wall of sound rose up and invaded the room. I recognised snatches of songs from Elvis to Elton John and through the window I saw people stop and look up. Two of the Irish maids from the domestic block heard what we were doing and put down the laundry basket they were carrying and began an impromptu dance.

Lyman Andrew got up and gave a wave through the window.

He turned back to me.

'Your go now. I want you to play these four notes with the right hand, exactly as I do,' he said, leaning over me. 'Don't try any fancy stuff to start with. Just stick to the four notes. Imitate. That's exceptional. Don't be fooled by a piano. It's just a drum with different tones. Then add the left hand.'

I picked out the left hand of the boogie-woogie, slowly at first. It was like starting an engine and then the rhythm took over. He sat down again beside me on half of the stool and I was conscious of his body next to mine. He began to improvise a tune with his right hand. I was playing in time but too carefully, too delicately. Then he stopped and my left hand went faltering on by itself.

'Keep on! Keep on! That's great, Smiles. Now imagine we're sitting by a jungle river and I'm teaching you the bongo drums. That's it. You are away, my brother. You are smoking!'

And I was, filling his rooms and the world outside with a thrilling sound. I went on until it became perfect and my four notes stood out above the rhythm and shone like jewels.

That was the effect Lyman Andrew had on me and others. He made you shine like a diamond. I believed in Lyman Andrew, Dr Kaplan, I always have, more than God or music.

FIFTEEN

Smiles was wading naked in the river, pondering the strangeness of the wedding night, when he saw the boat appear out of the sunny morning.

'Lola! Mr Smiles! Captain get a message from upriver. President's soldiers all going to Kisangani. We not got much time to get that piano up there and make the broadcast. We got to move!' yelled José.

St James was standing in the bow.

Lola had taken her bath and cleaned her teeth in the river but the paint still showed. Smiles hardly dared believe that it meant he was married to her.

The village had turned out when they heard the boat and Smiles felt passionately that he wanted to remain on that magical beach. He pulled on his clothes and so did Lola before they said their difficult farewells and the children waved: 'Goody, goody, bye, bye,' called one little girl, a phrase he had taught her. The adults stood motionless as reeds.

'Why can't we stay?' Smiles said, but Lola was hugging a reluctant St James.

She took hold of Smiles' shirt gently and tucked it into his trousers as the boat's engines reversed and they moved off. It was all too fast.

'We must take the piano to Fortuné,' she said. 'The broadcast may just stop the fighting.'

He turned around to wave to the villagers on the beach but the boat had already rounded a bend and they were among the shifting islands again, the walls of tropical forest higher and higher. The boat crossed the stream at the diagonal and then back again and all at once it was as if they were not on a river but on an immense lake, with the gaps between the islands opening ahead of them and closing up behind, like the jewels in a kaleidoscope. He had loved kaleidoscopes as a child, his father had bought him one. The hours had sped by as he gazed into the glass world, mesmerised by the changing patterns and colours.

Perhaps that's why the river seemed so timeless in this endless process of never getting to the other side and anyway, with the rapids below Kinshasa and more falls above Kisangani, this whole section of the country was cut off, a lost world that had drifted further back into the mists because of the war. It may have been the brush with death in South Africa or the soldiers in the botanical gardens but he felt he had done with all clocks.

All his life he had been governed by the number of beats in the bar, infinite variations in duration, and now this watery world made it all absurd.

Yet he still obsessively wound his father's wristwatch.

A large blue bird flapped over the soaring layers of vegetation which grew out over the river, covered in garlands of pink and yellow flowers. The trees rose like cliffs, yet there was something strangely familiar about their shape and they could be the silhouettes of elms or horse chestnuts from the wood at the back of the running track at his old school if he peered at them through half-closed eyes. Smiles sat, watching the grey-brown water slip past, and for a while he convinced himself everything was possible and he and Lola were still outside the tick-tocking world.

Lola felt the change towards her the moment she stepped aboard, the paint from the dance and the wedding ceremony on her face. The captain descended from his bridge and merely looked at her in silence, like she had been a naughty child, and then went back up and she heard him shout at the boy he had left at the wheel. She saw in the crew an expression that told her she had let them down.

After dinner Marie could not stand it any more. She brought the red plastic bowl that was for washing hands, the beaker for rinsing and the towel over to where Lola was picking at a pile of rice, red beans and fried banana.

'Let me get that stupidness off your face!'

'No.'

'Why?'

'It is the custom.'

'What?'

Lola glared at Marie but the huge woman did not flinch.

'It was a wedding dance. For a couple in the village. And for Smiles and me.'

The crew sitting at the table had gone completely silent.

Marie was outraged.

'We cannot let you make a fool of yourself. We cannot let you take part in the godless rituals of savages. Only a few years ago these people were accused of eating each other.'

'So were the early Christians,' said Lola. 'When they said they drank the blood of Jesus.'

Marie threw the bowl of water at Lola and dragged her out of her seat and pulled her towards the front of the boat, shouting at her in Lingala.

'You are not married! You are married already and you now marry the white man. You sleep with everyone and now you take this white man in a devil ceremony on some beach like a bitch dog. What happens when your real husband's patience runs out? What happens when the leopard kills us all? What do you do when you have to face your Lord Jesus and tell him all these bad things you have done? You cannot marry all the men you want.'

Lola felt a great sadness at the stupid words.

The crew were staring at her. She knew Smiles was about to come to her defence but she slightly raised one hand. If he joined in it might be fatal.

Marie's cheeks were red with anger.

'Xavier, your real husband, will follow after us and he will kill us. Look what happened to the boy. The boy at the gardens in Mbandaka.' The crew nodded. 'You are not married to the white man in the eyes of God!'

'I did not ask your god. I did not ask him about Xavier and I did not ask him about Smiles.'

'Then he will curse you!'

Lola laughed and pushed the heavy woman away: 'Well, then,

I won't ask him at all. He is not the kind of god I trust if he does not trust in love.'

Later, in an act of friendliness, José placed a bottle of cold Primus in front of Smiles and grinned at the arguments still grumbling around the boat. St James sat across from Smiles, regarding him differently. He was probably offended, too. Smiles had not understood much of what had been said except one name cropped up time and time again. Marie kept on repeating 'Xavier'.

Smiles finished his Primus alone as the crew got up from the table. Darkness was falling and when they stopped for the night even José would not help him pitch the remaining tent on shore.

He and Lola slept in the bow of the boat, half under his mosquito net and half under the piano. Smiles was wide awake before dawn; he looked at his watch and it was four-thirty and he was cold. In London he never woke before eight-thirty and was not fully awake until ten at least. But here it was different.

Smiles glanced down at her.

He kissed her hair and pulled on his Aid America jeans and shirt and shoes and slipped out from under the mosquito net. A dew had fallen on the piano tarpaulin and a wind had got up, ruffling the sheet on the hammock of sleeping José. Smiles went and sat at the front of the boat and looked to the east where the sky had begun to grow milky and he heard the call of a bird, far away. As the first red glow started to light up the shore beyond the reeds he saw they had stopped at a village and that canoes were bumping against the hull. The village smelled of woodsmoke but he could see the high trees of the jungle just beyond and caught the sense of that endless forest.

Then he saw a white skull on a wooden stake outside a distant hut.

'What is the matter, my love?' she said, suddenly at his side. He had not heard her.

'I do not belong here. I am making more problems for you.'

She put her hand on his face.

'Do not listen to this stupid crew. You're my problem now. You are mine, Smiles, nothing can change that.'

'Your husband and his men are following us. I am putting you in more danger.'

She shrugged.

'They are days behind us. We will get to my village and there we will have help. We will figure out something. I promise.' She kissed him on the lips and just at that moment at the back of the boat he heard Marie start her prayer singing, today in a martial and combative way, rising to a crescendo of disapproval and half-spat 'Amens'.

An hour later Lola walked with him around the battle-damaged village of Bolombo, which had been built for the Belgians in straight lines for a plantation long gone. Children ran ahead of them as she and Smiles helped José carry plastic bottles to get fresh water.

José was grumbling to her.

'Marie very mad with you, mama. She mad with you, because she like Xavier, who is a war hero.'

'We are all war heroes,' Lola said, yawning. 'Those of us who can still stand up.' She had no time for those who called themselves heroes. She had never been in awe of Xavier or of Fortuné for their exploits as soldiers: and she positively loathed Fortuné's carefully tailored uniforms and penchant for exaggeration.

One day she had fired her father's oily rifle through the kitchen window of her house when she saw soldiers running in the garden. The noise of the bullets had startled her like the sudden revving of the first motorbike she had sat on. The window glass had shattered and she was certain she had hit one of the darting figures. She knew. She felt it in the middle of her own chest and she could not breathe, as if the soldier's soul was stuck in there. They found a body at the bottom of the vegetable garden and one of her cousins took his leather shoes and a penknife that was in his pocket along with a kola nut and a purple custard apple. The boy soldier looked surprised as if he had not been expecting the bullet in the chest and his hands were cupped around the single wound, though she had fired off the whole magazine and burned her hands on the barrel. The fighting had been going on for three whole days and there was no electricity or water and she had been trying to read an Agatha Christie detective story by a sardine-tin lamp about a nice lady called Miss Marple in an English village, where even the murder was very polite. She had stared down at the blood but did not let go of the rifle, which was still hot. The boy was a Rwandan and she had been eleven years old. She realised she had to protect her brothers and sisters and that the dead boy and his friends would have raped and killed her, but she knew on the most basic level what she had done was wrong and she was angry when the local militia commander said she was a hero. It was obscene.

Only her father understood what she was talking about.

But being with Smiles was not wrong, however much Marie

mumbled in her prayers about painted and loose women, she had never been like that. No one, not even God, was going to tell her who she could love.

'Mama, come, come here. See the good *ngando*. The man has found his wife turned to the *ngando*.'

They went to the nearest hut and out into the back garden where creepers trailed down from a trellis and a man was kneeling on the ground, stroking the head of a ten-foot crocodile that had incredibly long eyelashes. The man was wearing a blue-and-white African robe and a hat and was talking to the reptile in Lingala and his own tribal language. There was no raffia string around the creature's jaws as Lola had seen on crocodiles in the market but it did not try to bite and the subtle oblong patterns on its back were beautiful.

'She is his wife come back from the war. Come back as a crocodile. She turn into a crocodile to survive,' explained José.

The man took Lola's hand and put it on the reptile's skin. It was warm and she looked into one elongated eye and was not frightened. Smiles reached over and touched the crocodile, too.

'She my wife . . . She is Flore.'

'That is what will happen to you, Lola,' said José, teasingly.

He clenched his fist at the reptile. But she leapt at him and her jaws snapped a warning. They all jumped.

José looked terrified and hurried back to the boat without them.

'Stay, mama, stay,' said the man in the blue and white robe. 'That fellow think bad of Flore. She likes you.' He took Lola's hand and placed it on the reptile again. Lola was scared now but she kept it there.

'Do be careful,' said Smiles.

But slowly Lola's fear seemed to fall away. She knew the creature was not going to harm her.

She ran her hand along the brown, ridged back.

Eventually the crocodile, with the help of the man who claimed to be her husband, even let Lola stroke her under the chin.

The sun was hot and Lola felt the creature's pleasure.

When they got back Smiles opened the piano. The children hung off the bank and every timber of the boat as he played Chopin, which they liked very much. Their eyes widened and several ran away from the strange music before pushing through the crowd once more, before they cast off.

The village vanished astern and the islands closed around them again. Under the deck roof it became airless and gaspingly hot; especially when they ran along the deep channels near the islands full of large, pink tsetse flies. Smiles saw a clearing and what appeared to be a shelter.

'The islands used by the rebels, sometimes,' said Gaston, one of the crew.

'Bemba rebels?'

'Oh, yes, papa,' he grinned. 'No Rwanda rebels get down here. These Bemba rebels. Forces Armées search for them. Much killings.'

Almost as soon as he said it, there was a cry at the side of the boat where a four-man canoe had come alongside and everyone ran to the rail. Smiles peered down, his heart thumping.

A large man with a shaven head sat in the bow, nursing a Kalashnikov.

He shouted in French: `We have a forest deer for you.'

The canoe was a large dugout and one of the paddlers tied it to the tender.

In the canoe was a deer with a red coat and white spots, its ears and flanks torn by dogs but still hanging onto life. The animal let out a bellow. José tossed a bundle of notes and the creature was manhandled onto the small tender, its feet all tied together. It was a doe and there was blood on its mouth.

Smiles was relieved. The men had only come to sell a deer.

'We keep it alive until we get to my village at Mombongo. The fridge is dead,' said José. But Lola, who had come up behind Smiles, was staring at the animal.

'No,' she said. 'You will kill the animal now.'

Lola had seen animals slaughtered when growing up in her village and that did not bother her. There was something about the doe and how the crew seemed to want to prolong its misery. Lola would normally have looked the other way. But the animal had its mouth open, panting, and made her think of her mother dying in the shallows at Kisangani.

'You must kill the deer now.'

'We do not take orders from you,' said Marie.

'You were talking of savagery only yesterday. To keep this creature alive is savagery.'

Then one of the crew said: 'We are not scared of you, mama. You are not your husband. And even your husband want you dead. You should not talk of killing things.'

She saw the mood turning against her.

'We should put her off. She will bring bad luck,' said another.

'What about that?' demanded Marie.

Lola sighed.

'You have been paid to take me upriver to Kisangani, or to where the rebels and Fortuné can be reached, with the piano. That's what Celestine arranged with you. It is all part of plans to make peace.'

Another of the crew stepped forward, a man covered in engine oil.

'Celestine is not here. He is arrested because we are travelling with you.'

Lola reached into her jeans and pulled out a roll of dollars.

'I will buy the deer and then everyone can eat it. But we must kill it now.'

'She is a witch,' someone muttered.

'I will pay you twenty dollars for the deer.'

José looked thoughtful.

'Do not give in to her,' said Marie. 'We will put the whore off at the next stop and deliver her to the police.'

Lola walked over to Marie and said very quietly: 'If you give me to anyone I will make sure that your name is known. Your name will be known in every village. The owls will be coming for you to peck the fat off your bones and the rest of your church.'

There was silence. The money was accepted for the deer.

'But she must do the killing,' said Marie.

'She must do the killing,' said the mechanic.

'No,' said Smiles.

Lola stood looking at them. She did not want to have to slaughter the animal but a part of her rebelled. She had never killed a deer though she had helped her grandmother with pigs and goats.

'I will kill the deer. Give me a knife.'

A sheath knife with a saw-edged blade was brought from the galley and she examined it for sharpness. She then stepped from the large boat into the tender, where one of the crew held the deer.

'Hold her tight. Tight!'

The boy obeyed her.

She did not look into the animal's eyes, only at the neck and the artery which, as she gently forced the head back, was exposed. She felt the deer's scorching breath on her hands and let it bellow one last time.

'Hush, now,' she said in Lingala.

And then she sawed into the artery and the blood spurted out and hit her in the face and filled the back of the tender. There was a cheer from all the faces looking down as she held the animal's head and the life quickly drained away from it. One of the boys moved towards her to start the skinning but she held up the bloody knife.

Like a cat at her kill, Lola did not leave the doe until she was sure it was dead.

Nor did she shed a tear. She was not going to give the crew or Marie the satisfaction of seeing her cry. She got back onto the boat and Smiles put his arm around her and there was a whoop as the doe's skin was already off and the intestines were being washed in the river. She had done her best and wiped the knife on a piece of cloth and slipped it in its sheath. She put it in her locker, just in case. It was dangerous to be called a witch.

Smiles was staring at her in disbelief.

'That was a very brave thing to do,' he said, and did not seem to understand when she was silent and ignored him and searched out soap and a towel and a water bottle for a shower. She did not want sympathy from the world of men, even of a man she loved. She attempted to shut out the baying shouts of the crew as the deer was butchered.

The peace and beauty of the island, Nganda Saisai, seemed a world ago.

SIXTEEN

St James opened the next packet of Smiles' story the moment he put the last one away. He still kept watch on his duck-quill fishing float. A boy soldier with an old rifle who sat next to him on the boat had caught a fish. But St James knew no octopus was going to climb onto his hook. He was going to learn more from Smiles' writings.

My Confession:
Stanley Miles-Harcourt: black book, packet five

I want you to understand, dear Dr Kaplan, that I was not a passive spectator in the business of Lyman Andrew. I tried to warn him. I really did. I could have told him right off, I suppose, but he would not have believed me. He just did not realise what people are like deep down. What they can become, I mean. I do not for one moment think mankind is wicked all the time; it is just some of the time that there is a distinct lack of kindness, and Lyman Andrew, as he went about his business in his snappy clothes and his shiny shoes, had no idea of the depths he was about to plumb or what was shifting in the darkness of others', less happy, minds.

A few days after he taught me the boogie-woogie I was up in Lyman Andrew's room, rubbing a special polish into the leather of his spikes to keep them supple. He even let me do his shoes now if I wanted to in return for lessons at the piano; not just blues and jazz but more complicated classical pieces. I played a few of the jazz tunes on the piano in the hall where we had assemblies, when we were putting out chairs. The other boys in form 3a were so impressed they let me go on playing while they did the work. It was the beginning of being paid for what I liked doing. I had finished one set of spikes and started on a muddier pair when he called to me.

'Smiles, come here, there's a movie on television.'

He had his own television in his study and this wasn't the first time I had watched it with him. This film was called The Third Man. *I remember being very sad at the end when Harry Lime was killed even though he was a bad man. He had a joy in life that I recognised in Lyman Andrew and I suppose there was the nearness of the names Lime and Lyman. But unlike him, Harry Lime knew how people actually behaved. You could see that in the way he wore his overcoat.*

'Did you like the film?' asked Lyman Andrew.

'Yes, thank you, it was really good.' I was about to ask what he thought of Harry Lime but he jumped up.

'Excuse me, Smiles, but I have to go. The headmaster is giving a dinner for the policemen who are investigating the ... murder. They seem certain it was a murder now, of your friend, David Wace. He wants me to go along and chat to them informally. Like a stupid American

I said I needed a lawyer to talk to the police the other day and it was the wrong thing to do. I had a few bad experiences down South when I was younger. It can't hurt. I got nothing to hide.'

I just stood there looking into his eyes. I wanted to say something. To tell him not to go.

'Thank you for letting me see the film.'

'A pleasure to watch it with you, Smiles. We must discuss it another time.'

Two weeks passed and the trees turned deeper reds and more spectacular yellows and I did not get the call Anderson had told me to expect.

I have never liked the autumn. It was when my father was found dead under the street light in his Jaguar. I did not like it before that. I have never liked the smell of cold rot. The stale scent at the very bottom of a pile of leaves that has a poisonous churchyard earthiness, a reminder that all things are limited by death. Only the smell of quince kept it away and that's probably why my father adored them. There were several quince trees in our garden. We always went on holiday in September before school and sometimes you could taste the leaf fall and the end of freedom in the wind. So I used to run around faster, making the most of every second of the summer, skinning my knees and getting green grass-stains on my shirt.

My friend Pinky Grey slept next to me in the dorm.

He leaned over and whispered: 'Hope you don't have a nightmare tonight.'

'What? I had a nightmare? I didn't.'

We hadn't talked all day because I had been practising. I did not remember even having a dream. The bell had started to ring and I had automatically got out of bed. It was like that every morning.

'You did have a nightmare. It was stuff about drums in Africa. And limes. I can't remember. You were really in a funk. Then you started talking about Wace. I always dream when I eat cheese.'

'What did I say?'

'You were talking about African drums.'

'No, about David . . . I mean Wace.'

'That was soppy stuff.'

'Tell me?'

He leaned out of bed so he was nearer to me.

He whispered: 'You said you loved him and you were sorry. Just that. I liked him too. That's what you meant, I suppose. I mean you were not queer on him, were you? You just liked him. You just said that and then you cried a bit. He was your friend. That's all it means, isn't it? There's nothing to worry about. It's just a word. Love.'

I took a deep breath. I heard the clock tower chime all the quarters and the hour through the night and could not sleep. I had a piece of tissue paper in which my mother had wrapped the quince she had given me at the beginning of term and I sniffed at it under the sheets. I tried not to cry.

In breakfast the next morning when one of the Irish maids dropped a tray in the dining hall I jumped a mile. But waking up in the dorm shouting did not matter as everyone thought I was brave for not blubbing when I was beaten by Anderson; although Pinky did not understand why I was not cut. I said Anderson had made me stand on tiptoe and you didn't cut that way but it hurt more. He believed me because the story fitted in with Anderson's habitual sadism.

I did not see Anderson around much. He kept out of my way.

At about five o' clock one afternoon I went up to visit Lyman Andrew and he was playing a really beautiful piece.

I now know it was his interpretation of Gassenhauer from Schulwerk Vol. 1, Musica Poetica, by Carl Orff and I made the shoe cleaning take longer. Among his best classical pieces I liked it almost as much as Franz Liszt's arrangement of Beethoven's 7th Symphony for piano and it was more modern.

He then turned to me.

'Can you help me with a few boxes from the clock tower?'

'Of course.'

'What is it, Smiles?'

'It's just that the things up there . . . The head forbids us to touch them.'

I did not like the room at the base of the clock tower, no one did.

'Oh, don't worry, I'll return them in one piece. I just want to look at them back here. You have no idea what's up there. It's real history.'

He was so enthusiastic I had to help him.

We walked around the cloisters to the main entrance and two third-formers passed us and sniggered. From the entrance hall with the cupboards full of cups and trophies the stone staircase led past a figure of the Madonna to the library and then another flight of stairs went up into the clock tower, which smelt strongly of mothballs. The day was very bright. We corkscrewed up the open spiral staircase with the sun dancing through the long, leaded windows, splitting the light into jewels; like climbing to heaven on a ladder of diamonds. A butterfly fluttered its failing, ragged wings against the bluish glass. Lyman Andrew went straight to the boxes that contained the papers of old boys who had been on expeditions to Africa. All around them on the floor were kudu and rhino horns and, in one corner, the head of a male lion had begun to go a bit mouldy. We waded in the detritus of imperialism.

'You know, I think my ancestors must have been from Congo,' he

said, holding up a picture of a man with a spear who did not look remotely like him.

I smiled and he appeared pleased.

'You would not believe the things I have found out up here. I never realised how the African was treated. It's all here. Written in the perpetrators' own hands. The things they did. But more than that, they put it all down in diaries as if it were no crime.'

Then he stopped and stared at me.

'You don't like it up here, do you, Smiles?'

'No.'

'Why?'

'Everyone thinks it's haunted. Don't you feel the cold?'

'Oh, the cold's just because of these old windows and the radiators don't work. You don't believe in all that. Do you?'

I shrugged and got the little ladder on rollers and pointed to one of the cupboards that was almost out of reach.

'The old doorman used to say that there were bad things in there. I have never seen inside.'

Immediately, Lyman Andrew was on the ladder and opened the cupboard. I could see past him and there was a baby in a bottle that I had heard described before. The infant was white and ghostly and seemed to be smiling. By it was another infant's skeleton and a row of earthenware jars. The infant's skeleton was partially wrapped with cloth and beads and shells and appeared to have been reassembled in a way that was tortured and twisted. There was no doubt of the evil surrounding those little bones. And behind them I thought I glimpsed a face. A human face. The skin grey. The eyes open and staring. I stepped back.

'We shouldn't go in there,' I said.

Lyman Andrew paused and then closed the door.

'I really must ask about these things,' he said.

He had taken a book from the cupboard and leaned against one of the old cabinets and started to read. He turned the dusty pages.

'My God . . . Listen to this! It's by a man who was on the second Stanley expedition. He wanted to see cannibalism. He bought a native girl for six handkerchiefs and paid his paddlers to eat her as he sketched. Here are the sketches. Here! This was the book he made the sketches in while she was eaten.'

He showed me a pen, ink and watercolour sketch of a girl having her throat cut. There was another of her insides spilling out.

'We shouldn't be here,' I repeated.

We climbed up to the small flagpole platform and looked at the blue school flag waving and billowing above our heads. I felt dizzy with relief to get out of the tower and would have preferred to climb down the outside than to descend the spiral staircase. To be in a place that was scary in the sunshine made you feel that everything was wrong.

'I had no idea . . . Are you superstitious, Smiles? Is that place truly haunted?'

I shook my head.

'I'm not. But I know what's in there is not good.'

The bell then sounded for the quarter-hour and we both held on as the vibrations rose through our shoe leather.

When the ringing died away he said: 'I'm sorry. You must still be thinking about your poor friend Wace.'

He looked at me with real sympathy. He rested his hand on my shoulder but only for an instant.

'Yes.'

Lyman Andrew was silent as we walked back to his study.

When I sat down on the sofa I noticed he was smiling at me. He saw I was looking at the book about Dr Martin Luther King.

'Do you think there are mostly good people in the world, Smiles? Or are we all wicked and fooling ourselves? We tell ourselves we are doing good stuff but really it's what we want. Are we just weak and self-deluding? They have not found who killed poor David Wace, have they? They have not found the murderer . . . I don't think they want to, do you?'

It may have been the effect of being in the clock tower and the pictures of the poor girl but I suddenly felt breathless and trapped. I did not want him talking like that. I had to get out.

I got up but Lyman Andrew caught hold of my arm.

If only I had told him everything about Anderson and the rest right then and there.

'Stop, Smiles, please. I was only fooling, asking those questions. The world is full of good people like Dr King. He made his great "I have a dream" speech about us all living together. The world is full of good people. Many more kind people than bad and when we examine the bad there is usually an explanation for what they do. I am so lucky to be teaching at this school. I don't think that even now in the north of my country I would get a teaching place at what we call a prep school, unless I was the sports coach. And in the South they would find me dead in a ditch or hanging from a cottonwood tree.'

It was then I lost it.

'You don't know anything!' I shouted out at him and ran.

SEVENTEEN

Smiles watched in the following days as the excited crew ate every part of the deer and drank much of the palm wine they had taken on board at the lovely island village. Even the hooves were gnawed and one of the kitchen boys ran around in the raw skin. All the anger they had worked up towards Lola had been channelled into the animal. Most of the crew had no head for alcohol and quickly fell asleep but the mood had been frenzied and he heard Marie grumbling on. Smiles had been offered a grilled plateful but he could not dissociate the doe from Lola herself, or the vile story of how one of Stanley's men arranged for a girl to be eaten that he knew so well from the haunted clock tower at his school. Lola refused to touch the meat or let any be given to St James, who sulked under the piano for an hour.

Smiles was sitting at the instrument in the dull heat of noon as they turned again out into the stream; the river was very wide now.

He was in the middle of an apt piece, Air de Diable by François

Couperin, and planned to get on to the great oeuvres of Bach in the afternoon. It was strange but the hatred did not seem to be directed at him at all when he was on the piano stool. It was as if the music made him invisible. She came up to him when he stopped.

'Was I doing OK?

'You know it was brilliant.'

'The crew seem calmed by it, thank God.'

'Was that Bach?'

'Couperin. Did you play music in your house? In Kisangani?'

Suddenly there was a carefree look on her face.

'We had a record player but mainly Congolese stuff and my father liked jazz and soul and there was white music like the Beatles. But there was a lady at the end of the street who had worked for a Belgian and had been his lover. I used to go to the house with my friends and she would give us sweets and make us listen to the music he left her. If we could tell her the composer we got a piece of jaggery sugar.'

He laughed.

'That's one way of teaching.'

Lola frowned.

'The market women said she was a sorceress. There was a horrible time at the millennium when people went around killing monkeys and frogs as if this was the reason for our bad luck. It was frightening. The crew are saying I am a sorceress. I killed the deer to take its spirit. The kind woman who gave me sugar was forced out and had a boy bring me all her records. We must be careful.'

'Yes.'

St James was watching them closely. Marie was constantly making threats now about handing Lola and Smiles over to the chief at the next village or just throwing them in the river. He had drowned the words out with Couperin.

'The crew went a bit quiet the other day when you mentioned owls,' he said.

'Owls?'

'Yes, I distinctly heard it. Owls.'

Lola frowned.

Then she laughed.

'I was talking about our secret police. There is a unit that breaks into the house in the day and waits for you to get into bed and then grabs you naked and spirits you into the night. These are called the owls. At least with them there is some political control. I sometimes feel my country is being forced into a state of continual fear, but by the foreign outsiders, the French and Americans who want to keep us in chaos so that they can steal the diamonds and coltan and anything else we have to offer.'

'So, no supernatural, vengeful owls?'

'No.'

'Pity.'

That afternoon they saw two large canoes racing out in the flow, loaded with Primus-beer crates. There were far too many crates on each and as barges covered in multicoloured anthills of humanity went past, powered by a squat pusher boat, one canoe went over and then the other. A giant eddy had been created, almost a small whirlpool. A man stood helpless at the spiralling end of his canoe, waving at them and then was sucked under, his right hand still flailing back and forth, even though his head had vanished beneath the enfolding water. It was so quick. They watched the other man holding terrified onto the second swamped canoe. Their captain, who had been sleeping while one of the crew manned the wheel, peered through his East German binoculars and shook his head. The pusher boat did not even slow.

The river was suddenly sleek and brown and empty again.

'They drink too much of other men's beer' was all the captain said, with a grin in Lola's direction.

The river had taken two men and there was not a murmur from the crew.

Smiles saw St James staring out at where the men had disappeared, as hunters from the bank paddled out to where the canoes had sunk and then turned fast back to the bank, out of the beautiful but fatal stream. There were no bodies or pieces of canoe floating in the river; the current had dragged them down to the bottom with the eels and the catfish.

'Do you think the octopus got them?'

'No, there are no octopuses in the river.'

'What got them, then?'

Smiles paused. He saw the alarm in the boy's eyes at the speed of what he had just witnessed.

He repeated his father's wartime learned words when confronted with a meaningless tragedy in the morning paper: 'I suppose it was their time to die.'

St James raised his eyebrows.

His stare changed from haughty indifference to one of unsure sincerity and alarm.

'Does everyone have a time to die? Is it written down?' St James almost whispered the words.

The boy looked pleadingly at him.

'When will I die, Mr Smiles? Will it be soon?'

The question was both childlike and philosophical. It was the kind of question everyone asks, although in Congo it had more immediacy.

'No one knows.'

'Then why did you say it was their time?'

'It is something people say.'

'We do not say things like that here. It would mean we know.'

'All I meant was that . . .' But his words ran out. 'No one knows when they will die. It's part of the excitement of living.'

'So it is not written anywhere? Like the secrets of the octopus?'

Smiles sighed.

'Some people believe our whole life is written down. I don't. Those paddlers were just unlucky to capsize in that particular bit of river where the current dragged them under. There was nothing that said they should be there.'

St James seemed troubled.

'Not even God?'

'No, if there is a God, I don't think he fixes things for us.'

'But you will tell me the secrets of the octopus?'

He smiled at the boy.

'I will. I promise.'

Lola had never liked Mombeka and as they drew in it was half-obscured by great clouds of smoke and reminded her of the war, when the riverbanks had been ablaze. The village was more like a small town of about fourteen thousand people with a chief who kept a fierce band of mai-mai to demand tributes from anyone who landed. Yet Marie was dressed in her best blouse and jeans and ready to land when the boat slithered along the bank and the boys tied up to a palm tree. She tottered on the high gangplank as she had been drinking the last gourd of palm wine and shouting 'Whore! Whore!' at Lola.

The wine became stronger the longer you kept it in the heat and the gourd she was drinking from had been up on the bridge under a sheet of hot corrugated iron.

On the high muddy bank there were tall palm trees dotted here and there and in a clearing stood solidly built huts made from branches, wood and mud. There was laughter and shouts, and armed men, in green fatigue trousers and blue T-shirts, emerged from the smoke like a leisurely group of demons, ten of them, with scarves knotted around their heads; each carrying an AK-47. All the men had a ragged, swaggering air. They grinned at the boat and nodded. The tallest of them rested a fat reefer in the sights of his AK-47 and called for one of the ridiculous blue plastic chairs visible on *Le Rêve's* deck and a crate of Primus beer, which one of the crew hurried to them and a kick was aimed at him for his pains.

Marie, whose red blouse was too small for her and who had put on layers of make-up, told them off in Lingala and then began to ask one something in a whisper, while taking a sip of his beer, but then there was a shriek of laughter from the mai-mai and both of her arms were grabbed.

At first, it seemed a joke.

But she turned round to the boat, struggling and shouting in Lingala, fear in her voice.

Marie screamed and screamed as she was dragged off through the rising, swirling smoke.

The crew all stood at the rail but no one moved.

The young faces did not betray any more emotion than when the canoes had sunk that afternoon.

Lola instinctively crouched down by the piano.

'Stay down there, mama, stay down. The chief here is not a good man. You stay down there. I keep the engines going. She got drunk and was going to give you up to this chief,' whispered José, as smoke drifted towards the boat. The differences he had with Lola now seemed forgotten.

One of the mai-mai who had gone with Marie then came running back and shouted to José.

'Chief wants you to come. He take your woman for his compound. He likes fat women.' The man chattered his teeth together in a biting motion. 'He give you good price.'

'Tell him we will come immediately,' replied José. 'Can you pass the rope from that tree stump? We have to tie up better.' The man did as he asked.

'You tell the chief I have a bottle of Portuguese rum I will bring for him. I will make good price for the woman,' added José. 'But she is good and fat.'

The mai-mai giggled.

As soon as the man had gone the rope was hauled on board and, with a wave to the bridge, *Le Rêve* slipped out into the stream. A string of canoes and a boat pushing rafts crowded with people came down the river at that moment. It cut between their boat and the shore, shielding them.

'What will they do to her?' asked Smiles in a whisper.

Lola just shook her head.

'If we meet Xavier I will tell him.'

José laughed.

'If we meet Xavier we will probably see her again quite soon.'

Smiles looked back, swallowing hard, and the sunlight was dancing on the water and made the great clouds of smoke at the other end of the village seem alive. There was a rain shower and the forest glistened again. He had not liked Marie yet he was frightened of what might be happening in that smoke. But the boat rounded a bend and the trees grew even higher. The great, healing calm of the forest returned. He felt a little giddy. It was people who made time and death and all the fear in the world.

Lola tended Smiles for the next few days.

He had a fever and she suspected he had malaria as he had lost his pills and the cook's little silver bottle of Deet insecticide was empty. Her father always said it was better to accept malaria as one of the facts of life like rain rather than mess about with nets and chemicals. But she kept Smiles under the net to stop him being bitten by the tsetse flies or anything else. He was shaking and shivering and last night had started to tell her a long story about a boy having his throat cut in a dark place and about Lyman Andrew, but it had not made sense . . . And he kept talking about a girl on a bed.

When they moored at the little village of Pimu, the witch doctor gave her special herbs to make Smiles stronger and as she watched the fireflies in the beds of reeds she realised how much her love was growing for him. The village was on a sandy island like the one downriver where they had become man and wife. She felt that now, nursing him under the stony eyes of her little brother. The fireflies over the river were a different species: as big as shooting stars. They flashed above the boat like fireworks and she made a wish and petted a yellow dog and went back to Smiles and St James, who was trying to read one of his sister's schoolbooks, *Madame Bovary*, by weak torchlight, while inland drumming started at a neighbouring village. Another huge firefly zipped over the boat and she prayed they would survive tomorrow. Whenever she felt that wartime day-to-day, hour-to-hour, way of thinking had gone for good, it flared back into life again. It was always present underneath, like the drumming, or the soft darkness of the night. She looked down at Smiles' delicate features. Perhaps she was not meant to escape what was coming. Perhaps she must take her happiness with this man while she was able, like the star-flash of the great firefly, and accept what came after with good grace. Like her poor mother.

The threat of the crew turning against them seemed less without Marie but Lola remained watchful. Smiles did not get a full fever and his headache passed.

He gripped her hand. He seemed troubled.

'I keep remembering the faces of the crew when the mai-mai took Marie.'

She nodded.

'Here a child in the city is treated as a prince or a princess for a year and then has to fight for food. There is no pity. It was not like that in the villages. My father said this lack of pity makes us into beasts.'

He took a sip of water.

'They reminded me of my school,' he said.

The next morning they put into Lisala for fuel.

To Lola the small port of Lisala had always been a most beautiful spot and she liked to visit her mother's relatives there when she was a child. Tall, flowering trees had shaded her while she made crowns for her hair with the other little girls from the fallen white, gold and blue blossoms. Beyond low hills were acres of head-high long grass to play hide-and-seek in. Everyone was safe in those days and her father had a cousin there and talked politics with one of the local bosses. The land rose from the river and fine European houses looked down on the jungle islands and channels. It was the birthplace of Mobutu, the big man in the leopard-skin hat who had ruled the country for so long and taken it to bankruptcy and civil war. Her father said Mobutu once was a good man and very brave but that power had changed him into a creature less than human. He had let the roads and the rail services go and be overrun by the jungle. He encouraged people to steal from each other and the state in Article Fifteen ... `Vous êtes chez vous, débrouillez-vous.' This is your home, fend for yourselves. He stole men's wives (her own grandmother had to be hidden once in a car boot) and murdered the husbands by throwing them from helicopters into the river. She did not know the truth about the stories that he ate the hands of rivals; he certainly encouraged all the horrible tales about himself. He was a black Kurtz far beyond anything in Conrad's polite imagination. The cook's son who became Mobutu Sese Seko Kuku Ngbendu Wa Za Banga, the all-powerful warrior who goes from conquest to conquest, leaving fire in his wake. What he had left was a ruin.

The waterfront now was a joke. Most of the larger buildings had been burned out and the beach, which had once had a port, was clogged with rusting hulks of barges and carpets of blue flowering water hyacinths so thick that children were turning somersaults on them. Her family here were all dead.

'We do not have any fuel left,' said José. 'I have to walk up to the high town near the palace if you want to come. It's safe, no one is going to leave you. You will come?' She nodded and so did Smiles but St James went under the piano.

'I still feel a bit groggy,' said Smiles.

'Take my hand,' Lola said, and they went down to the large beach that had been nearly washed away in heavy rains. Here and there were pieces of concrete and at the top of the beach was what had been a warehouse next to a hotel. The Hotel California had taken a direct hit from a rocket or a shell and with its upper floors removed there were families camped inside under a tarpaulin. The walls were pockmarked with rifle fire and black-ened with high explosive.

'We are exiles in our own country,' she said, voicing her thoughts. 'Refugees. Perhaps that is the future for the whole world. You must have a low opinion of Congo.'

'On the contrary, I love your country.'

'Why?'

'It's beautiful. And I love you. And you are beautiful.'

She sighed.

'But it is such a mess.'

'Yet, as you said, everyone gets on with things. You have had this huge war and everyone is just getting on with the next day. There is no weeping and wailing. I like that.'

Mobutu's palace was a looted two-storey white building in a semicircle and in front of the doors was an immense kitsch statue of an African woman cradling a child, cast in bronze. But there was a view of the river and the islands that was the most beautiful she had ever seen. The dictator had dined with his eyes on heaven.

'Come on,' yelled José. 'I must go and see my friend for the fuel and we will buy St James some blue pear. This is the best place to get blue pear and green pigeon on the river.' But there was no fuel and they had to trail back to the port and on the way an albino girl with red hair shouted at Lola in a language that wasn't Lingala.

'What did she say?' asked Smiles.

'Oh, she is a fortune-teller. It was just fortune-teller's rubbish.'

'Tell me.'

'She said we would never finish our journey. It's a Swahili way of saying we will always be in love. '

José led them back to a makeshift bar overlooking the muddy beach and they sat drinking beer with a fat army captain who kept playing with his large diamond ring.

'He wants two thousand dollars for the fuel,' she told Smiles.

'What?'

'Two thousand dollars. The price is going up all the time. It's the last of the fuel in Mobutu's birthplace. The captain says soldiers have gone up to Kisangani in force and Xavier has totally destroyed two villages on his way. I have some money and so does José but we do not have all he is asking. How many dollars do you have?'

Smiles turned to her.

'What I have I thought was for us to get out. I hardly have sufficient for the air fares.'

She stared at him.

'We cannot leave the crew here. None of them are from this region. They don't speak Swahili.'

Given their behaviour, he could not believe Lola was defending them. He reluctantly unzipped a pocket in the Aid America jeans and dug out a roll of damp bills.

The army captain insisted they stay for a Primus beer as he was still unsure if he could sell the petrol to them. Then he waved his hand at two figures in the road. One of the men was very tall with a wooden crutch and a tattered black raincoat and the other had greying hair.

With a mixture of growing fear and anger Lola realised it was Celestine and Thérance who were approaching the table. Thérance began to hop quicker, an irrepressible happiness on his face, while Celestine had that air of quiet triumph that was the look of businessmen all over Africa and which she had always distrusted. She still was not sure who had betrayed her and Smiles in the botanical gardens at Mbandaka but there were great welts under Thérance's eyes where he had been beaten and his left leg dragged uselessly at an angle, causing him much pain. Under his breath he was humming a tune that she recognised from *The Mikado*, one of the Gilbert and Sullivan songs he had on his mobile phone.

Celestine had cuts on his face as if he had been whipped with a pistol and his left eye was closed.

'*M'boté, mama,*' said Celestine. 'We have come to warn you. Pray God that we are in time. And to help! The good captain of supplies here is a friend of mine.'

Eighteen

The next packet St James took out from Smiles' leather bag on that last afternoon was stranger than he had ever expected. He ate a roasted peanut from his top pocket and then took the pages from the envelope. There was a salty taste as he licked his thumb and turned each page.

My Confession:
Stanley Miles-Harcourt: black book, packet six

We all get glimpses in this life of what we think at the time is wholly good or completely evil but it is so hard to judge, is it not, Dr Kaplan, when our face is in the mud or down the toilet, so to speak? And where does your expertise fit into all this? Would you make a bad person well? Would you help a monster, an all-round rotter, succeed? (I hope it would not depend on the fee. A little joke, Dr Kaplan, my little joke.)

*

I had not felt safe for a second that autumn term after the death of my friend David Wace. I was waiting for something to happen and it did when I least expected.

Before house games, the day after I had run out of Lyman Andrew's study, I was eating the last piece of my tuck-shop bar of Rowntree's chocolate when the head prefect of Devon House wagged his finger and beckoned me in the cloisters.

He was the one whose ear Lyman Andrew had taken hold of during army corps. The prefect was doubly annoyed with Lyman Andrew because several boys in Devon House had refused to be beaten and were having their cases reviewed by the headmaster, who would inevitably beat them himself because of 'bad attitude', but it was embarrassing for the house. Lyman Andrew's disapproval of beating and bullying was spreading to other houses. As a backlash there had been a revival of blacking balls with boot polish if juniors were cheeky and, specifically aimed at Lyman Andrew, making boys black their faces and act as slaves for a day to their own year. This was called 'Niggering' and was meant to have been outlawed.

'Follow me, Smiles.'

'Where are we going?'

Normally he would have been angry at my asking him. But he just paused, smiled and said: 'That will depend on you, Smiles. Have you been down to the catacombs before? I know they are out of bounds but you must have been tempted. If not, a treat lies before you. Only you might not come back.'

The catacombs were not really places where skeletons were put as in Mediterranean countries, but rather a network of passageways, under the cloisters and the houses, for which there was no logical explanation. They carried pipes and electricity but most schools buried theirs in the earth. There were rumours of great halls full of dusty old furniture and oil paintings, and others with seats for special Masonic Lodge meetings. I heard, much later, that these passageways were all part of Templar tradition and the subterranean rooms, their floors laid in chequerboard tiles, were like the old commanderies where the Knights Templar met. One of the maids who had been down had told me that there was a big chamber where the heating boilers were but she had heard 'church singing' and run out fast.

The prefect led me to a door at the bottom of the tower between Derby House and Devon House. He took a key out of his pocket and turned it in the lock. He had to push the heavy door open with his shoulder. A musty smell came up from below.

'Follow me closely, Smiles, and do not stray. You do not want to get lost down here.'

Our footsteps echoed along the stone-flagged passages, dimly lit with creamy electric light. The white-painted walls gave way to old brick and the air became warmer. We descended into a long, dark room. A fire had been lit in a chimney grate but the place was illuminated with large, flickering candles probably taken from the chapel. There was the burned-sage tang of dope being smoked.

In a pool of reddish light was a boy I did not know.

He was naked and his hands were fastened to a rope above his head. He was trembling. Even in the half-light his skin was incredibly white, like paper. His pleading eyes were wide and tear-filled.

Around him stood figures in black robes.

One wore the mask of a leopard.

On a small table there were bottles of French wine and glasses.

A voice said: 'Brothers, we are going to enact the death and rebirth of Hiram. Our inspiration is the young apprentice of the temple's great *architect. The builder of Solomon's temple. The most secret rite of the Universal Brotherhood of Freemasons.'*

The black-draped figures were chanting around the boy and he was sobbing. It seemed to me obvious what they were going to do. He began to cry out as two of those present held him while a third parted his robes to expose his taut-veined erection and, taking hold of the boy's buttocks, forced it deep into him. The boy let out a scream but there was no one to hear who would help him. He tried to struggle and the rope twitched. I looked for a way to escape but, wherever I looked, my path was blocked.

'Not yet, Smiles.'

It was the voice of the prefect who had brought me there. I could not see his face now. The boy was yelping with pain and they left him alone. Then one of his tormentors went back and beat him with a thick rope.

The figure with the leopard-skin mask took out a knife, walked over to the boy and cut his throat.

I backed away but hands held me.

The blood spurted everywhere and I thought I was going to faint, but I could not stop watching. The boy coughed, gasping for life. His white skin was cut from ear to ear and the bubbling, bright red tide ran down his naked body. It had the rank iron smell you get in a butcher's.

I was hardly able to breathe.

He hung there with the rope bound round his wrists, the life pumping out of him. The figures closed round him again and I saw the flash of the knife. They then turned to me and I was hemmed in against the wall. The one with the leopard-skin mask came close. He had the knife in his hand. It was a bayonet from the school armoury.

I opened my mouth to say I would not tell and not to hurt me, I'd do what they wanted, but no sound came out.

'Well, that was the death of Hiram the apprentice, though not exactly

as at your local Masonic Lodge meeting. I do hope we can pack the young boy in magic moss and bring him back to life.'

It was Anderson.

He clasped my left wrist and pressed my hand on his and I felt something warm, wet and pulsing.

'This is that poor soul's still-beating heart.'

I half-fainted.

'Don't be worried, Smiles. We are not going to cut your pretty throat. Or remove your bits. At least, not if you help us play a little prank on your good friend and mentor Lyman Andrew. He has been getting too big for his boots, has Lyman, and, anyway, I don't like his silly name. You cannot imagine the fun I have planned for him. Don't worry, he'll not come to such physical harm. At least, not from me. Not if you cooperate. You are going to help us, aren't you, Smiles? I did you a good turn the other week and you have always struck me as an obliging boy.'

In chapel the next morning the headmaster read an account of a nun in Africa who was made to eat her own kidneys but still prayed for the souls of her tormentors. The headmaster said this was an example of how we should love our enemies and pity those savages who had not found the light of Jesus. How we must forgive even those who killed David Wace. Everyone knew he did not mean it but it was the sort of thing you said in chapel.

We all faced each other down a central aisle and the address was given from a huge brass-eagle lectern.

I was in the choir stalls next to Derby House, dressed in my white-and-red surplice. I had not slept. I felt the gaze of Anderson on the back of my neck. But across from me I saw that all the boys were looking at

Lyman Andrew during the head's address, not in an accusing way but with that long blank stare that was typical of the school.

I prayed to God that Lyman Andrew might decide to return to America. Even to the South.

We had stood up to sing the closing hymn when I noticed one of the junior-school choirboys across the aisle staring at me. He had glasses on now but I was certain it was the boy I had seen in the catacombs, the apprentice in the ritual of Hiram. The muscles of his neck were straining to the highest descant notes of the hymn the choir alone was meant to sing. There was not a mark on his throat, even though I had seen blood running down his chest and onto the floor. I had smelt the blood. I had seen him white and dead. Felt his beating heart.

I had spent that night imagining the boy was dead, but the fact that he was now restored to life was more frightening. I knew it was a trick but it preyed on the deepest, darkest of fears of unstoppable forces that went beyond life and death. Anderson had controlled it all.

The boy was smiling at me and singing.

I thought of David Wace.

We were not meant to turn round in chapel but I did. Anderson was gazing right at me and raised his eyebrows and gave a little grin. A few paces along, Lyman Andrew stood bathed in a shaft of sunlight, singing each word for all he was worth.

NINETEEN

'You must understand, Lola, that it was not us who betrayed you. By the light of heaven, why would we do such a thing? Wasn't it my idea to charter the boat and take the piano? It makes me sad to hear the ridiculous notion that we conspired to have you cut up by the mai-mai,' said Celestine, and Thérance nodded and grinned an idiot grin that told Smiles the ambitious assistant had been beaten too hard and too long. He felt very sorry for both of the men but like Lola he completely distrusted them.

Celestine's smile was in place even though his gold tooth had been knocked out.

'One of the things those monkeys in Mbandaka tried to get out of us was where you were, Lola. A spy had seen us going out to the mission earlier and the new commandant in Mbandaka is an old enemy. Then they just hit us and attempted to make us say where Fortuné is hiding and that we were responsible for the bomb in the kitchens of the Intercontinental. Eventually they let us go after beating us up one last time and said we had to report to the police in Kisangani, my official place of business, for further questioning by the army. Then they laughed. They said that Xavier is going upriver with a big force. The city is threatened by new rebels coming from the east.'

Lola shook her head.

'Fortuné would never join up with the Rwandans and the Interahamwe.'

Celestine shrugged.

'I don't know who these rebels are they were talking about. We only heard snatches between the blows, didn't we, Thérance?'

Thérance's eyes were far away and scared, his back hunched, as if still expecting the lead-weighted clubs of the interrogation cell at the military prison outside Mbandaka. She saw Smiles reach out and put a sympathetic hand on Thérance's shoulder. Lola had felt so sure in the botanical gardens that Celestine and Thérance had betrayed them. There were others, though, who knew they were going to the botanical gardens; the old priest, for example.

'How did you get here so quickly?' Smiles asked.

His voice told her he was still suspicious.

Painfully, Thérance answered.

'Papa Celestine convinced a white Baptist preacher that we had been wrestling with the real devil, Satan himself. The preacher is a very stupid man. Papa Celestine asked him to put us on a Mission Air flight from the little airport in Mbandaka and he does and here we are. We sing hymns all the way . . . "Onward Christian Soldiers".'

'What do you want?' Lola asked Celestine.

'To take the piano, of course.'

'And?'

Celestine's confidence wavered for a heartbeat, then he said: 'To ride on the boat. Our money and food have run out and we can get no further. Thérance needs a doctor and if we do not report in Kisangani we will be posted as enemies of the state, like Smiles. Then we will be caught and handed over for questioning to Major-General Xavier and you know how that ends . . . We have done our best not to be followed but could be being watched even now. You and Smiles must not go to Kisangani, you will be walking into a trap. Get the piano to Fortuné and broadcast the Peace Concert. We must plan together. It will make it so much more difficult for them to do things in silence and the dark if the world listens. It can be sent out on the Internet or to the BBC. To America. I know you do not think much of me, Mademoiselle, I know that you are your own woman and I respect that. I know you will not allow yourself and what you believe in to be trampled on, but the piano is more important now than ever.'

After he had finished his speech Celestine took a deep drink of beer and folded his arms. She saw the sores on his wrists where he had been shackled or tied.

Lola sat for a long time staring at the table in front of her, not moving, even when the army captain, who with the intervention of Celestine had now finally let them have the fuel, bade them goodbye and good luck.

Eventually she turned to Celestine and said, almost in a whisper: 'You may come with us but if I even think you have betrayed me or mine then you will wish you were in the hands of Xavier because I will kill you myself. I will cut you while you sleep.'

Her eyes were wild at that moment and he looked away. 'And I have my own plans for the piano.'

At first the crew did not want Celestine and Thérance on the boat but she persuaded José to take them.

For an age Lola sat in the bows watching the trees change and become darker-leaved and mightier, in particular on the northern bank of the river. The boat stopped at Mombongo overnight and it rained and rained so she and Smiles slept on the deck under the piano, and Lola stayed awake listening to the toads and frogs and other night creatures. The last time she had been back to her village was with Xavier.

At breakfast she chewed on a roll and watched the islands in the stream open and close until she stood up with excitement.

Smiles was behind her.

'*Mittakenamittake!*' cried the *profondeur*.

The engines stopped.

The bow slipped into the soft sand of the beach. On the shore were a group of girls with hair teased into spikes and bobbles. Once Lola had worn her hair like that. She was probably related to all of them yet they stared at her as if she had arrived from another galaxy.

She turned to Smiles.

'This is my village. This is where I was born! This is me, I suppose. I am a little village girl. This is Bokondo-Rive, and that's my tree!'

Before José could put the gangplank in place she leapt over the side and splashed in the cool water and then ran up to the tree with spreading green leaves and looping roots that no one knew the name of at the edge of the beach – which she had climbed every day – and kissed it.

A young girl came sprinting towards her.

'Lola! It is Lola!'

A crowd was soon surging around Lola, wanting to hug her.

'My uncle . . . I must see my uncle,' she said to Smiles, who had to fight his way to her side. 'My uncle is the chief, after his cousin, Jean, drowned.'

'I'm sorry.'

'That was a long time ago.'

But then she was looking into a face that reminded her so much of her father, whom she missed.

Her uncle was a smiling man, done up in a raincoat against the chill of the morning.

He embraced her and took her aside a few steps. Smiles, mobbed by curious children, did not follow.

'You have not brought your soldier boy this time?'

'No,' she said. 'But I have brought an Englishman and a piano.'

She felt the mood change almost instantly.

'I heard things. I heard that you were no longer with your husband.'

She took a deep breath.

'I am with the Englishman,' she said and saw the chief's face grow sombre.

'Your poor mother would not like this,' he said. 'I cannot offer you the hospitality of the village. As chief I must rule you cannot sleep even one night in our compounds. You must understand this. Xavier brought gifts to me. It is not because I fear him, even if I do fear him for the village. But unless those marriage debts are repaid you cannot sleep here.'

Lola felt the tears well up in her and stopped them.

'I understand . . . But it is ended with Xavier. I was married to the Englishman downriver at Nganda Saisai. I love him so much . . . He is a pianist and he was due to play a concert in Kinshasa but there was a bomb.'

Her uncle nodded.

'We hear on the radio.'

'The concert was meant to be for peace. But there are many people who do not want peace. We are trying to get a piano to Fortuné's base, where there is a transmitter and he can broadcast it. I believe he is in Pendé, near Bokoli. Will you help me?'

To her delight his face broke into a beaming smile. The chief had become her uncle again.

'That I can do, Lola, with the greatest of pleasure. That I can do. Return to me when your things have been brought ashore.'

Smiles sensed there was a problem between Lola and her uncle but they were speaking quickly in Lingala and he could not possibly understand, except by the way she hung her head for a moment, her shoulders fell forward and the gentle and intelligent chief cast a sad look towards him, standing a few yards away under the shade of Lola's tree. Whatever it was, Smiles immediately liked the village. There was a market behind the beach with straw shades for the stalls and beyond that a few huts in the elephant grass and a cleared space of grazing land for goats and a line of planted trees. He was told by a man that at the other side of the goat meadow was the village proper and that was where they were going to carry the piano when they took it from the boat. The whole community seemed to appear and form a ramp of muscle and the heavy piano was plucked up and first deposited on the beach, where Smiles had to play a tune while the children cheered. It was then carried, with much singing, across the goat field and into a building that had open sides and a thatched roof, which the chief announced was a new church. The village around was made of neat, mud-walled houses with palm-thatched roofs, but there were none of the straight lines, or equal compounds, of the plantation villages. Smiles watched a child chasing after a hen and suddenly realised he was looking into Africa as it must always have been.

'We must go back to the boat. It has to leave,' said Lola. 'To kiss my little brother goodbye.'

Smiles returned quickly with her.

But José had already cast off and St James was standing in the bow.

Lola was speaking to a pretty girl, who then leapt up the side of the boat and was pulled aboard. The girl had a panga slung loosely around her shoulders.

'St James, you hear me?' Lola shouted from the shore. 'Yvette is one of your cousins and she will look after you, you will mind her now. Go to our house in Kisangani and stay there until I reach you. It is safer for you this way.'

Smiles was not so sure. He was also anxious about the contents of his precious music satchel he had left in Lola's locker. She assured him it was better there than losing it in the jungle.

At the rail next to St James were Celestine and Thérance.

St James held up a hand to wave and the ramshackle boat turned out into the stream and was gone.

'It is only two days,' said Lola, mainly to herself, as she was left alone with Smiles under the big village tree. 'He will be all right.'

'He is close to becoming a man,' said Smiles, in French.

A woman, overhearing, shrieked with laughter and said: 'Men never become men. That is why Congo is in this mess. That is why the world is in this upset. Most men do not even become cruel-hearted boys, killing frogs. They stay as babies playing with their own doo-doo and howling like tyrants. That is the way of our good men in Congo.'

Smiles and Lola walked back up to the church and sheltered from the sun with the chief.

'It can hold two hundred people,' he said proudly. 'We built it to celebrate that the war has stopped. It has not ended yet, though. We hear shooting in the jungle. The fighting is spreading from the east again.'

'I hope not,' said Lola.

'We had a raid not long ago. They were Rwandans, maybe Interahamwe. They look for the women refugees that flee to where Fortuné is. Whatever people accuse him of, he has made that place a safe one for the refugees but that is why the Rwandan rebels want to kill him and the women. They say he has taken them into slavery. One of the men from our village has been up there and it is not true. Many of the women are dying anyway after the rapes. The Rwandans infect them with the Aids. It is a terrible thing.'

His quiet words seemed to blow through the church with the dusty wind.

Smiles took hold of a wooden post.

'What denomination is the church?' he asked nervously, just for something to say.

'Anyone is free to worship with us. We like to sing, as Lola will tell you. But if people come here with a different way, Catholics or such, or they worship baby Jesus, or a crocodile, we don't care. I went to Yangambi when it still had an agricultural university so I do know a little of the outside world. But you must excuse me if I have to abide by our custom in the matter of marriage, our African custom. It is most important to get our society running again on the right lines, not the imperial way. Nor the path of corruption and Mobutu, laws must be obeyed. Now, enough of the lecture. Please could you play us some more of your beautiful music? Then we will eat before you set off in the forest for Pendé and Fortuné's base where you will make your broadcast. I am afraid you must go too quickly. There are many things I would have liked to discuss with both of you. But you do understand, don't you? There must be new beginnings.'

Three hours later the piano was being carried between high stands of trees down a track that was just wide enough for it to fit through.

Smiles was out of breath and the sweat was pouring off him and he had not even touched the instrument, except to play Mozart.

Fight men took it at what was almost a run.

They had been going for what he calculated was two miles.

It was then they suddenly plunged into the forest to the right and came to a halt by a huge fallen log.

'We have to walk along that,' said one of the men to Lola: 'Piano too big.'

A giant tree, hung with creepers, had toppled over and formed a pathway into the darkness that was only a yard and a half wide. The jungle leaves seemed to reach out towards Smiles. He was panting for breath.

Lola hugged his arm.

'There is a stream down there, a small, shallow river, where we can float the piano on its side in a canoe and push it along. The river goes most of the way to Pendé. If we can just get it down this log.'

The men stopped and looked at him.

Smiles stared at the piano. It was one of the best he had ever played and the dappled sun glinted on the black lacquer. For all he knew it may have been one of those confiscated during the French Revolution by the infamous Bruni. It was a piece of history. Yet European history was no use whatsoever to people making the categorically new.

'Cut the legs off.'

The men hesitated.

'What?' said Lola.

'Cut the legs off.'

'But you love that piano.'

'Yes.'

He sighed.

'We will not get it an inch further with its legs. They can be put back on again when we get there. Can you ask them to do it carefully?'

The men from the village removed the legs of the piano

delicately, cutting and levering with their pangas and using great strength to uncouple the original joints. (A man had run back to the village for a saw but it was not needed.) Then they tied the lid down. The tarpaulin had unfortunately been left aboard the boat. A small canoe was being carried as well.

Smiles followed the chief's son along the rotting log into the gloom, to a stream bed of luminous white sand.

Smiles just turned around and around looking up at the canopy. He had entered another world.

This was different from the palm forest. He walked onto what he thought was a path at the edge of the stream and in a few steps could go no further, the leaves and twigs and small branches crowding and pressing against his face. At every level the vegetation was thick and lush but Smiles noticed another characteristic as well. Apart from the occasional gurgling of the stream and the drip of the water from the canopy above, there was near complete silence. He heard the voices of the men as they started to bring the piano down the sloping face of the log, but when they did not speak the silence took over; it forced out the melodies and snippets of Mozart that were moving in his own head and replaced them with a more gradual, subtle music of its own.

He stood in awe.

Lola had scrambled after him and her shirt and jeans were wet from the moisture on every leaf.

'You like my forest?'

'It's incredibly beautiful.'

There was a shout from above and a cry as one of the men fell off the log and plunged twenty feet down into the jungle and the piano slipped and Smiles heard something crack. The chief's son had to hack his way into the vegetation with his panga to reach the fallen man. When they were able to get to him it was clear that he had broken his leg, which was twisted at a violent angle, and Smiles had to restrain himself from running up the log and checking over the Zimmerman.

'Boys take him home,' said the chief's son. 'We get more people.'

Two villagers carried the injured man up the log and they disappeared into the forest. Those remaining edged the piano slowly down the rest of the fallen tree to the forest floor where, turned on its side, it was placed precariously in the old canoe and half-floated, half-dragged upriver.

Even with eventual reinforcements, after only a few minutes Smiles had to stop, panting again, but the men of the village went on and so did Lola. A huge black, white and yellow butterfly glided off a leaf as they rounded a corner and ahead was another fallen tree, which they had to wrestle the canoe and the piano over.

But at the far side of the mossy trunk there was enough water to float the boat once more.

The village men wore shorts and T-shirts and were mostly in bare feet.

They stopped as they came on a waterfall that had slowed to a trickle over and around a dam of fallen trees.

Smiles climbed up to the still pool beyond the lip of the falls, which was more than six feet deep. Delicate bamboo grew at the water's edge and he saw a red flower in the vegetation, like ginger but more bulbous.

Ropes were attached to the piano and the canoe and they were dragged up the face of the falls.

At one point the wood caught and part of the piano lid splintered. The men stopped for a second and looked at Smiles. He nodded and they hauled away.

The clogged lip of the waterfall was full of smaller logs and pieces of rotting debris. But they managed to drag the piano over it without more of its black-lacquered wood breaking, although there were scratches and there was a deep indentation in the lid where the piano had slipped on the initial tree trunk.

Everyone paused for breath and went to the other end of the pool, leaving the roped piano turned on its side in the canoe, floating on the still water like a yacht sail, surrounded by delicate white blossoms that had dropped from the canopy far above.

Only Smiles was near by on the bank.

At first he thought nothing of it as the piano began to drift slowly, almost imperceptibly downstream.

But then he heard a sound like paper tearing and caught sight of logs falling away and a rush of water.

As the dam at the top of the waterfall began to break he grabbed frantically at the tangle of ropes trailing behind the canoe. It was no good. He then plunged in and swam around the piano, putting himself between the log dam and the Zimmerman.

The water surged around him in a roar.

The canoe and the weight of the piano were threatening to trap him against the log wall. Without thinking, he scrambled up on top of it.

'Help him!' he heard Lola shout, just as the logs he was standing on gave way with the force of the churning water.

Smiles toppled backwards and there was a thud as he hit his head on the sand in the shallows ten feet below and the sky between the trees far above started to spin. Then, as he looked up, the piano teetered on the brink of the half-broken dam.

There was nothing he could do if the piano fell. Except not lose consciousness and try and get up and out of its way.

He thought of when he was in the car with Emma and that horrible sensation of being frozen in an impossible moment for all eternity, of Emma's red hair tumbling over his arm, the beauty of her face and her perfume.

Lola then screamed in his ear.

'You idiot! You stupid fool, Smiles! You could have been killed for a piano!'

She started to cry and kissed and kissed him.

He moved his legs and his arms and his back and then crawled out of danger.

His chest and ribs hurt.

It was painful to breathe.

But the soft white sand had broken his fall.

The men from the village were all smiling and singing.

'They say you are a hero. They say you are like a holy man because you will give your life for your instrument. Believe me, these men do not suffer fools or pay compliments easily, not that I agree with them. I think what you did was mad.'

She kissed him again.

They helped him back up the waterfall and pushed the canoe and piano to the edge of the deep water.

The pool joined a network of swampier, muddier streams on a plateau of jungle. Smiles was told that at the other side of the hill these streams flowed into another large river, the Aruwimi. The chief's son said that Pendé was below them.

His head hurt like hell and he felt groggy and watched as Lola and the men made a camp of sorts.

Smiles looked up at the colouring sky between the many-fingered leaves and felt the light-headedness that had preceded his bout of fever. If anyone had told him he would be risking his life in the middle of the jungle six months ago he would have politely excused himself and walked away, convinced they were insane. And now? All this had been for Lola and for something he had lost a long time ago among the neat quads and red brick of his school. Now, as the country took him over, there was more and it frightened him. He could make a real difference by playing the piano in the concert broadcast from Pendé.

TWENTY

St James opened the next packet in Smiles' leather satchel. At first he was surprised by what he read and then chuckled to himself. It was hard to imagine Smiles doing such things, even as a masquerade. And although he did not understand everything that was written down he was sure the story was moving towards its climax.

My Confession:
Stanley Miles-Harcourt: black book, packet seven

The head matron threw open the door.

'Your breasts, Smiles. Your titties! Your last titties were in tatters. These are the real thing. The real thing!'

I was in the green room beneath the stage at school, putting on my make-up for our production of Salad Days.

'There you are, my dear Smiles. Breasts! Not just the cardboard ones

like everyone else but real fake ones. Savill's. The Rolls-Royce of false female kit . . . They belonged to a former matron in Connaught House who had hers cut off by our friends the Japanese. Chop, chop! Salad Days *is one of my favourite musicals and you are a superior Jane, Miles-Harcourt. Looking at you now, I think you'd have made a much better girlie. You are a beauty! Quite a beauty, in the manner of Her Royal Highness, the Princess Margaret, when young!'*

'Thank you, Matron,' I said. I was doing what I do best. Trying to please. I think I learned a little about women from being Jane in Salad Days *and I certainly loved them more. It was a good idea to be on the right side of Hag Grey, the head matron, who swept around the school like a schooner, upholstered in floral prints. She was a woman of immense enthusiasm who had a title and a great house in Norfolk but had chosen to devote herself to the school and us.*

I was still getting used to the reflection in the mirror, to the slightly over-coloured image of myself as a girl. I had no idea I could change so completely, Dr Kaplan.

The other 'Jane' had broken his nose in a game of basketball refereed by Anderson and had a large white bandage over the front of his face. I had protested that my voice was too low when the part became available. But Lyman Andrew said that though I was no longer a treble, my voice had not broken in the classic sense, I could still sing soprano and my speaking voice was all right . . . He was so pleased I could do the part. He had worked night and day on the musical, trying to get everything perfect and he really trusted me where music was concerned.

When I still attempted to refuse he became angry and said: 'You must take the opportunities life offers. You can't avoid life, you know.'

I bit my lip.

'I know that . . . I do know that.'

His face was immediately sad and concerned.

'I am so sorry, Smiles. I did not mean . . . Losing your father, that must have been . . . I'm the one trying to avoid life, sitting in this nice school, playing games.'

'It's OK. I'll do the part. I'll be Jane.'

There was a slick inevitability about what was going to happen next.

I was left alone in the star dressing room, surrounded by sticks of stage make-up and the real thing. I loved the smell of the greasepaint. My mother had liked amateur dramatics and always organised a Christmas play. My father had been enthusiastic, too. I revelled in the art of transformation.

Tonight there was not just the performance to consider. There was afterwards. I had to look better than ever. I had to be more than just a boarding-school-stage 'girl'.

'You must,' repeated Anderson, 'be the object of his complete desire. To everyone who sees you tonight. Leave the rest to me.'

I put on a pale blue eye shadow and carefully brushed the black mascara onto my long lashes. I applied a far more subtle shade of lipstick than the carmine red from the stage make-up box and dusted around the face powder and last of all pulled on a black curly wig of real hair.

It was a strange feeling. I had only sung or said the part before in rehearsal. Now there was a girl in front of me and I found myself getting an erection. The metamorphosis must have been working as it crossed my mind that I might actually fancy Lyman Andrew but I dismissed that. I wasn't queer. I wasn't.

On a coat hanger was a short blue dress and a pair of hold-up stockings. In front of the mirror was a pair of black-silk women's panties Anderson had provided. I took off my shoes and socks, trousers and underpants and left them in a cupboard with my blazer and shirt and tie.

I pulled on the panties, which held back my waning erection. I had to concentrate.

Next, I put on the bra. The clip was on the front and I inserted the two gelatinous breasts in the cups. I then pulled on the black stockings and stared at myself in the mirror, pressing my knees together and pursing my lips.

I did not look foolish.

Then I slipped the silky dress carefully over my head. I should have put the dress on first and then the wig, but the wig fitted so well it stayed in place. I stepped into a pair of black, patent-leather tap shoes, not high heels, which fastened around the ankle. I gave a skip just to make sure I could dance in them as Hag Grey swept back into the room.

'Perfection, my dear! Perfection! You could marry a viscount! Hurry along now. Curtain up in five. The breasts are a triumph! You look splendid, my dear! You'd fool your own mother!'

When I went on stage I felt the great vaulted Gothic assembly hall go pin-drop quiet. I heard a senior boy in the wings say: 'It's a girl. It's a real girl.' Lyman Andrew was there in the first row, staring up at me, but the footlights were so effective I could not see beyond.

I just threw myself into the musical as Jane. When you are frightened of making a fool of yourself, it's best to become someone else. The person that everyone wants to see. I became Jane. It was the only way I had of keeping my mind off what Anderson had planned.

The entire school rose for a standing ovation after I sang `You Never Saw A Saucer So Saucy As Mine'.

There was clapping and stamping and calls for an encore, which I duly did, and then they clapped and stamped all over again.

At the finish there were endless curtain calls and a very small boy *from the junior school brought me a bouquet of flowers. A strange, moon-faced man from the* Watford Observer *was beside himself and slobbering as he clapped and jumped up and down.*

'You . . . you are incredible,' said Lyman Andrew. He threw his arms around me. I thought for a moment he was going to kiss me.

'Thank you,' I said.

'You really gave your all. I'm so grateful.' There were tears in his eyes and I noticed immediately we were bring watched by Anderson and the other prefects and by the headmaster.

Anderson gave me an almost imperceptible nod and I took a step nearer to Lyman Andrew.

'I'm really glad you liked it,' I said, still out of breath.

'Liked is not even in the ball park. Loved! Adored!'

'I'm sure it wasn't that good.'

He was drawing attention to us.

'It was a superlative performance, Smiles. When I see something as joyous as that . . . it gives me so much more hope for humanity. That is what art should do! Inspire!'

I gave him my biggest smile.

'Well done, Miles-Harcourt,' said the headmaster.

'Yes, jolly well done,' said Anderson. 'But now it's time for bed. Don't forget it's a cross-country run in the morning. A good run before break-fast and one day you will be running the country. Isn't that true, Headmaster?'

St James put back the packets. He knew of certain bars in Kisangani where men dressed as women but could not imagine it happening in a school play.

TWENTY-ONE

The single rifle shot came after the sound of the breaking twig and she saw the white flash of the muzzle and there were shouts and running and a hush, although any moment she expected the endless explosion of automatic fire, the flares and the green tracer, the red tracer, the clump of grenades, spreading like the web of a malicious spider that left spinning whirlpools of knives and pangas and spears in her fatal wake. Lola listened so hard she discerned the rustle of a small frog that hopped between her shoes.

Then there was a surprised, dying scream as an attacker ran into one of the village men in the darkness.

The silence and the jungle leaves closed with a gentle, velvet totality around the man's cry and there was quiet again, she could not hear the frogs or the insects, there was nothing in the blackness and she hardly dared breathe, it was as if all existence hung in a void above the still water like the evening mist. She moved slowly along the bank and crouched next to Smiles and put her hand on him.

He jumped but she kissed his hand and pulled him down with her and towards a bush.

Above her and reflected in the pool she could see several small stars. She waited like that for what seemed an age. It was hot even by the stream and she longed for a drink from one of the water bottles up at the other end of the deep pool. She could not see what was there. She shut her eyes tight to get them better used to the night and when she opened them she caught sight of movement.

'Don't worry, mama, it me,' whispered her cousin, the chief's son. 'The men will go back to the village. To lead whoever it is away. I will go on to Pendé for help. It is not far. Stay here. Stay right here, mama.' He then touched her nose in a gesture of affection and blended into the night.

Her pulse was racing.

Lola remembered hearing a lone rifle when she was with a friend having a coffee and a *pain au chocolat* in the gardens of the Académie des Beaux-Arts on a table under the scrubby acacia trees, as they were saying it was time to get rid of the tortured war sculptures in front of the modern building she had always regarded as a happy place. A single shot had grown into two or three and then a burst had stitched itself into the full-scale battle in Gombé cemetery with the shock of mortar explosions shaking the ground and a cloud of smoke rising over the city.

At first people had actually said it was some kind of exercise or even fireworks for a religious holiday but then the firing came nearer and everyone ran. She had gone back to her aunt's and tried to 'phone Xavier but there was no reply.

Xavier and the government were victorious and Fortuné had fled for his life upriver. The battle sparked riots and the mob set on anyone they deemed rebels; loan sharks, outsiders, immigrants had been set upon and beaten or, in the worst cases, killed with a panga or covered in petrol and set on fire. A short time later Bemba himself had fled the country. The UN and the NATO force had stayed safely in their compounds and their white Land Cruisers were not even seen at the pizza restaurant in Gombé, where the chef wiped the steaks of the unwanted Europeans around the toilet bowl.

She expected troops to come to her door and arrest her.

To drag her and beat her and shame her in the street for being the cause of it all.

She had watched the scaled-down, sanitised version on TV in between the gospel music and the commercials for real estate in parts of town yet to be built. Bemba had been accused of an attempted coup and Fortuné was named as one of the people who had assisted him, about which the President was said to feel deeply as Fortuné had been a brave fighter against the rebels. The report did not go into further detail. The television also did not show too much of Xavier, who did not like publicity. Instead the screen was filled with the chubby, shy face of Kabila, who loved the limelight even less.

After Xavier had burst in and she spat at him and he threatened to hunt down Fortuné, Lola was sure she would never hear from him again.

But soon the notes had started arriving.

He sent her a poem about two flowers twined together which was in her pocket now. But she had not gone to see him.

There was something so adolescent, and white, about what the brothers had done. So self-indulgent.

Instead, she had stayed in a quiet world, reading and hoping for a time when she could go back to the university, until Celestine had pursued her with the plan for the Peace and Reconciliation Concert that had the support of the top people in the land and she had believed him. He had said Fortuné had fled to a plantation near Kisangani that had become a sanctuary for refugee women. He wanted to see her again and she felt she owed Fortuné that.

And then she had met Smiles, which she did not intend or expect.

She stared out at the soft darkness.

She never thought of the darkness as evil; when she first saw the title of the Conrad book she thought of the forest and the very centre of the forest as a good place, a place of safety, a place to run; to her the heart of darkness was not evil, it was Africa.

More stars shone in the strip of sky.

Smiles had lain back against the bank and his breathing was regular. She doubted he was asleep but he must be exhausted.

The night in the forest held no terrors for her.

She had always gone hunting with her father and his ragged pack of yellow sharp-nosed dogs and slept out in the middle of the bush and he told her stories of magic and talking honey badgers, but also tales of Europe, where a cousin had been, and Nairobi, where he had been himself. She would go out with him when it rained and her brothers would not. She was only six or seven the first time he left her totally on her own on a moonless night by a tall tree and went running off with his dogs and commanded her to watch and not to sleep and to crawl between the buttress roots of the tree with the long knife he had given her. She had watched for hours in complete calm. She was not afraid. When he asked her why, she had told him it was because the forest was her friend, as he was. On another occasion she had seen a ripple in the darkness and heard the throaty call of the leopard himself, who had stopped, scenting her, but padded on and she always thought he did not eat her because she was part of the forest and part of him.

Lola did not shut her eyes once.

As the sky started to lighten far above her she did not feel tired.

When she went out hunting with her father she might only snatch a few hours' sleep. Yet she came back refreshed.

The light spread across the pool and the piano and she stood and looked down on Smiles, who was now fast asleep.

The piano drifted out in the pool, secured to a tree with a piece of rope.

She wandered to where the men had made camp and in a plastic bag inside a pack found a few bread rolls and a piece of dried fish. On both sides of the stream the jungle was impossibly thick but she saw a path and went carefully along the trail. First, she noticed the blood on the leaves and then the body of the man, his neck sliced open, his eyes staring up and his hands hooked around the branches and the creepers. His rifle had been taken but she knew by his face and his heavy jungle boots that he was not from near Kisangani or downriver, he was from the east. He was one of the eastern tribes or a Rwandan. At his waist was a panga and with a lot of trouble she loosened his belt and slid it from under him. The man was thin and sickly and far from home. It was hard to think of him as one of the feared Interahamwe. What had brought him to this?

She heard Smiles calling her name and went back to the pool.

'My God, I fell asleep,' he said. 'I don't know how . . . and you were gone. My God, where did you get that panga?'

'There's a man back there, dead. One of the attackers.'

She went to him and he hugged her and hugged her, like a child. She wondered if she deserved the love of this good man.

Dawn penetrated the forest slowly for Smiles and he could hardly move his limbs.

'Why did they leave us?'

She reached out and pushed back a lock of hair which had fallen onto his forehead.

'They have to defend the village.'

He glanced around him. He still was very scared.

'They have no rifles.'

'The chief does in the village. They do not make a show of them and because of that they are seldom bothered. The men here grow up hunting and fishing, they know the jungle. But because they do not seem to be a military camp, that is why there is a market and people trade with us. We have to think beyond the war.'

He was surprised she was so calm.

'Who was it? Who attacked us?'

She shrugged.

'I don't know. The man who was killed is over there. Don't go and look. He is not from this region. He may be Interahamwe.'

'My God. They just kill everyone . . .'

'Yes.'

Smiles walked around the bank and pulled on one of the ropes holding the piano.

'What do we do?'

'Wait. My cousin, is trying to get to Pendé. I just hope it has not been attacked.'

An hour later Smiles looked up from a bread roll he had been nibbling and, for no particular reason, began to whistle the *Missa Luba* Sanctus. Lola put her fingers to her lips. He then saw a crouched soldier in camouflage gear, pointing a rifle straight at his chest. He took a deep breath.

But at that moment the chief's son stepped out of the wall of jungle.

'*M'boté*, Lola. Please go with this man, he is from Pendé. Fortuné's men will come for your piano. You can trust them. Now I have to return to my village. You must go fast. Fortuné is sick, Lola, and the enemy is all around. He has been wounded and has a fever. Go now. Go quickly.'

They hurried along game paths and the sweat poured down her face as they crossed swampy ground made up of a network of pools and little streams and then a bigger one which fell gently through an area of very tall trees to a wider valley and she saw a string of blackened, brick-built houses. There was wild cocoa in the bush near by and the place had once been a plantation. The man with the rifle stopped and called out and they were surrounded by others, who, after an amazed discussion about the piano, went back up the hardly visible trail for the instrument.

She then saw a soldier she recognised as being one of Fortuné's lieutenants.

He came running up to her.

'Mama Lola! We never thought ... we never thought for a

moment that you would find us. That you would get here. And with a piano! A piano!'

'Where is he? Where is Fortuné?'

The man's expression changed.

She felt herself go cold.

'He's not dead, is he?'

'No, mama. But he badly wounded. Better prepare yourself. Try not to show too much. I don't think he realises . . . how bad.'

Lola walked ahead of Smiles along the long avenue of houses which slanted up a hill. The houses were packed full of women and children. Some of the women had bandages on their faces and bodies and the children ran screaming between the brick shacks, a few of them burned out, many of them with crude pictures of soldiers in sunglasses on the walls. There was graffiti praising Bemba and his mai-mai. The women had the expression she had seen many times before: a fixed stare into a future that had failed them.

She and Smiles were led up to a green and white-painted house built in a European style, partly of brick and wood with a slate roof, which looked a little like a Swiss chalet Lola had once seen in a book. Behind it were buildings and this must have been where the plantation owner had lived back before independence. There were steps up to the door and on either side stood a guard. They were ushered inside to a high-ceilinged, downstairs room with a four-poster bed on which lay Fortuné with a large wound plaster on his chest and his arm connected to a blood drip. She felt like crying out and running to the bed but she had to keep control. Poor Fortuné. How could this have been done to him? There was a bandage on his head too and around his right hand. Yet, badly wounded though he was, he still managed to luxuriate on a mound of old silk pillows and there was a twinkle in his eyes. On one finger was the enormous diamond ring she remembered.

'Hello, beautiful Lola . . .'

'Hello.'

'I'd have tried to look a bit better if I'd known you were coming. I hear you ran into bad people in the forest.'

Lola smiled. She went over to the bed and kissed Fortuné's cheek and slowly, painfully, he took her hand.

'We brought the piano.'

The wounded man was staring at Smiles.

'My men told me and I said it was impossible. And this is Mr S. Miles-Harcourt, the pianist? I am so pleased to meet you. I'd shake your hand. I am what is left of Fortuné.'

Smiles glanced around at the other soldiers in the room.

'Lyman Andrew . . .?' he began, and she felt the mood change.

'Is a traitor! He betrayed me! He betrayed everyone!' shouted Fortuné. He gasped for breath and, clutching at the sheets and pillows, he tried to pull himself into a sitting position. A nurse attempted to help him but he waved her away. He started to cough and slid back down to the pillows, his body shaking as he managed to control himself. Slowly, his breathing calmed down but there was fury in his eyes. He was no longer playful.

'But we brought the piano for him,' said Smiles.

Fortuné managed a shake of his head.

'You will please play the broadcast. I cannot tell you how we need peace. We may be attacked at any moment by these Interahamwe devils from the east, or even my idiot brother and his *Garde Républicaine*. Or both!'

Lola saw Smiles was aghast. He was not really listening to what Fortuné was now saying.

'Lyman Andrew betrayed you? And all these women? I . . . I cannot accept that. Lyman Andrew could not betray anyone . . . He . . . he betrayed you?'

TWENTY-TWO

There was a cold and hostile silence and Lola moved towards Smiles.

'What happened, Fortuné?'

Fortuné lay back on his pillows. Each word hurt him.

'The women, everything here, was Lyman Andrew's idea. Helping these poor women. I did not want to be involved but he got me involved and there are always more of them, coming from the east, displaced by what he called the big chill. Money is paid by rich American bankers and some in Europe to keep the eastern half of our country on ice through terror, especially against women. Small acts of total brutality have depopulated parts of North and South Kivu so that mineral rights for the coltan, that makes mobile 'phones work, and gold and diamonds can be bought cheap and sold dear when the Chinese build us roads. It's like the old clearances in the rubber days only better hidden . . . No one is going to work his land if hardly believable acts of savagery will happen to his wife and family. Then, after the bomb in the hotel, Lyman Andrew changed. Suddenly, next day, he was gone from here and

233

someone must have given the whereabouts of this place as we were attacked . . . He is helping the enemy. His own people have got to him. That is what I am told.'

Smiles stood there, silent. He wished he did not, but he understood exactly how one can go over to an enemy. He thought of Anderson at school.

He took a decision.

'I will do the broadcast,' he said. 'I am so sorry about Lyman Andrew, though I can hardly believe . . .'

The handsome face set hard.

'Believe me, he is a traitor.'

Smiles took a deep breath.

'I'm sorry. You know your own business. It's such a shock. It just does not sound like the man I know. Of course, I will try my best and play the concert.'

Fortuné's face broke again into a charming smile.

'Thank you,' said Fortuné. 'Now, my friend, can I have a minute alone with Lola? I promise I will not run away with her.'

Smiles left with the soldiers, who seemed happier. Only a nurse remained.

'I heard about your escape in Mbandaka. That was Lyman too, it was not me or my brother. It was Lyman Andrew. He is an American. He is working for the Americans.'

She kissed him gently on the forehead.

'You did not love me, you loved my brother.'

'I am with the Englishman.'

He laughed the laugh of the friendly, popular boy she remembered from parties in Kisangani.

'But you love my brother. I do, too. It was the money men who forced us apart, Bemba and his crowd. Do you remember how he bought me a Ferrari? Gift-wrapped with a red bow outside my house?'

She stared at his face.

'When I first saw you, in Kisangani, I think it was at a basketball game . . . I thought you were gods.'

He giggled and then shuddered with pain.

'There are several Rwandan bullets in me that prove you wrong.'

'I remember you bought me an ice cream. It was a chocolate chip.'

He sighed. There was blood on his long eyelashes. He gazed pleadingly at her.

'I loved you. I was prepared to die for you. To kill Xavier. My good brother.'

They fell quiet again.

'You will get better.'

The nurse looked hard at her and then withdrew.

They were completely alone.

He took her hand.

'I am all shot up, Lola. You must get out of here once the concert is over. You must leave. I am finished and the Rwandans who attacked you will come again and we do not have the men. I have only three hundred. Please promise me you will get out and, if you meet my brother before he comes for me, make him listen. I will try.'

She had tears in her eyes. She opened her mouth.

He gripped her hand tighter.

'Please do not say anything more, it is easier. I loved you, Lola, I really did. I do!'

'I loved you, too.'

'But only when my brother did not . . .'

An hour later Smiles watched the hurried preparations for a concert as they set what was left of the piano up on a concrete platform under a frangipani tree. He felt slightly miffed at being dismissed from Fortuné's presence and could not believe that Lyman Andrew would betray any adopted cause. The Zimmerman was first put on an old table to dry out and then on coffee chests but in each case the sound was altered so the legs were retrieved from the canoe and hammered back into place with four-inch nails that split the precious wood. Once Smiles would have cared about the piano, felt every hammer blow, but now he only cared about the broadcast. The Zimmerman stood at a drunken angle but the sound was surprisingly good, given a small hole in the right side where it had fallen on the huge log and that several of the higher note strings had been taken, probably for fishing line. He sat on one of the old coffee chests and started to play a snatch of Borodin.

The sunset was red as rubies.

He was given a plate of manioc with a little chicken-and-peanut stew but though he felt weak and exhausted he was too nervous to eat and returned to the piano. An elderly man then walked up carrying a staff and began to scatter water over the Zimmerman.

Smiles reached out to stop him but Lola grabbed his hand.

'No, he's a witch doctor. It's magic water, the piano is now mai-mai. It is like the water we put on ourselves so the bullets will not hurt us.'

He was surprised she said 'us'. But he could see by the way the troops were dug in to camouflaged holes and trenches around the main buildings that an attack was expected. His nervousness increased.

'I'd better try and play well, then,' he said.

When the witch doctor had finished, a simple microphone was linked to a transmitter and a laptop. A man wearing earphones nodded to Smiles and he made himself as comfortable as he could at the piano. He looked out over the clearing and, apart from soldiers, his audience seemed mainly to consist of seven children, a small dog and a goat until, to his surprise, Fortuné was carried out on a stretcher and lifted into an old armchair which was placed on the ground near the microphone.

Fortuné raised his hand and there was a cheer from his men.

'I've never missed a party in my life and I'm not going to miss this,' he said and winked.

Despite the danger from the Rwandans or from Xavier's forces, hurricane lamps were being put in front of all the huts and their lights formed a bright, flickering perimeter in the deep shadow of the trees.

Smiles had not decided what he was going to play. He did not know until the moment he touched the keys splattered with the witch doctor's water: it was Beethoven's 7th.

He had considered playing the Beethoven sonata he was halfway through in Johannesburg the day he had blacked out and everyone thought he was having a heart attack. But on this occasion only Liszt's arrangement of the 7th Symphony could measure up.

The music built slowly and delicately: he began working and

reworking the notes, which, for him, were the most moral in all music, and sent them out over the eternal forest.

He let the epic absurdity of the moment wash over him with the cooler night breeze.

Then he saw the first figure emerge from the jungle and the shadows behind the huts.

It was like witnessing life itself being created: out of music.

The theme grew stronger and the shadow stepped tentatively into the light, moved back into the forest and then out towards the huts. The shadow was a long-limbed girl born out of the darkness and the swirling woodsmoke of the fires under the tall trees.

The cliff-edge blackness of the forest shifted slightly and became another girl and another, holding an infant. Very soon, ragged groups of ten shadows were breaking away. Slowly, hundreds began to slip into the lantern light and all the newcomers were women. These were not the women from the huts, they were refugees who had been in the forest all the time, waiting, watching and scared.

They came clutching a bag or a child, a chicken, a tarpaulin or a plastic water container but never very much. They came reverently, as if entering a church, and, once they were finally visible, pressed forward to get a better view of him and the piano. When they were among the huts or in the open around the piano they sat down close to each other, leaving room for others to pass. There was no talking, no jostling. The dogs that followed did not bark and the babies they held did not cry. A few of the women had had a hand cut off by a panga, or had scars on their bodies, or walked in a way so tortured it told its own dreadful story.

They listened intently as he performed better than he ever remembered. There was wonder in the eyes of those closest to him.

Tears began to run down his cheeks.

The notes spoke of human strength and dignity and he realised he had never suffered as these people had, never gone hungry, never had to drink filthy water, never endured the blind, animalistic nature of war. The nameless, savage fears.

Lola watched, proudly, as the strange and beautiful music filled the clearing.

There was a glow of sheer happiness on Smiles' face.

At times he lifted his head to the stars. He was playing as a man possessed now. The impossibility of the journey through the jungle seemed as nothing when she looked around her.

She was sad and angry that Smiles' friend, the American Lyman Andrew, had betrayed them but in a way she understood. A good man who had tried to help the refugees. Why were people like that driven out into the wilderness in the first place? Did society fear that their goodness would disrupt the primitive order? Or was it even worse? Was it that their goodness shone like a light and illuminated the horror in the hearts of the rest of us? Then everyone felt so much better when, like Lyman Andrew, they went bad ... And she had seen many good people go bad in Congo.

When Smiles stopped playing there was a deep silence. Lola clapped and slowly the soldiers and then the women joined in and began to stamp and they made a noise, a low, shimmering 'Hooooooooo ...' that rippled out into the forest. The applause and stamping went on for ten minutes.

Smiles stood and bowed and bowed.

Fortuné then began to speak to the crowd.

'What does he say? Is he calling out your name?'

Lola shook her head and put her lips close to Smiles' ear.

'*Na loba* – Can I speak? That is what Fortuné is asking them.'

Then she heard the refrain.

'*Loba* – Speak!'

It reminded her of the question-and-answer style of preaching she had seen at a black Baptist church in Kisangani. Everyone began to shout '*Loba*'.

Fortuné was speaking quickly, breathlessly from his chair, telling them they were safe, as soldiers began to pass among the women, handing out food. The women, and it seemed the whole jungle, began to sing and a woman soldier was pulling at her arm.

'Please come with me, mama. A girl in the hospital wants to see you.'

She followed the woman behind the green-and-white main house to a series of outbuildings, one of which had women with bamboo crutches sitting on the ground outside.

'You come in here with me, mama. Her name is Céline. She know you from the Lycée in Kisangani. She has been in the east near Goma.'

'Yes, I know Céline . . .'

She was clever and pretty and always came top in *maths* and *histoire*. She had had a short fling with Xavier.

Lola remembered a bright day as they raced to a Lebanese shop for a mango water ice and a piece of sugar cane.

She blinked at the gloom lit only by a few hurricane lamps.

There was the smell of antiseptic, blood and gangrene in the hot, cramped room. In the entrance was a row of empty rocking cribs, carved out of a single piece of tree like the canoes, which knocked against each other with a low and hollow wooden sound that sent a shiver through her.

She knew the raped women often broke the necks of their newborn babies.

The woman soldier picked up a lamp and carried it to the end of the ward. A few of the women were moaning and one was covered entirely in bandages. In the corner was a bed shut off behind wooden screens. There was a halting singing coming from the other side, like that of a child trying to remember nursery rhymes.

Gently the soldier touched Lola's arm.

'It is very bad. She should be dead but she refuses to die. She was taken on the road by the Interahamwe. I think they used a rifle and a bottle.'

'I have seen bad things,' said Lola, and stepped to the other side of the screen.

The corner was dark and at first she could not make out the naked form on the bed. The sheets were stripped back and there was no part of the girl's body that had been spared. Holes had been made in the soft flesh of her stomach for the continuation of pain and pleasure. The girl's singing stopped and a broken, claw-like hand reached out for hers and the word `Lola' came from what was left of lips that had once kissed her on both cheeks.

'Céline?'

The reply was a whisper at first.

'Lola? Lola . . .'

The hand gripped hers and she forced herself to look, to remember.

'Lola!' It was a cry for help. 'You tied the ribbons in my hair and I took yours. Oh, Lola, do you remember the flower I gave you to say sorry? Do you remember the flower? There is no flower like it. Do you remember the flower? You must . . .'

She did not. She could remember no flower.

Suddenly, it was as if she could not breathe. A hand was pressing on her chest. She could not remember the flower. She could not remember the flower. She wanted to run.

The claw of a hand still held hers. A fingernail cut into her skin with the passion of the moment. Bones were out of line. Lola thought of all that had brought Céline here.

Lola felt the dark-green walls closing around her.

Her knees had started to fold under her when there was the roar of guns and the sound of an explosion. Céline's hand squeezed hers and then let go.

The woman soldier was pulling Lola around the screen and out of the door and there was the percussive shock of more explosions. The shutters on the windows were being closed behind her as she saw Smiles running towards her.

A man who was with Smiles said: 'We are under attack! The Interahamwe have come for the women. You must get back to the jungle! Get back to your village if you can!'

A building in front of them erupted in a sheet of flame but the words Céline had said echoed in her mind.

'Oh, Lola, do you remember the flower I gave you to say sorry?'

And then her body did not seem to work and she collapsed like a rag doll and Smiles was trying to carry her to the forest with the help of another. The bullets were thudding against the white bark of the trees and the women were screaming and screaming. It was like nothing she had heard before, not in Kisangani or in the civil war. There was a terrible, frantic edge to the sound, a note that said they had come to the end of everything, yet only moments before they had all been listening to music of such beauty. In the past, when all around her fell apart, she had had a dark and quiet place deep inside her to go to, like the forest, but now the annihilating cry had reached there too.

It was a cry from the end of all worlds.

Twenty-three

St James opened the next packet with great anticipation as he fished from the boat. He knew that a border was going to be crossed. He sensed that what was called civilisation, in the school, was going to be challenged. He had seen it many times. He was surprised only by the exotic background and customs as he kept one eye on his fishing float and turned the pages.

My Confession:
Stanley Miles-Harcourt: black book, packet eight

So, my dear Dr Kaplan, after being complimented by the headmaster I did not return to the green room. Instead, I slipped into the music school and from the cocktail bag I had with me adjusted my make-up and face powder. I then sprayed myself with the Chanel No. 5 perfume Hag Grey had left and waited until the lights were switched off in big school, as we called the assembly hall.

I smoked a cigarette from the little cocktail bag, just as Jane would have.

My heart would not slow down.

I had never felt quite like I did after that night on stage. I had become a different person completely. At least, that is what I told myself.

I stubbed out the cigarette and put it in a piano and then made my way to Devon House. One of the windows in the domestic block opened at the clacking of my heels on the cobblestones and a high-pitched, female Irish voice called out: 'Is that you, Clare? Oh, ignore me, then, you fucking Jesus whore . . .'

I walked on. I dreaded bumping into a master but I took the footpath up to the back of Devon House and Derby House and went in by the tower door. I slipped off my shoes so as not to wake Hag Large's nervous sheltie.

When I reached Lyman Andrew's rooms I paused outside the door.

If I did not do what Anderson wanted there was no telling what he might do. My mother would be devastated if anything happened to me, or if I were suddenly expelled.

Anderson was also part of my world at the school. I understood his cruelties and rituals. I knew Lyman Andrew was right but he was from so far away. I did not want to hurt him, but I had no choice.

I looked at my watch. It was the time agreed.

The handle turned and I walked into the familiar rooms. Mozart's Cosi fan tutte *was on the record player. It was one of Lyman Andrew's favourites. He got up immediately.*

'I couldn't just . . .' I began. 'Just sleep.'

He smiled. He seemed delighted to see me: almost expecting me.

'I don't doubt that.'

He was drinking a glass of red wine.

'I know I should not offer this to you, but would you like some? It might calm your nerves. I . . . I know what it's like! Performance, I mean. When I've given a concert my mind will not let me sleep even though there is nothing else left to do.'

'Yes, please,' I said.

I perched carefully on the sofa with my knees together, as I had been shown for the part and Lyman Andrew came and sat next to me. He handed me a large glass and I took a sip. On the coffee table and under it were documents about slaves and Africa and several ageing cardboard boxes.

'You'll get into trouble if you hang onto those things from the clock tower,' I said.

'I'll get into trouble?' He seemed angry for a moment.

Then his smile returned.

He said: 'I can't get over it. You really are a looker in that outfit, Smiles. In the audience they were saying we had cheated and got a girl from the girls' Masonic in Rickmansworth. I didn't know there was one.'

'Perhaps a proper girl would have been better.'

'No, no, most certainly not. You were a girl. You were Jane. That's what I wanted.'

'Wanted?'

Lyman Andrew seemed tongue-tied.

'For the play,' he said at last.

I took a sip of wine. It warmed as it went down. I took a larger gulp. His leg was resting against mine. I could feel the tension.

'You should think about doing this as a professional career. Acting, I mean, Smiles. If you can become Jane this easily, what would you be like in a male role? I am so happy for you, Smiles. But . . .'

'But?'

'I have personal news. I will be returning to the States. I think I am going back to playing the piano. The Chicago Conservatory made me a fantastic offer. I am about to accept. They are a wonderful institution, especially for people of colour. I know this is a quick decision and I feel our friendship is only beginning. But it's just this place. And the vile things I have found here. In these records I've been reading, my God, they make me trust in America. I never had the first idea. It doesn't change what I believe but . . . It gives another perspective entirely on civilised humanity.'

He gestured at the papers and boxes.

There was a knock at the door.

'Excuse me,' he said, getting up and touching me on the knee as he might have a girlfriend, and I turned my head away. All the caller would see was long, black, curly hair. It was one of the junior house prefects asking where I was. Lyman Andrew told him he did not know. The prefect then asked if Lyman Andrew would come and attend to a boy in the junior dorm who had stomach pains. Lyman Andrew sighed but went. He took every duty seriously.

After he had gone I walked into the bedroom as Anderson had ordered me and stepped out of my shoes. Anderson had told me to lie face down on the large, wrought-iron bed and to lift my dress so my bottom was exposed. 'It's easy,' he said. 'That's all I want you to do . . .'

I lay stretched out on the covers, wondering what Lyman Andrew was going to say when he returned.

I pulled up the dress over the silk panties.

(You may think this insane of me, Dr Kaplan, but I felt more comfortable going along with Anderson's plan, with the devil I knew, rather than the unknown of Lyman Andrew. Like the young men of Stanley's expeditions who did terrible things in Africa, I suppose.)

I pushed the panties down slightly.

Did Lyman Andrew fancy me? I was pretty sure that he did. The thought made me shake. I wasn't queer but I liked Lyman Andrew and if anyone . . . I raised myself on my elbows and shook my long, fake curls. I heard a movement behind me.

'You little fucking slut, Smiles.'

The voice made me jump.

The next thing I knew I was hit again and again very hard on my back and shoulders. A knee was against my neck. I could hardly breathe as my hands were tied to the bed. My panties were torn off. My dress!

I blurted out: 'Anderson said.'

But it was no good. My legs were being forced apart. I struggled and bucked. I started to cry out. I tried to turn to see who it was. There was a knife at my throat. Shit, they were going to kill me! Then a blow to my head made the lights go out.

When I came round there was a dull pain between my buttocks and blood on the covers and sheets.

The dress had been ripped from my shoulders and as I moved there was a sharper hurt from my ribs.

I tried to get up but my hands were still tied and the room spun around. I was gasping, with relief.

At least I was alive.

'Smiles, Smiles, Jesus, what the hell happened, Smiles? What are you doing here? Who did . . .?'

Lyman Andrew put his hand on me and, instinctively, I pulled away.

'Smiles . . . Smiles . . . I am so sorry . . .'

He began to stroke my hair. My wig was missing. I was sobbing. My eyes stung from the mascara.

There was a loud noise and the bedroom door was thrown open.

Then there was another voice:

'Stay exactly where you are, sir. I am a police officer and my colleagues will want you to explain yourself.'

The lights were suddenly switched on. They seemed very bright. Brighter than the stage spotlights. I felt guilty and ashamed and exposed in girl's clothes. It was suddenly for real. I was going to be for it. I glanced around and saw a uniform over Lyman Andrew's shoulder and a second policeman. The headmaster was there. He had an expression beyond horror. But it was Lyman Andrew they were concerned with, not me.

'My God, Mr Andrew. You disgust me. I never thought I would say that to another human being since the war but . . . My God! To encourage a promising boy to take part in a harmless musical entertainment like Salad Days *and all the time your infernal mind is preparing to satisfy the most bestial of urges.* Salad Days, *for God's sake! If it were up to me I'd wake up the cadet-corps armourer and take you out and put a bullet in your brain pan. You should be shot down like a dog, sir. You are no better. We offered you our trust and brotherhood and this is how you repay us.'*

At first there was anger on Lyman Andrew's face but then all the breath seemed to go out of him. I felt his body slump forward. He probably saw that the prefects behind the police and the headmaster had the unreasonable anger of any lynch mob in Alabama and only needed an excuse. The police would not have been able to stop them even if they had wanted to. Lyman Andrew lifted up one of his hands. My blood was all over him.

Lyman Andrew turned to me.

'How . . . ?'

'Get Mr Andrew out of here. Best put him in my study,' said Anderson, taking over from the constable.

Before Lyman Andrew was able to say another word he was dragged away in shock and I lay face down on the bed, sobbing.

'The poor boy's in a bad way,' I heard a voice say. 'Keep Matron out. This is not for her eyes. Get Sister from the infirmary. This is a job for Sister, the doctor is being woken. Best leave the boy alone.' There was the flash and then a double flash of a camera.

'Yes, leave him for Sister and the doctor,' said Anderson. The voice did not permit room for argument. It was the crisp, clean voice of command. The other policeman went down to see Lyman Andrew and wait for his superiors.

But Anderson stayed, sitting on the other side of the bed. He untied my hands. His voice was tender.

'Gosh, Smiles. I am truly sorry. I, in no way, intended this to happen. Someone has gone too far. Do not worry. This will be paid for. I deeply, deeply regret what has been done to you. But you must be strong and silent. "Aude, Vide, Tace", eh?'

I lifted myself up and looked in the dressing-table mirror. The wig was on the bed like a dead animal. My eyes were black with mascara and the lipstick had been smudged across my chin. My mouth tasted . . . I knew what my mouth tasted of and the pain throbbed between my legs. Blood trickled down my thighs.

Anderson put his hand on my shoulder and I reached up and held it, trying to stop crying.

It was strange, so strange, but the person I felt most anger with at that moment was Lyman Andrew.

After what seemed like an age there was a shout from the next room. One of the constables had returned.

'Gordon fucking Bennett! You in there? Mr Anderson? Sir? Come

and have a butcher's at this lot while I go and get the Detective Sergeant. Your boy there may be feeling bad but it could have been a lot worse. Look at this fucking lot! In a civilised country! That nignog has been up to some jungle jinks. That animal should swing from the nearest tree!'

St James looked around him as he finished the packet as if worried anyone could see what he was reading. From the market he heard the shouting of an angry crowd.

TWENTY-FOUR

Smiles left the firing and fighting and the Zimmerman behind him and frantically dragged Lola away in a small canoe with a rope through a hole in the prow. He had found it with the help of the soldier at the hospital, who then ran back to the battle. Smiles, too, wanted to stay and help the women and felt a coward. But he had to save Lola and was quickly floundering in a network of half-remembered streams and channels which made pulling the canoe easier but became a maze. Night closed over the jungle and he still could hear the occasional single shot in the distance, or a scream. He thought he had no energy left but he went on: his arms were shaking with fatigue which fought against a primeval desire to get away. In the end he had to rest and in a cul-de-sac of vegetation he pulled the canoe to the side and hauled himself out onto the bank, his fingers numb from tugging on the rope.

He stroked the side of her face but he could see that she was just staring at the heavens above, her eyes unblinking, and she would not hold his hand, even a proffered finger like a baby. Her skin was quite cold on the blisteringly hot night. He wondered what it was, what she had seen in the hospital that had had such an effect on her, to send her into such a state at the moment a battle started. He had not followed her into the hospital, intentionally. Even his eyes were cowards. He leaned down and kissed her on the forehead but she did not kiss him back.

'Please, Lola, speak to me . . . Speak to me, Lola . . .'

But she remained silent and unmoving.

He poured water into her mouth and closed her jaws with his hands to make it go down. He gave it to her from the one canteen the soldier had left him and he drank from the river. The tepid water tasted of forest and the blood on his fingers.

Smiles thought for a brief moment of the piano.

He was still thinking about bloody pianos!

At least he had managed to play the Peace and Reconciliation Concert.

Before the fighting started.

It almost made him laugh.

He watched the fireflies high up in the canopy.

Painfully, he tied the rope from the canoe to a tree to wait out the night. He was exhausted, utterly exhausted but he could hardly bear to close his eyes. She could not leave him now. She was unscathed and perfect.

To his right a sudden growling tore apart the silence. A shudder of fear went through his entire body. It was more than a sound. It was the dark vibration of pure horror. He had no idea what it was but he had the sensation that there was something savage watching him closely. Could it smell the fresh blood on his hands?

Was the beast going to eat them first, metacarpal by metacarpal, and did a pianist's hands taste better? He could not stave off the sudden wave of dread.

All he had was a knife.

His fruit-and-cheese knife from the concert in Rovigo.

He wondered if Lola had anything. One of Fortuné's soldiers had taken the panga. But in a long side pocket of Lola's jeans he felt something metal. Smiles took out the knife she had used to kill the deer and slid the blade from its sheath. He hadn't a clue what to do with the knife and the prospect of sticking it into whatever was out there revolted him. If he moved along the bank he might draw the creature off but that would mean leaving her and that was impossible. His emotions wrestled with practicalities as they did at the piano. The creature did not make another sound but he knew it was there and, unlike him, part of the forest around him, not having to think for an instant, the relationship between predator and prey as familiar as a Bach sonata was to Smiles.

He was sure it was coming for them now.

Smiles tried to stop trembling.

There was a sudden twig-breaking movement to his right, the smack of leaf on leaf and a small animal fleeing over the streams and pools, and, whatever lethal creature it was, followed and he thought for an instant that darkness moved against darkness and he caught the subtle sound of a cat's paw slipping across a giant lily pad, taking its tightly sprung anger away for the present and the world rolled forward again, leaving Smiles gasping.

In the morning he pushed the small boat on and hauled it over trees and tree roots, talking to her all the time, but she did not move. Her limbs were limp. The day was hot and he took off his T-shirt and put it on her face and smeared himself with a pitch-black mud he found at the base of a tree. When the sun penetrated the clouds, the mud protected his skin and stopped the insects biting. He rubbed it all over his body, on his face and on his legs. At about noon he gave her more of the precious water and still he seemed to be no nearer the river of gentle white sand which led down to her village.

He wondered if anyone from her tribe would hear the shooting: would come to help them. Smiles then realised how absurd the idea was. He was beyond exhaustion now and his hands were bleeding again.

The air had become suffocatingly close and he tried not to think of Lyman Andrew. If Lyman Andrew had betrayed them, it was Smiles' own stupid fault. How on earth was a good man to retain his goodness in the middle of a war and a jungle? But he must not think of that. All he must think about was keeping Lola alive and getting her back to the village.

He was lost and all he cared about was in a rotten canoe which he no longer had the strength to pull.

The stream ahead of him turned a corner and lying across it was a huge fallen tree that had brought down a stand of bamboo.

He tried at first to get through the bamboo to the tree.

The fallen bamboo shifted and reared, groaning and he could not find his way out again. He realised too late he was making a cage for himself and Lola.

He was going to die with her in the middle of nowhere.

The trouble was it was not nowhere. He realised that, smeared in drying mud, he loved the place like no other. Even in the middle of the jungle he felt a calm and a peace that he had never known before.

He was outside of time with her.

He looked down at Lola in the canoe.

'Lola, we have to try to get out of here ... You have to help me. I cannot do this alone.'

She was breathing gently and her eyes were open.

He gave her the last drop of filtered water from the canteen and then carefully filled it from one of the clearer pools.

Smiles felt he was getting a fever but it was probably his imagination.

He pricked himself on a toddy-palm thorn and then, reluctantly, snapped one off the plant and pushed it into the skin of her hand between the thumb and forefinger. She did not react or jump or cry out and hot tears of anger and frustration started to run down his face. Yet he also realised he was trying, really trying, at something with every fibre of his being, probably for the first time in his life.

Lola felt the small thorn in her hand but she did not acknowledge the pain. She knew he was there and heard his voice and he was helping her but it did not make any difference. It was not the women in the hospital that had made her retreat into herself. She had known all about the dirty war, this so-called chaos war, in the east. The Belgians had done the same thing in the era of King Leopold. She knew this, the women were targeted, but it was not that. Such was the documentary of the war. What kept going through her mind were the words spoken in a voice that still had the discernible pitch of girlhood.

'Oh, Lola, do you remember the flower I gave you to say sorry?'

She could not remember which flower, frangipani, flamboyant, or hibiscus. She used to like yellow hibiscus. But the phrase grew into a chorus until all the women were repeating: `Oh, Lola, do you remember the flower I gave you to say sorry?' It came from everywhere and all the energy had gone out of her body.

The enormity of what was being done to those women was enough to stop the earth turning.

Smiles stayed in the bamboo grove for several days and then he lost track, getting weaker and his fever growing. More than once he thought he saw men coming towards them through the misty jungle in the early evening, not knowing whether to try and hide or to greet the apparitions as saviours. But mostly he realised there was no hope and, whatever he did to revive Lola, there was not a flicker in her eyes.

He attempted, comically, to catch a lizard but it was just out of reach and he gave up.

That morning he had forced himself to eat a live giant snail and had been sick. The snail survived and crawled away.

He thought of opening his veins so she could drink his blood. He had read that somewhere in a glossy magazine, in a private jet, going from one concert hall in Australia to the next.

He used her knife to cut down two different lengths of bamboo and, beating them with another slimmer length, discovered he could get notes out of them, like on a xylophone. He cut other pieces of different length and picked out a scale. Then he attempted the *Missa Luba* Sanctus. He selected a second drumstick and played more. He began to sing. He wanted anyone to hear him, even if it was the enemy, any sort of rescue was a chance. He banged on the bamboo and sang at the top of his voice until he passed out from heat and fever, slumped on the tree roots in the shallow water, by the gently drifting canoe.

'We must kill him. He is a man who turns into a crocodile, *ngando*. We must kill him now. Look how his skin has turned black and is in a pattern like a crocodile.'

'The skin is white underneath. He is a white man.'

'If his skin is white it means he is dead. Everyone is white when they are dead. The bodies of the drowned are white.'

'They truly are.'

'We must kill him now. I want the knife and the canoe and whatever is in it. He is *ngando*.'

'You must share.'

'We will kill him, then.'

Lola experienced a complete panic. She could hear the hunters. Was it hunters? It was like she was hearing voices from the bottom of a well. She had been in a dream sometimes and could not wake up to get away from the bad things that were happening. But she had to. She had to save Smiles. Yet she felt she could not breathe or move and she could still hear the empty cribs knocking together in the half-light of the hospital.

TWENTY-FIVE

St James was getting used to being on his own. It made him feel like a man. Now he was a man. He was sure he was a man and so was Smiles but there were things in the white man's confessions that confused him and which he would not talk of in the market.

My Confession:
Stanley Miles-Harcourt: black book, packet nine

A week later I was out of the small hospital that was the school infirmary and the doctor, a divorced man who devoutly believed that gonorrhoea was divine revenge on evil women like his wicked wife (who had run off with a trumpet player in a jazz band) and was forever telling us that it originated among 'banjo-playing blacks' in the American South, the West Indies and Africa, produced his neatly typed medical report for the police, whom he had helped on several occasions, including

over the murder of David Wace. You would have loved him, Dr Kaplan.
The doctor, who also had a pathological hatred of worm casts ('mother
earth's shameful discharges'), had my blood samples sent off to a hospital
laboratory and was disappointed they came back negative. He put this
down to the good food and 'plenty of Christian fresh air' at the school.
In a few more days the bruises on my body were an angry purple but
the pain in my bottom was starting to go. Everything snapped back
into place with the school routine. I became the housemaster's fag again
and, apart from showing me how to tie a 'Winchester Duchess' fishing
fly, he did not go beyond trying to suppress a kind of awkward sympathy.
Sister, at the infirmary, told me I could talk to her at any time as long
as I was clean and properly dressed. She said I was at liberty to seek
professional help but that was up to me. She, being in the profession,
would advise strongly against it. 'In the war, when this happened to
one of my nurses, I put them on a double linen round and checked every
one of their hospital corners. After an upset, it's best not to think too
much and work hard.' Back from Scotland, the Colonel stopped me in
the cloisters. He was not looking me in the face. He seemed almost in
tears. 'Just remember, boy. If you drop your rifle on parade DO NOT
PICK IT UP! Don't move and no one will bally notice. Be quite, quite
steady. D'ye hear? Quite, quite steady. I see you are cheering, sir. This
is but a passing cloud.' Hag Grey blamed herself for making me look
too much like a girl and the padre preached a strangely tortured sermon
about 'Afghan friendships' and the difficulties of Everest from the rear.
The rave review from the Watford Observer *was pinned on the school*
noticeboard with a large picture of me with a winning smile and my
arms open.

The headline was: 'Saucy Saucer Girl Jane Steals Show'.

Two weeks later the head of Devon House suffered a broken jaw and two broken legs while on an exeat to the village. He said he had been hit by a Green Line bus and went home because of his 'nerves'.

He was not expected to return.

When this was announced in chapel, Anderson gave a slight nod in my direction.

Finally, I had to see the headmaster, who, after talking about the travels of Herodotus, giant, gold-digging ants, travelling hopefully and what may have happened to Cervantes when captured by a corsair, said: 'You must endeavour to put the whole thing behind you.'

I tried hard not to smile nervously.

The headmaster stood up, angry.

'I did not mean . . . I did not intend that to come out as it sounds. Drat! You know what I mean, Smiles! I mean, Miles-Harcourt,' he said. 'Go back to your lessons.'

But in the school at large, among my friends like Pinky Grey, being bummed against my wishes was not out of the ordinary, really, except I had been dressed as a girl. The latter made unconsenting sex almost inevitable and out of my hands. What happened to me was a rite of passage, so to speak. (And nothing like what women have to endure in Congo, Dr Kaplan. Absolutely nothing.)

On the night it all took place Lyman Andrew had been marched down to Anderson's study but had apparently tried to leave.

One of the constables caught Lyman Andrew on the stairs and he was locked up in the school mortuary before being taken to Watford police station.

What excited the police most was that the signed, bloodstained exeat and off-games 'fudge' from Sister that David Wace had been carrying on the day of his murder were found among Lyman Andrew's sheet music for Salad Days. *Also, there was a smoked human head in one of the cardboard boxes.*

Policemen came from all over England just to see the smoked head.

Lyman Andrew had been staying in a hotel in Bushey village the day that David Wace had died.

It was said it would be easy for him to take the body through the school's side entrance and put it on the rubbish tip and . . . Everyone immediately accepted that Lyman Andrew was obviously the murderer. The entirely unconnected human head clinched it and I almost began to believe it myself.

The headmaster, seeking to deflect any blame, fuelled the rumour in the school that Lyman Andrew was not only a rapist and a murderer but a possible cannibal due to David Wace's missing heart. The fact that the smoked human head turned out to be an 'anthropological specimen' brought back by an old boy from Africa and normally hidden in the clock tower, well, you can see how the hunt was quickly in full cry, can't you, Dr Kaplan? It probably brings back memories of the less progressive South Africa of your youth.

The matter was thought so serious the school was addressed by Viscount Burwood, chairman of the board of governors.

'It is best not to talk of this. It is heinous that this wicked man, crazed by his obsessions, perverted the rituals of our brothers in the lodges around the world. When one comes across a case like this one knows what evil is: it is darkness visible!'

And the smoked human head was put quietly back in the clock tower.

I last saw Lyman Andrew when he was returned to the school to account for his movements on the night of the play. We had been told not to speak to him. I was coming out of the library on the first floor by the main entrance below the clock tower. He stood very straight on the chequered floor of the hall in his own clothes but handcuffed to a uniformed policeman. Two detectives in leather jackets were nosing around the silverware in one of the cabinets. I dreaded having to give evidence in what would be a murder trial, though there had been few details in the papers. Lyman Andrew glanced up and his face was caught in a beam of light from the stained-glass windows. He looked every bit as good and honourable as I remembered him.

He still had the same dignity.

Then he saw me and I half-stepped back towards the library door.

I was terrified he might start shouting `Why have you betrayed me?'

Instead he just smiled, closed his eyes and nodded his head.

'How did filth like you ever get to a posh place like this, Andrew? How come they let you in here?' said one of the detectives loudly.

'Luck, I guess,' said Lyman Andrew.

It was either pure luck or the long arm of the Masons not wanting a scandal which would involve the school, their secret rituals and cannibalism, that some weeks later a prison van was left open and unattended. The prisoner was in his own clothes. He had seen a lawyer and was about to plead not guilty, against the lawyer's advice, which is probably why he was given the chance to escape.

Lyman Andrew was completely disgraced but intelligent enough to make his getaway.

Mysteriously, the police never found his passport and after a bank reported a Wells Fargo traveller's cheque being cashed, it was rumoured he had gone back to America.

The FBI began to look for him and his gentle, smiling face was in the press there.

For weeks the papers talked of a hunt for a brutal child murderer.

*One referred to him as 'the possible cannibal'; another, worse still, as
'the piano-playing cannibal'.*

*His parents even admitted he was prone to depression and a case in
which Lyman Andrew had been questioned, the killing of a white boy
in Mississippi at the time of a civil-rights march, was reopened.*

*But a month or two passed and there was no more interest. (The
police publicly dropped the case a year later, Dr Kaplan, but Lyman
Andrew never came back. He had gone too far.)*

*Anderson was very nice to me after all the upset and, because Anderson
was very nice, so was everyone else.*

*When it was time for him to go for an interview at Sandhurst, having
sat his A levels, he insisted on taking me to the Copper Kettle in Bushey
village.*

*It was a very pleasant tea room full of rich old ladies and horse brasses
and chintz. All around us the women gave admiring glances at our
blazers and greys and remarked how boys from the school were all so
well-mannered and a credit to themselves.*

Anderson took a bite of toast and put it down.

*'I have always been very fond of you, Smiles. I always thought there
was something special between us . . . Not like that. I don't want anything,
I don't want anything at all, you understand, although . . .' He smiled.
'I just want to be friends. We have unfinished business, you and I. I
just know it.'*

*I hadn't a clue what he meant. Except for the obvious. Perhaps he
did want to be friends. I suddenly had the impression of great loneli-
ness. But I had helped him utterly destroy a good man I truly cared for
and I was lonely too.*

*He had made me believe in the beating heart of the choirboy whose
throat I 'saw' him slit. I wondered how he did that. Had he taken a*

sheep's heart from the kitchens and put a mouse inside? Or was it just suggestion, what I expected to witness and feel?

After our hot, buttered toast and cakes and tea we went to the church-yard by the village pond. Our reflections rippled past in the water under the church tower and a high blue sky. We walked along to where the graves were overgrown. He kept patting me on the back and I wondered if he wanted to have sex with me and what I was going to say and do. (After what had happened, a lot of seniors thought they could have sex with me.) I could run and he would catch me. I couldn't report him because no one, right up to the Masons who ran the country, wanted to talk about Lyman Andrew any more. My name had been kept out of things. Even if I told the truth, they would not want to hear it. I imagined a great room with a polished table and not even a clock ticking in the icy silence. They preferred to lock away the African smoked head even though the man it had belonged to had been murdered brutally. So I carried on down the path. I told myself that my personal truth was not going to benefit anyone.

I was trying to please again.

Myself, as much as Anderson.

At the bottom of the churchyard we wandered onto the bridge over the little stream and he produced a packet of French Gauloises Disque Bleu cigarettes out of his pocket. He offered me one. I took it.

'Friends?'

'Yes, Anderson.'

'Call me Paul.'

'Yes, Paul.'

He was silent for a long time and then flicked his cigarette ash into the muddy water. He took hold of my shoulders, gently.

'You do remind me of my sister, Smiles. She was a sweet and good *person too, just like you. Don't lose it, Smiles. Don't lose it. Stay away from chaps like me.'*

So you see, Dr Kaplan, just what a self-serving little shit I can be. But you do not know it all yet. There is more poison to come out of the wound.

As he put the packet back into the satchel St James tried to guess.

TWENTY-SIX

She could not let Smiles be butchered. Fighting back from the bottom of a very deep place, Lola sat up in the canoe, pushing off the shirt that Smiles had spread over her and screamed at the top of her voice. She screamed so loud she felt the jungle shy away and birds fly in panic.

The men heard her blood-freezing cry and saw a rag-clad figure rear up in the canoe and they ran off, as quickly as they could, into the bush.

'A sorceress! A sorceress! She will turn us into crocodiles like that poor dead man!' cried one, and then they were silent. Not a leaf moved and she heard a bird sing close by. It was a small blue bird like those she had fed in the forest on peanuts as a child.

The hunters had vanished with the completeness of terror.

She gulped in the air: her head ached and then she saw Smiles, floating, face down.

Lola got unsteadily out of the canoe, her limbs stiff and cramping, and waded in the water, turned Smiles over and weakly pulled him to the bank. He was breathing! He was breathing! The hunters had not cut him. There was not a mark on his body below the black mud. He was covered in neat rectangles of dry, black, flaking mud and looked very like he had transformed himself into a crocodile and she could not help but smile. Especially as she had recognised one of the men from her village by a scar on his nose from when he had been fooling around and pretending to bark at one of her father's hunting dogs.

'Pascal, you come back here now! This is Lola! We were together in *deuxième*, do you not remember? Please come and help me, Pascal. This is not a trick. I am not a witch. I know you played for Notre-Dame soccer team in Kisangani and went on a trip to Gabon with them, and your aunt used to hit you on the knees and elbows with an old wooden spoon and you were in love with Miss Ilunga.'

But it was a good hour before the hunters re-emerged from the forest and came up to her. They stood close and she could feel their breath on her face. To make sure that she was real and not an apparition, they sniffed at her suspiciously because everyone knows that a ghost smells of grave earth and ginger. She was given a water gourd and drank greedily as one of the men tried to pour water into Smiles' mouth and washed some of the skin on his cheek white again.

'Look,' she said, tears of relief coming into her eyes as she hugged Pascal. 'Mud.'

But the hunters were not convinced as, sweating, they carried Smiles back towards the village on lengths of bamboo lashed together and Lola heard them say that he was in that state between identities: that he was neither one thing nor the other. That was why he had such a fever and a witch doctor would have to be summoned to make sure he did not turn back into a *ngando* and drag their children into the river. They all agreed that this was the first time it had happened to a white man. A white man who became a crocodile would probably be hungrier and meaner than any normal human being. But if the white man had not become a crocodile he would not have been able to survive and protect the wife of Xavier, the wife of Chui, the leopard, the Major-General who everyone knew, even in the villages, was to be President one day. It was foretold. And if a chief holds all the magic of his village in the palm of his hand directed by the witch doctors, what power must a President command?

Lola smiled. She was touched that neither Pascal nor the rest even imagined there had been any impropriety with Smiles, whether man or beast. She was not sure Xavier would see it that way.

She remembered the flower that Céline had talked about.

It was the light-blue blossom of the water hyacinth.

Céline had loved it because it travelled.

'I want to travel some day,' she had said. 'I want to go places in the world! I want to go to Paris! I want to drive around Paris on a warm night with a handsome boy.' Lola dreamt of Paris, too.

She staggered a little as she mounted and walked along a huge log with a waterfall at one side. Céline had set off an explosion inside her that shifted everything and now, perched on that log in the glorious forest, she felt so alive, purged of her petty stupidities.

'Did you hear the battle in Pendé?' she asked.

Pascal laughed.

269

'We listen, Lola, we hear, but we not go near. Much fighting. I am not sure who wins, not even who it between. But the *Garde Républicaine* is moving upriver to Kisangani in great numbers. They took over one of the pusher boats and many barges.'

Abruptly, the jungle plunged into a creek and she smelt the smoke of a brazier and cooking on a pirogue. Lola came out of the forest, not by the sandy-bottomed stream but on a track she did not know. At first the people in the large canoe were suspicious. But after long explanations about Smiles' appearance and assurances he was not a *ngando* and would not bite, the hunters propped him in one end of the boat. He was still only barely conscious and drifted off after he had taken a little water. She drank more as her mouth and the back of her throat were dry and felt blistered. The woman who was cooking offered Lola a dish of river fish with some manioc and she took several tentative bites before being sick over the side and washing her mouth out with the water. Pascal and the hunting party were arguing.

He turned to her. He was a tall and powerful man but there was a dilemma which showed on his face.

'It is too far to the village for Smiles. Better you go in this canoe. They go to Kisangani. Stop in Yangambi if you like, only a day away. See doctor, we will never get back to the village, Lola, it is too hard for him and for you. And . . .'

She raised her eyebrows as he hesitated.

'And what?'

'He is already in Kisangani.'

'Who?'

'Your husband.'

270

She turned away.

'Your husband, Chui, the Major-General, Xavier. Perhaps he has come to battle with Fortuné. Perhaps he has come for you?'

She nodded and fought the tiredness in her limbs as she said goodbye to the men who had saved their lives. They shrugged their way into the forest and in a few moments had gone and could not be heard. Only the green wall of vegetation hung over the canoe and then the paddlers picked up their long paddles from the bottom of the pirogue and they slipped out of the little tunnel of leaves and into the dazzling grey brightness of the main river, heading for Kisangani. All wars sooner or later come back to Kisangani and hers was no exception. She must go straight there. Smiles would get much better doctors and even if she had launched less than a thousand ships, she had to end the conflict between the brothers; if poor Fortuné was still alive. She must try and help Céline and all those other women.

Smiles woke with a start, a buzzing in his ear, and he wondered at first if he was in a police cell. He could see the room only indistinctly through the gauze of a mosquito net. There was no window and light came from a single bulb. Yet they would not have mosquito nets in a police cell, nor any television. The low buzzing came again. A hornet was trying to get into the netting. There was another one further up. His head felt as if it were about to come off and there were bandages on both his hands. It was then he noticed that a man in an ill-fitting army uniform was sitting in a green armchair by the table the television was on at the end of the bed. The dishevelled soldier came over and peered down at him through the netting and, with the Hollywood film magazine he was holding, killed both of the hornets and stamped them into the floor.

'*Guêpes*,' he said, mistakenly, and left before Smiles could ask where he was.

The soldier did not come back, so, slowly and with a monumental effort, Smiles managed to heave himself up and sat there for a few moments, breathless. He did not know what day it was. The fever was gone but his hands were hurt and swollen. He pushed his bitten and scarred legs out from under the netting and brushed it away from his face as he saw other hornets bouncing off the walls of the room. He did not pay them any attention as he once would have. Stopping at regular intervals for breath, he pulled on the trousers and T-shirt that had been left on another chair. They did not fit and were not his, nor did the slippers he found under the bed. He opened the door out into the sunshine and blinked.

Ahead of him was a pebble path and a bamboo fence. His room was in a block of others with air conditioners in various states of decay outside.

At the other side of the fence he heard a splash and saw the tops of conical thatched wooden huts you do not see in the bush. He was in a hotel. He walked slowly and painfully until he could peep around the fence.

A man was doing breaststroke up and down a pool.

He was very like the swimmer at the Hotel Memling but there was a Congolese woman this time on a sun lounger, speaking into a mobile 'phone. The effect was still surreal. Smiles looked past her.

Beneath a spreading tree was a group of soldiers.

Seated on a chair with her back to him was Lola. His spirits soared. She was alive and so was he. Then Smiles saw whom she was talking to.

Lola was drinking a Coke and chatting to Xavier and he and his men were laughing. They all wore the camouflage jackets and the red neckerchief of the *Garde Républicaine*. Each man was slung with ammunition pouches and grenades and had a rifle around his neck. Their laughter carried across the swimming pool and he dodged back behind the screen and made his way over the pebbles into his hornet-haunted room. He sat under the mosquito net watching one. The men who stood by Xavier reminded him so much of those who surrounded Anderson at school, but the comparison was flawed. Xavier was far more dangerous.

Smiles watched a fat-bodied hornet climb his mosquito net to one of the more obvious holes. He could picture Anderson here, all bony knees and khaki and his Eumenidean Society: it also occurred to him that the Eumenides or Furies often turned themselves into hornets to sting the sinful. His sin was pride and the fiction he could make amends. He thought of Lola and tried to imagine her with Xavier, tried to imagine her and the Major-General: the distant king who had been present at even his and Lola's sweetest feasts.

She did not come and join him in his room. In fact for the next two days she avoided him and he did not see her by the swimming pool. A hornet stung him but it was not so bad. He was distracted.

He had begun to wonder how she had won her life and his.

*

273

When Lola finally went to see Smiles, to her surprise and delight he was swimming up and down the hotel pool and the staff all stopped and watched him because there was a rumour that he had turned into a crocodile in order to save her; the rumour had already travelled upriver. There was no other way, it was claimed, that a white man could survive in the jungle and save someone who had played in the forest as a child. One of Xavier's *Garde Républicaine* was by her side.

Smiles hauled himself out using the ladder. He was still weak.

'How are you?' she asked.

'Missing you. Where have you been staying?'

'On the boat,' she said. 'It seemed best.'

'Certainly cooler.'

'Yes.'

'And the piano and my notes?'

'Everything is fine,' she said, as the guard watched, his hand on his rifle.

Lola felt the same dislocated urge to hold Smiles as she had on the first day she met him. But she sat down under a sunshade, where Smiles had left a hat and an iPod she had sent to him.

Xavier's soldier sat at a nearby table and birds darted between the flowering bushes. On the other side of the swimming pool were more small trees and then a football pitch on which a group of Russian coltan dealers were kicking a ball around.

'Did you send the doctors?' he asked.

'No.'

'Well, someone did,' Smiles said. 'The first was a bitter little Frenchman who said he did not want to be involved in politics and left. The second was a witch doctor who put a fetish on the bedside table with a bottle of beer and said: "God Save the Queen, Bobby Charlton and Margaret Thatcher." Then he left.'

She knew he had meant the story to be funny but it sounded plaintive and they both fell silent.

'You saved my life, Smiles,' she said.

He could not disguise the longing in his eyes.

'And what now? What now? Where is Xavier? Did he attack his brother? And the women? Has he killed his enemies? Killed them all? Is he President yet?' he said. The words tumbled out.

She shrugged. She could see Smiles resented what peace she had been able to make in the ever-changing circumstances.

'I do not know,' she said, glancing over at the guard, who could hear every word. 'At least you have some music, Smiles. The iPod.'

'Yes,' he said. His eyes were sunk into his head from the fever.

'It belongs to Xavier.'

Smiles looked surprised. He fingered the small piece of technology that had witnessed a time when she and Xavier were first lovers.

Smiles then laughed.

'I would have thought he was the last person to like Mozart,' he said.

'You don't know him. Look, here is St James. We have a car and we can take you up to see the Wagenia fisheries at the Chutes Boyoma and go around the town a bit. I want to show you. This is where I went to school, Smiles. Can you imagine me as a school-girl?'

He stared at her and then, she thought, forced a smile on his face.

'Yes, I can,' he said. 'That would be nice. A trip out. They have not allowed me out of the grounds, you know.'

They drove the short distance to Wagenia and walked out on a series of bridges made from canoes balanced precariously between rocks to where the fish traps were set on great scaffolds of wood above the wide, brown river, which roared over falls and rapids. There were only a few fishermen as the water was not high and they could not get the tiger fish at this time of year. Smiles stood at the furthest point and looked out at an island on which there was no settlement. He was glad to get out of the hotel but he still could not talk properly to Lola with two soldiers and St James always there.

'That was where Stanley had his camp,' said Lola.

'Smiles had a camp on the island?' said St James.

'No, Stanley, the English explorer.'

But St James only shrugged.

'Who?'

'You know that huge statue that is now face down in front of the Ministry of Planning? It used to be on the top of Mount Ngaliema. The army went and took it down,' explained Lola.

'Why?' asked St James.

'Because Stanley claimed to discover a land that was already there,' said Smiles. 'No one likes a pretender.'

They drove back to Kisangani with the mesmeric greens of the jungle at both sides, past an empty mosque with a whimsical minaret and into the town. They stopped briefly beside a piece of soot-covered ground about the size of a soccer pitch. A sign declared it to be a mass grave for the fighting of 1999 and 2000. 'I think our father is in there,' said St James, and they drove on. To Smiles it was as if the holocaust had been scorched into the ground from somewhere below, from hell itself. At the limits of the barren cemetery field a man was capering in the road, tears running down his face.

Everywhere there were buildings with holes in them or the signs of fire, and compounds surrounded with painted, corrugated-iron murals which showed poor men and women taking diamonds in by one door and coming out of another rich and beautiful and eating tinned corned beef. The diamond buyers competed over the size and beauty of the stones they painted. One of the figures was skipping with hands full of dollars, a girl on each arm, a cigar in his mouth.

'The buyers are the most dangerous men. They are our downfall, those diamonds and the gold and the coltan,' Lola said. 'There is blood on it all.'

Watchful youths with shiny new guns guarded both portals.

'Can we stop here, please?' she asked the driver at the next junction. 'We want to eat.'

Smiles and Lola and St James sat at a bar near a roundabout and ate grilled fish and listened to Fally Ipupa, and one of the twins who ran the bar pulled Smiles up to dance and he looked back at Lola, sitting at the table, where she began talking to an old friend from school. Little boys were break-dancing in the street and everyone seemed to want to touch him. Yet he felt more lost than he had in the jungle. There was a difference about her now, after Pendé. There was a look in her eyes; a stare that went to infinity and beyond, and she laughed more than she had before. He was so frightened that he might be losing her. He was losing her. He talked to her but it was not like it was before. The more she tried to be nice to him the more it hurt. He must get her away from here.

TWENTY-SEVEN

The next morning at seven Smiles' door was thrown open with a huge crash and he was instantly terrified. Half-asleep, he had been thinking about Lola, of course. How she had said it was better she stayed away for the present and he hardly had the courage to ask, to bring up the delicate matter of her leaving Congo with him. He saw the scruffy soldier, who had returned and slept at the end of his bed (Smiles was not sure if he was guard or jailer), leap to attention. The room was noisily full of troops with combat-wide eyes and guns which reeked of cordite. One stepped forward and pulled back the mosquito net.

It was Xavier.

His face glistened in the overhead light and there was that fierce look in the man's eyes Smiles had first seen in the grave-yard.

A hint of a smile crept onto the Major-General's face.

'I meant to come here and thank you before, Smiles, I hope I may call you that? Smiles . . . I want to thank you for saving the life of Lola. There is no one more precious to me in the world. I have loved her from the first moment of seeing her and, of course, she is my wife. And I heard your piano concert: Beethoven's 7th, one of my favourites. You play brilliantly.'

'Thank you.'

Everyone in the room smiled.

'Of course, due to a power cut in Kinshasa and an unfortunate electrical storm it was only heard by those lucky enough to have a radio in Kisangani, which compromised its political effectiveness. But your touch was incredible in the circumstances.'

Smiles did not know what to say.

'I have never heard Beethoven played with the composer's own passion and I have many recordings downloaded from the Internet,' added Xavier.

Smiles found it very strange and sinister discussing music with a man who broke open coffins and was said to eliminate whole villages.

The soldiers merely stared at him. They were covered in river mud and at least one tunic was stained with what looked like blood. The soldier was not wounded. It was the blood of the enemy. Smiles said nothing.

Xavier behaved like a cat who had stolen the cream and Smiles hated him but felt quite powerless. It was rather like school, when he had faced the Eumenides.

Xavier took his hand as if they had been friends for years. The Major-General sat down on the bed.

'There was a battle last night, what a battle! Thousands of our men were involved against some of the pro-Bemba rebels and mai-mai and Interahamwe from the east and renegade units of our own Forces Armées. It was across the river at the Tshopo Falls, beyond the ones you saw yesterday. The rebels wanted to take the old dam and power station and cut the main road to the east and, if they had done, Kisangani would have fallen and the country would have been sliced in half. We had a hard time defeating them, they had been well-trained and had new American rifles. I hope it will be different under the new President in Washington.'

There was menace and resentment in his voice as he said 'American'.

The soldiers parted and Lola swept into the room and strode straight over to the bed. Xavier rose and she looked alarmed.

Smiles saw the field dressing under Xavier's jacket.

'You've been wounded,' she said, angrily, as if talking to a child.

But the elation of battle was with him and Xavier let her.

'Are you well enough to come with us, Smiles? I am going back there,' said Xavier.

Smiles was staring at Lola.

'And why do you want me there, General?'

'You will see' was all Xavier said, and strode off with Lola following him, arguing in Lingala, and Smiles' fear returned.

They drove quickly and bumpily out past the empty mosque, where two vultures played on the steps, and the medical school and the two sprawling breweries, which as usual were a hive of activity, and past houses with papaya saplings and vegetable gardens full of waving children. From underneath mango trees men leapt out into the road and cheered them like liberators.

The children shouted Xavier's family name and his nickname 'Chui', the leopard, and occasionally the open-topped Mercedes slowed and he stood up. Lola sat next to him, dressed demurely in a black skirt and white blouse, borrowed clothes that made her look like an office worker. Smiles wanted to hold her, right there, with the soldiers in front watching, their hands tight around their rifles. He hated Xavier now all the more for being so accommodating to him and never once acknowledging him as a rival.

After about half an hour they came to a crossroads and drove past a modernist power station in dark concrete and then clanked across a bridge over which women were carrying great loads of grass or cylindrical panniers of corn cobs on their heads.

The women all were singing and Smiles wondered if it was because of the battle.

The iron bridge seemed to have been constructed out of a giant Meccano set and the women's song was drowned out by the fearful roaring of the falls. The water surged through turbine sluice gates and onto a rock ledge just downstream from the rusting structure, before plunging into a wide pool. On the far side of the pool was a sandy bank and a sloping escarpment of jungle. Spray hung like mist in the still air.

About a quarter of a mile the other side of the river they drove down a gravel track and parked by a collection of vehicles on the beach he had seen from the bridge.

A body under a green, bloodstained sheet was being loaded into an ambulance. It was one of many laid out in a neat line.

Exhausted soldiers all with the red neckerchiefs sat on the sands, their rifles on the ground, gazing into empty space. One man had taken his shirt and boots off and was paddling listlessly in the water. The soldiers stood up as Xavier got out of the jeep but he said something to them in Lingala and they smiled and sat down again, smoking their cigarettes. A soldier held up his fist and shouted Xavier's name as they had on the road.

Xavier just nodded and then turned and began painfully to climb steps which led up the jungled hill.

At the top of the escarpment were more soldiers and then, to Smiles' utter surprise, a zoo.

In one sturdy cage a large chimpanzee was smoking a cigarette held between the forefinger and middle finger of his left hand and the soldiers were laughing. Then Smiles noticed that past them, other cages, whimsical iron constructions from the early Belgian era, held men in them. In the trees were monkeys and a man in a yellow jacket shot nuts at them with a catapult. At his foot was a bucket full of small crocodiles.

'He shoot food at his monkeys that get out,' said a soldier. 'He don't want to lose his friends . . .'

The enemy faces stared back at Smiles, sullen, resigned or just plain scared. Several of the men had the green uniforms of the renegade Forces Armées but others wore jeans and T-shirts and trainers; these were obviously the Interahamwe. 'Those who kill together'. To Smiles they looked like beggars.

One prisoner was giggling hysterically to himself, another was smoking marijuana. Smiles noticed that at the other side of the cage was another line of bodies. He was about to ask what was going to be done with the captured men when Xavier motioned to him to follow and he saw, out on its own, an enclosure like an oversize Victorian canary cage with great loops and flourishes of metal.

One man was inside and Smiles stopped.

'My God!'

He knew now why he was here.

'This is what you came for,' said Xavier.

Smiles had the sudden desire to run. His mouth was dry.

He immediately recognised Lyman Andrew, even though the American's hair had turned grey. An angry wound in his neck had been partially bandaged and his angular frame was much thinner.

But his eyes were steady and Smiles was the one who felt like a traitor.

When Lyman Andrew spoke, his voice was somewhere between tears and bitter laughter.

'Oh no, for fuck's sake, no. Take him away, can't you? Take that little fucker away. Just put a bullet in my head, why don't you, *mon general*? He's shooting everyone else, is the General. He likes things orderly.'

Xavier did not say anything at first. When he spoke it was softly as a truck groaned up the track towards them and on it were the remains of the shiny black Zimmerman.

'Your friend came from England to see you, Mr Andrew. He helped bring you a piano, this piano, a very early piano from the French revolutionary period I oversaw the restoration of in the Académie des Beaux-Arts. He played a concert at Pendé. Smiles did all this for you, before Pendé was attacked by the scum you now support. You helped those women for years and, now, I cannot begin to tell you what your new friends got up to. They are not music lovers.'

The sense of menace behind the Major-General's matter-of-fact words made Smiles feel queasy. It reminded him of when he first saw Xavier in Gombé cemetery.

'Aren't you interested to know what they did to those women?'

Lyman Andrew said nothing.

Smiles spoke.

'Celestine was taking the piano to you. But you weren't there and I thought . . . I just thought . . .'

Lyman Andrew smiled.

'You thought? You were always so thoughtful, Smiles.'

Xavier went up to the bars where Lyman Andrew was standing.

'We followed Smiles and his piano. We got to my brother Fortuné in time. He told us how he was betrayed by you, that you have now sided with these creatures who are in the pay of the Americans, or whoever owns the mining companies these days. Now we have captured you we have proof of that link. I have seen war for many years but I do not understand what happens to a man like you. I can see how you can break with my brother. But the women? After you did so much for them?'

Xavier walked away from the bars and Smiles stepped up to where the Major-General had been standing.

'I suppose you are righteously ashamed of me too, young Smiles. I wanted you that night, you know. That night the prefect Anderson tricked me. For years I laboured in Pendé . . . Helping the women who fled there . . . Helping them at what became that useless fuck Fortuné's place in the jungle. Then, do you know what happened?'

'No, Lyman . . . Don't . . .' said Smiles.

The American smiled mirthlessly. There was a long pause.

'Fortuné's soldiers began raping our rape victims. When I went to confront him with this I found him hoovering up cocaine with the same men and planning to grow the stuff in the plantation. I had spent years trying to build a moral life again and for what? The whole fucking business of helping is futile.'

Lyman Andrew paced around the cage.

'Then I discovered that the world-famous pianist S. Miles-Harcourt was on the same bill with yours truly at the Peace and Reconciliation Concert. I ask you! An even bigger joke than the concert itself, which was pointless, a smokescreen to hide an unstoppable tide of cruelty with each side as bad as the other. I wanted none of it. So I calculated, when the dust had settled, that American money and influence would win and more people would get food and medicine and the right not to be violated. I gave the location of Pendé away to someone who is euphemistically styled an American adviser.'

Lyman Andrew stopped pacing and shook his head with a wry chuckle.

'This adviser's Interahamwe recruits were meant to take care of Fortuné, not the women, and after the love-sick Major-General had been lured upriver by the well-meaning Lola here, to fight his brother, Xavier's *Garde Républicaine* was to be zapped by a large force of Rwandan regulars, Interahamwe and renegade Forces Armées and then blamed for his brother's massacre, all very neat. The trouble was the Major-General was not meant to win! You can rely on nothing in Congo. Even you should remember that, Xavier. Even you!'

A tear was running down Smiles' face and Lola moved towards him.

'I came to say I am sorry. I came to make things . . .' he began.

Lyman raised his eyebrows.

'And what precisely does that mean here, Smiles? To make amends? This is not a British public school. What does it mean, Smiles? Perhaps, we should go to my study and put on *Cosi fan tutte*?'

Smiles sighed.

'I . . . I really do not know any more. At school I could not save you, they hated you. It was not just because you were black, it was because you were too good for them.'

'Well, you can't say that now. And, as usual, you get the sympathy.'

There was a look of anger in Lyman Andrew's eyes, all the greater because it was partly suppressed. Lola could see the effect it had on Smiles. She began to wonder at what Smiles had told her about the idealistic Lyman Andrew and the school. Can a man change, so much?

To her, Smiles looked frantic, as if he were waking from a bad dream into a worse one. He stood awkwardly by the cage.

'I came to tell you. I came to confess, I wrote it all out. I collapsed in South Africa and realised I must come and see you . . . You do not understand.'

Lyman put his head back and laughed so loudly it made monkeys dart around the trees and the birds fly. The chimp came up to the bars and began to scream and jump, scream and jump, scream and jump.

'You think I don't understand?'

'Come away,' Lola said sharply to both Smiles and Xavier.

Lyman Andrew looked at her angrily.

'Spare me your whores, Xavier.'

He walked to the middle of his cage and squatted down.

'Look, the victorious General trying to restrain himself. He shares everything with his brother when he is not trying to kill him. But Fortuné is such a nice man. He is loved by his soldiers. He was so indulgent with them they thought it might not matter when they raped the women we were helping. At least with Xavier here there is no moral confusion when he gives an order to slaughter. Are you going to kill me here or throw me to the mob? Smiles has seen the mob set on me before, haven't you?'

Lola put her arm on Smiles.

'Come away . . . Come away. Your friend is not here. He died a long, long time ago. He would have forgiven you.'

Lyman Andrew suddenly grabbed through the bars at Smiles. He then began to shout at Xavier in French and Lingala, cursing him and calling him a woman and a fool.

'All cowards hide behind being the hero, don't they, Xavier?'

Several soldiers by the cage were watching the expression on the Major-General's face.

'Get him ready to move,' said Xavier, and the soldiers smiled wryly. Lola knew that smile but she found it hard to have sympathy for the American.

Sunlight burst through the trees and illuminated Lyman Andrew's greying hair. No one said a word in the green clearing and even the monkeys were quiet and the chimp had gone right to the back of his cage. Every eye was turned to the American and he was, for Lola, the apotheosis of all men; the quintessence of humanity in his overreaching ambition and his epic hatred in failure.

She wondered what Xavier was going to do.

'Come on, Major-General, let your men get it over with. Don't pretend to be any less than you are,' taunted Lyman Andrew

A flicker of a smile lit Xavier's face.

'You will go back to Kisangani and then we will take you to Kinshasa to stand trial. Perhaps there are charges you have to face in England.'

'No, he doesn't,' said Smiles. 'They were dropped ages ago.'

'Well, following what happened in Pendé, there might even be charges in The Hague,' said Xavier. 'What I found when my brother had been attacked after the broadcast was beyond belief. What had been done by friends of your new friends.'

Lyman Andrew was taken out of the cage and dragged onto an open truck and he started to shout again. But even a few of his fellow rebels yelled at him to be quiet for their sake. Two guards got in and a soldier nodded that Smiles was to follow. He climbed on and walked to the front, near the cab.

Xavier came over to the truck and looked up at Smiles.

'I am sorry, I thought you might want to see him one last time. I am sorry.'

Even to Lola the words came as a surprise.

On the way back over the iron bridge the leap from the back of the truck happened without any warning.

The truck had slowed to a crawl and the two soldiers guarding Lyman Andrew had got off and were trying to herd the men and women carrying baskets of grass and greens and *chikwangue* alongside. Smiles' eyes strayed to where water gushed from the great sluice gates underneath and then hit the rock shelf with an arc of white spray that rose in a mist over the river ahead. He had never seen water explode like that and the power of it was frightening. Smiles looked back into the eyes of the man who had been his friend, whom he had loved and believed in and betrayed. Lyman Andrew stood before him with handcuffs around his wrists and the boots taken from his feet, in fawn jungle trousers and shirt, and he saw his old friend's desire to damn everyone was waning, perhaps in remembering the good times at school, or the realisation of what Xavier had in store for him. In that instant he became again the man who had taught Smiles to play the piano. Lyman Andrew stepped forwards and kissed Smiles full on the lips and then, without so much as a word, jumped from the truck before the soldiers knew what was happening, and threw himself through a hole in the gantry and into the annihilating flow.

There was confusion and the bridge was cleared. At the other side Smiles was taken down from the truck near a large hoarding that warned of picking up mines and other ordnance. Smiles rested his head against one of the hoarding's supporting poles. He found he was breathing very quickly and Xavier, whose open-topped car had screeched to a halt, was snapping angry commands and was saying something to him but he did not quite hear at first, the roar of the falls was in his head as was the silent kiss of Lyman Andrew.

'Sit down, sit down. Here is a paper bag. Blow into it. It will help you. You could not have done anything. I am only glad that my troops following did not open fire. I am sorry.'

Smiles blew into the bag and his breathing came under control.

'Are you? Are you sure that . . .?'

The Major-General was gazing at the bridge.

'No one survives these falls. We will not find the body. It is held under and torn to pieces against the rocks, he would have been unconscious in the first millisecond. A whole army has been thrown over that bridge at one time or another and I cannot remember anyone ever finding a body.'

Xavier put his hand on Smiles' shoulder.

Lola had her arms around him but was staring at Xavier.

'It was so quick. So quick.'

The awful sound of the water seemed to grow louder as Smiles made to get up.

'I must go out on the bridge.'

'No,' said Xavier firmly. 'No, I do not think that is a good idea. Lola can go. Lola can go and throw flowers. That bridge is not a good place to feel too much sorrow. It is well-known in this village by the bridge. I have stood there.'

The words were gentle and intimate and there was compassion and empathy in that strong face, a reaction again Smiles had not expected and at the bottom of his heart made him hope that Xavier would let Lola go. To fly away with him to Europe and leave the Major-General's bloody world and the river. The soldiers who stood by were in no doubt that Lyman Andrew was more frightened of the fate that awaited him at the hands of Xavier than jumping into the roaring mouth of the falls but Smiles now did not believe that his old teacher's motives were that simple or selfish. Lyman Andrew could no more cross that bridge out of his dreams, out of Africa, than he could play on after a symphony or a concerto was finished. He recognised the majesty and beauty of the simple end notes when they came and he did not recoil from playing them.

Smiles was crying now. He was crying so the tears streamed down his face. He did not care who saw.

Lola broke an armful of frangipani flowers off a nearby tree and took them out onto the bridge alone and threw them down into the roaring, misty abyss.

Around Smiles people watched and waited; those who lived there had rebuilt houses and replanted gardens reclaimed from the war. Who was he to feel that his loss was larger than theirs? The crowd cheered Xavier, and with his wave the traffic started again, crossing the bridge and disappearing into the trees at the other side where not so long ago there had been fighting. Smiles climbed back into the truck. He wanted to be alone. And then, as they passed a lorry loaded with dead bodies, a soldier pulled a piece of plastic sheeting off two who were clutched together in a final embrace. Smiles felt so sorry. He only glimpsed them for a moment but he was pretty sure it was Celestine and Thérance.

TWENTY-EIGHT

St James had not liked being left alone on the boat, fishing while Smiles and his sister went to see Xavier and this triumph in the forest. Why would they not let him see the dead rebels from the battle upriver? The market people said Xavier had killed many. St James toyed with Smiles' leather satchel and took out the last packet of papers.

My Confession:
Stanley Miles-Harcourt: black book, packet ten

Well, you nearly have all the truth from me, Dr Kaplan. Every last drop. After Anderson I did well at school and when I was a sixth-former I was made a prefect and had my own study. It was as if Lyman Andrew had carried away all the guilt with him, wherever he had gone. I was even allowed a piano in my study for practice, as long as I did so in the daytime. Only occasionally did what happened come back to haunt me. I was in the middle of a difficult piece of Chopin one day and I started to think of David Wace, of his curly blond hair, his soft brown eyes and the way he used to pat me on the back and I would chase him, laughing; how we sneaked up to Merry Hill fields together and smoked cigarettes and planned what we were going to do with the endless vista of our lives which stretched out in front of us like the American prairies or the Russian steppes. David Wace was always playing tricks on me and that was why he took the quince my mother had given me from one of the trees my father had grown. A tree I remembered in our garden from my earliest years. I knew he had the quince because he had put his hand under my nose and then hared away again. He had this exuberance for life and did not understand the small rituals and tribal passions of others. I had raced after him, through the back gate of the school and up towards Bushey village.

It was a really sunny day and I remembered how red his lips were and how rosy his cheeks. He looked like a girl that day.

He stopped where the road that ran round the back of school met the road to the village.

'What have you done with that quince, David? Please?'

With a smile he said: 'You shouldn't be mooning over that stupid thing in your tuck box. The others are beginning to think you are a loony. We all had our things from home ... Roberts even had a secret teddy. You should chuck it, we are friends now and that's what's important. It's all about our dads dying, that's what my mother says and ...'

'Where is it?'

'You don't need it.'

'I want it. It's mine. Don't you understand?'

He nodded his head.

'I understand.'

'So where is it?'

He laughed.

'I ate your mouldy old quince.'

He was standing at the kerb just by a lime tree and I was right next to him. In that instant I thought he had taken from me everything that I had left in the world. I remember him shielding his eyes from the sun and then out of the corner of my eye I saw the car coming towards us. David Wace was my friend and I loved him like the brother I never had, yet I pushed him smartly under the right wheel of the Colonel's speeding Daimler, knowing in some vicious, animal part of my brain that even if he was going to stop, the brakes of the old car would not bite in time. There was no change in the last expression I saw on David's beautiful face, as if this was all part of the rough and tumble of the game and he did not blame me, and the pain in me was as instantaneous as the shock. The Daimler threw him forward onto a grassy bank before the back entrance and skidded to a halt. The Colonel got out and stood there as I went over and looked down at my friend. His eyes were closed, his body in the foetal position and he appeared to have just gone to sleep.

'I am so sorry, David . . .'

Then I heard a wailing noise from the Colonel and another voice. It was Anderson.

'It's all right, sir.'

'I've run over a deer, haven't I? They are all over the estate . . .'

'Yes.'

The Colonel was obviously drunk with his head in Scotland and Anderson was trying to calm him down. Anderson turned round and looked at me.

'Wait there, Miles-Harcourt. Stay exactly where you are.'

The voice was commanding, an order. Orders were the familiar

currency of the school and I obeyed gratefully. It freed me from thinking
of what had happened in terms of David Wace and the hair that hung
over his forehead.

I did not move. I fully expected the police to be called and to have
to go with them in handcuffs and spend the rest of my life in prison.

Anderson persuaded the Colonel to walk back to his house in the
school grounds on foot, staggering a little, turning round to look back.
I saw Anderson had his fingers to his lips. He then jumped into the car
and reversed it back to where David Wace lay.

'You are going to help me, Miles-Harcourt. I saw exactly what
happened. You are going to help me and then a veil of silence is going
to descend over this affair. Well, it may. If you cooperate. What we are
going to do is not very pretty but we are not going to tell a living
soul.'

We put the body in the car and he drove it into the school grounds
and onto the rubbish dump. I did not know Anderson was able to drive
but he was good at most things. He left me there with the body in the
back of the car while he went off to get something and I thought he had
tricked me and he was going to get the police. But he came back with
a little bag that had belonged to his father, who had been a doctor.

He dragged David Wace onto the rubbish dump and took off all of
his clothes. He put them on a smouldering fire and then, without warning,
he started to cut down the middle of the body with a scalpel from the
medical kit and everything fell out like links of sausages and I was sick.
The smoke and the smell went up my nose and I began to faint but he
shook me awake. Even now I cannot remember the details clearly, although
I can 'see' a music score in my mind any time I want to. The angels
close their wings about us for good purpose at times, Dr Kaplan, but I
can hear Anderson's voice.

295

'I want you to see this, Smiles. I want you to see all of this. It has to look like a murder. A piece of voodoo by a local Masonic loony. We are in this together, aren't we? "Aude, Vide, Tace"?'

TWENTY-NINE

The piano was brought back to the boat with Smiles and Lola.
Xavier left in a hurry for an outbreak of shooting on the other
side of the city. A soldier who helped get the Zimmerman aboard
said it was being taken back to Kinshasa for repair. Smiles only
cared about Lola now. The day was baking hot and as he went
up the gangplank he received a curious look from St James, who
was fishing. Smiles' leather music satchel was in Lola's locker
with all of the packets of his journal, the inside smelling of quince,
and he was sorry he had once doubted the boy would take care
of them. He should destroy his black book, his confessions, but
half-wanted to keep it as a link with Lyman Andrew. Smiles was
sitting silently gazing out at the river when Lola said she wanted
to buy herbs and a chicken to build him up and get the port official to stamp their exit papers, which then would have to go to
Xavier. Smiles started to go with her. He saw an airliner come in
low over the river like a craft from another world. They could
fly out of the country from the city's small airport. A breeze was

blowing from the north into his face as he picked his way among the drying clothes and she turned towards him, her face so beautiful. He was determined he was not going to lose her.

'Be careful, the crowd in the market is looking for rebels,' shouted José from the boat. 'They are taking any stranger. There is a rumour that there are many spies and rebels in the town. They are trying to please Xavier. Don't worry, they will not touch St James. I maybe going to get fuel.'

Smiles did not feel like a stranger. The strangeness was in his overwhelming sense of belonging.

It was then he saw the mob.

It was as if a wave was coming towards them through the market along the top of the riverbank. He could hear the shouts. Dust rose from corrugated-iron stall roofs as they went over like breaking surf.

Even Lola looked frightened and there were no soldiers to be seen, only the blue-uniformed policemen, who seemed to be stirring up the crowd, and a boy from the youth militia, fishing on the boat next to St James. There was a scream as the mob caught someone.

Lola turned to him.

'I must go alone. I will be better alone.'

'Don't go. Don't chance it,' he said to Lola.

'It's all right, this is where I went to school. We must have those papers. I hope Xavier will not object.'

Lola glanced over at St James and then headed off among the stalls.

But a crippled boy ran after her and began to shout.

There was a roar from the mob, which turned in her direction. He could not let them take her.

Smiles stepped to the middle of the mud road.

'I'm the one you want! I helped the American who loves Bemba! I am the rebel!'

The crowd stopped for an instant and then they tumbled towards him down the muddy bank and he tripped turning to step on the gangplank. There was such hatred in the mob and a few of the boys he had seen around the boat carried or rolled tyres and a man had a can of what looked like petrol.

He felt a dizziness.

But there was a grin on his face.

How small his existence had been but for her. Even his piano-playing was only interpreting the soaring souls of others.

A man towered over him, a panga raised, and then his mind flew off into the brittle sunshine of Kisangani and the slab-like clouds. Lola was running. She was running towards him. She flung her arms around him, kissing and kissing him, and then there was an explosion of more light than he thought possible.

She saw the mob heading for the boat and knew she had done the wrong thing in leaving him. She thought of her mother. She thought of Céline and the hospital and screamed from the very bottom of her soul.

Lola could not see Smiles for the crowd now and she shouted and fought her way through the people whom only seconds ago she had been terrified of. A man grabbed her, called her a rebel and tore at her dress.

Then there was the gunshot and she was left standing alone on the grass with everyone else running away.

A man with a panga was on the ground and so was Smiles.

She looked onto the boat and St James held a rifle. He was pointing it up the bank at the crowd. The boy soldier, younger than him, whose gun it was, stood helplessly by him.

St James had known what he was going to do for a long time. He did not want to be a hero. He had seen all his life that such ideas led to the cemetery. Lola had cried out. She had not got away. He was not going to let his sister be taken, like his mother, whatever it cost. Yet he felt a fool as soon as he grabbed the rifle of the boy fishing beside him, flipped down the Kalashnikov's safety and shot the man with the panga, who now lay wounded in the leg. St James had aimed for the middle of the body but the man had moved. Xavier had told him one day on the beach when the Major-General was teaching him how to shoot that he must always aim for the middle of the body and never fire over people's heads as they did in films. St James knew, if he shot to kill, the crowd would run. Or thought he did. In fact he had gambled. That was stupid, even though he was right. His mouth tasted of metal and the gun was hot where it touched against his bare skin because his T-shirt was too small for him. But he felt little more than that. He looked over the side of the boat and there was Smiles, clutching at his chest, his lips blue.

The Englishman Smiles was still going to die, he was sure.

He had seen it clearly before now. Like the woman who told prophecies in the market saw things.

The wounded man was trying to crawl up the bank. José ran down from the wheelhouse.

St James shook his head and put the gun down on the deck. He had saved his sister Lola and the Englishman was going to die and . . . and he never was going to learn about the octopus. The trouble was he liked the Englishman, he really did. The boy soldier was shouting at him for taking his rifle. St James just stared at him. St James was not going to cry, he was not going to show his tears because he was now a man. He then heard sirens and shouts and prolonged bursts of fire and saw the crowd melting away and the boy soldier scurry to the other end of the boat. Soldiers raced down the bank and he recognised Xavier striding after them. St James peered over the side of the boat again and saw his sister bent over Smiles, kneeling in the muddy water. He wondered what Xavier was going to do. The man St James had wounded had reached the top of the bank when one of Xavier's guards turned, and, almost as an afterthought, shot the man twice and continued walking. St James swallowed hard. He hoped he would not face a firing squad.

Xavier was angry as he came down the bank.

'I thought I gave orders that . . .' he began to say, but stopped. He went straight to Lola's side. She was rocking back and forward and he saw that the Englishman was trembling.

'Has he been hit?'

'No, St James shot a man who was going to kill him and . . .'

'He's having a heart attack. He's not breathing,' said the Major-General.

Immediately, Xavier propped the Englishman's head back and started to give him mouth-to-mouth resuscitation as his men stood around him. It did not matter to him, he told himself, if she had had an affair with the pianist. He must not give in to his jealousies, he must not. He blew air into the man's lungs, hoping for a response.

He wanted him to live and to leave and if Lola was going to leave with him there was nothing he could do to prevent her.

All the armies in the world cannot stand before love. He knew that now.

The Englishman was the sort of civilised man that he had longed to talk to after years of fighting in the bush. It was quite strange. He did not feel jealousy towards such a man and he knew Lola's emotional needs. In better times Xavier hoped they might have become friends. He admired Smiles. There was a romantic quality in the Englishman's quest that he recognised.

It was then the Englishman clutched at him, it was only a second, and inserted his questing tongue into Xavier's mouth. The Major-General froze and then he realised what was happening.

He gently let go and with a last cough and then a long exhalation of breath the Englishman died.

All Smiles saw was Lola running towards him and flinging her arms about him . . . He did not know where they were. It was a place of such amazing light like the sun on the forest leaves after it rains along the river. His arms were around her and they were kissing and she was going to be with him for ever.

Lola watched as Xavier stood over the body.

'I should have saved him. Our doctor is with the wounded. I should have got him to the UN base.'

'They would not have opened their doors to you.'

He shrugged.

'Then I should have knocked them down. I should have saved this man.'

302

His words made her lose her temper and she rounded on Xavier.

'Do you still think you are God?' said Lola. 'Because you have a few soldiers? You don't control any of this any more than he did.'

He saw how upset she was.

'No.'

'You are trying to play Caesar to the white man. He was my lover. We were married.'

Xavier stared at her. The men who had been standing near them started to inch back up the bank.

'He is dead, the white man,' Xavier whispered. 'I did not think I was going to be sorry, but I am. I am sorry. He was a good man.'

Slowly, he reached out his hand and Lola took it.

With the other she touched Smiles' face.

Lola then went up the bank with Xavier, the whole world in her chest. She wanted to shout, she wanted to cry out, but she did not. José and St James caught up with them. She let Xavier lead her through the still-angry crowds to his car while two guards were left by the boat with the body of the Englishman, her lover.

Epilogue

A week after the death of Smiles two rioters had been shot and twelve were in prison and St James watched as Xavier, Chui, the leopard, became the conquering hero of Kisangani. St James was happy for him as everywhere he went the crowds waved and cheered. Now Xavier could be pleased his brother Fortuné had survived and he had spirited him out of the country to a very good hospital in Gabon. But already he was arguing with Lola, who had moved back to the boat.

'Smiles should have had a proper funeral,' St James heard her say angrily.

'I am very sorry,' said Xavier, who stood on the gangplank of the boat. 'The body was accidently burned with the others. 'I am sorry.'

It was unusual to hear Xavier apologise.

St James also knew that this burning story was not true. St James could go anywhere among the soldiers and listen to them talk after he shot the rioter. He heard them say that Smiles' body had been taken on a truck after curfew and cast into Tshopo Falls with Lyman Andrew. They said Xavier threw no flowers but that he stood there a very long time.

One man said the General just liked to watch the waters. Another said the General was jealous of Smiles but did not say why. A third said Xavier was sad for the Englishman, who had saved the General's wife, Lola. Many more said it was unusual for Chui, the Leopard, to be sad about anything. The soldiers did agree, however, that it was fitting for the two musicians to be for ever in the music of the falls.

Xavier followed Lola up the bank to his waiting car and St James went with them. They drove a short way along the road to where units of his victorious troops were embarking for Kinshasa on great barges. With them went the rebel prisoners Xavier's troops had not killed, who were glad to be spared and given the choice between jail and joining the Forces Armées if they renounced their past and changed. A thunderstorm was forming to the south. That had not changed.

'Come with us, General. Come with us and march on Kinshasa!' shouted one of the officers, as Xavier stood behind Lola outside the car. All the troops cheered.

St James then heard Lola say: 'If you move on Kinshasa, I will leave you for ever.'

Lola and Xavier and St James had waved and waved as the pusher boats shepherded the crowded barges into the middle of the river, the troops singing songs from the time of independence. 'We will wait for you, Xavier!' they shouted.

St James believed for a moment, as he looked at Xavier saluting in his uniform, that was what would happen. But for several weeks he had hesitated and argued with Lola.

'If you are to stop this endless cycle of war in our country you must act in a different way,' she said, and St James saw Xavier start nodding in agreement with her. He had changed. Something to do with the business with Smiles had unsettled Xavier. The truths the Englishman had brought were not always as welcome as his music. Perhaps that is why Xavier threw his body into the waterfall. To make sure his ghost could not be heard.

On the Monday of the third week, Xavier came to see Lola, who was sitting on the grassy bank above the boat, among brilliantly coloured mammy cloths drying in the sun. St James sat by her.

She stood up and kissed Xavier on the cheek.

'What is wrong?'

He glanced up at his car and soldiers on the road. A button on his tunic was undone. St James knew that Xavier was anxious.

The Major-General spoke softly.

'I have been told to take all the leave owing to me. You know what that means! They are spiriting my victory away. The President's office has ordered that the battle of Tshopo Falls be struck from the records to avoid revealing that Kisangani was ever threatened.'

Lola held Xavier's hand.

'Don't worry, you still command the *Garde Républicaine*.'

He shook his head.

'No. I thought I would be asked to fight around Goma, but no. There are even suggestions that I may have to face charges.'

'What charges?' asked Lola. Her arms were around him now.

Xavier managed a laugh.

'Well, there is the death of an American Baptist preacher who was trying to convert the Interahamwe, the businessman Celestine Mbando and the internationally famous concert pianists Stanley Miles-Harcourt and Lyman Andrew. There are accusations that I have destroyed villages, including the centre for raped women at Pendé, and bombed the Intercontinental Hotel. It might all land me in a cell next to that creature Bemba, on trial for war crimes in The Hague. All those who were for me in the government are now against me. If I had just had one live American prisoner . . . Perhaps Lyman Andrew was right. You can rely on nothing in Congo.'

Lola shrugged.

Above them on the bank the Major-General's car then left without warning.

It was obvious even to St James that they were in danger and had to flee. The next morning *Le Rêve* moved off into the stream through the mist with the old piano still aboard. Xavier was sitting on the piano stool. He had the American passport of Lyman Andrew open and was looking at the picture, possibly, St James thought, wondering if he could take the man's identity. The passport would not help him play the piano. All the strings had now been stolen for snares and not a note could be played.

Xavier pressed the ivories and there was no sound.

St James went up to him. He felt sorry for the General.

'Mr Smiles can still play that piano?'

'Yes, I am certain. Better than ever,' said Xavier.

Xavier put his hand on St James' shoulder. He could not remember him doing that before.

'Can Papa Smiles still turn into a crocodile?' he asked.

Xavier sighed, but then his stern expression softened.

'Yes, I think so.'

'And an octopus?'

'Eight arms will certainly help him playing the piano.'

St James laughed, too.

'It will.'

St James knew deep inside that all of them were going to travel soon, far away, he knew not where, and he welcomed the chance to see the octopus and many other wonders of the world. And after that they would return to the timeless river. He had seen it all very clearly.

ACKNOWLEDGEMENTS

I would like to thank Sarah Hochman, David Rosenthal, Andrew Kidd, Mike Jones, Sally Riley, Nadja Poderegin, Bryan Ferry, Paul Kasongo, Kathleen Wyatt, Maria Aitken, Xavier Maret, Antonia Willis, Sir Nick and Susan Kay, Paul Ross, Thérance Mwanza, Marleen, Hilde and Lieven De Rouck, Catherine Clarke, Didiane Kongolo, Alice and Persephone Pickering and all who helped me in Congo.

ACKNOWLEDGEMENTS

AUTHOR BIOGRAPHY

Paul Pickering is the author of four novels, *Wild About Harry*, *Perfect English*, *The Blue Gate of Babylon* and *Charlie Peace*. *The Blue Gate of Babylon* was a *New York Times* notable book of the year. He was also chosen as one of the top ten young British novelists by bookseller WH Smith. As well as short stories and poetry he has written several plays and is a columnist for *The Times*. He lives in London with his wife and daughter.